"I'm taking the midnight shift with Noah. If danger strikes, it will probably be then."

So Seth would be with Noah. Rebecca had to admit that knowing this made her feel a little better. "Look, I don't mean to be a pain, Mr. Armstrong, but these are my children. I have a right to know that they are safe. Or at least as safe as you can make them."

He nodded. "I agree you do have that right. But you have to trust me to keep them as safe as I possibly can."

Did she trust him? No, why should she? Rebecca told herself she didn't really know the man at all. Still, Pony Express superintendent Mr. Bromley trusted him, so what other choice did she have? She'd have to try to trust Seth Armstrong to watch after her boys.

How did a mother release that kind of trust to a stranger? She reminded herself that to keep her family together, she'd have to try.

Rhonda Gibson lives in New Mexico with her husband, James. She has two children and three beautiful grandchildren. Reading is something she has enjoyed her whole life and writing stemmed from that love. When she isn't writing or reading, she enjoys gardening, beading and playing with her dog, Sheba. You can visit her at rhondagibson.net. Rhonda hopes her writing will entertain, encourage and bring others closer to God.

Books by Rhonda Gibson

Love Inspired Historical

Saddles and Spurs

Pony Express Courtship

The Marshal's Promise
Groom by Arrangement
Taming the Texas Rancher
His Chosen Bride
A Pony Express Christmas
The Texan's Twin Blessings
A Convenient Christmas Bride

Visit the Author Profile page at Harlequin.com.

RHONDA GIBSON

Pony Express Courtship

⬥ **HARLEQUIN**® LOVE INSPIRED® HISTORICAL

Recycling programs
for this product may
not exist in your area.

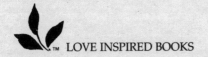

LOVE INSPIRED BOOKS

ISBN-13: 978-0-373-28351-4

Pony Express Courtship

www.Harlequin.com

Printed in U.S.A.

A man's heart deviseth his way:
but the Lord directeth his steps.
—*Proverbs* 16:9

This book is dedicated to the men
who rode the Pony Express routes.

To my husband, James Gibson,
my best friend and strongest supporter.

And to my Heavenly Father,
who helps me to reach my dreams.

Chapter One

Dove Creek, Wyoming
February 1860

"What were you thinking?" Rebecca Young demanded of her youngest son, Benjamin. She tossed the water bucket to the side. Her body shook as fearful images built in her mind. "You could have been killed." The acrid smell of smoke in the early-morning air almost choked her as she fought for control. Benjamin might be adopted, but she loved him as much as she loved her daughter, Joy. The thought of losing him in a fire tore at her heart, leaving her feeling raw.

Black soot covered his young face and tears traced dirty tracks down his cheeks. He coughed, echoing coughs from others around them. The eight-year-old boy wrung his hands and shook his head from side to side. "I didn't mean for it to happen, Ma."

Fear and anger warred for control of her emotions. If Jacob hadn't seen the flames tearing through the barn and gotten Benjamin out, her youngest son would have died in the fire. She couldn't—she heaved a deep sigh—no, she *wouldn't* let her fear take the sting out of her scolding. "But it did happen, Benjamin. How many times have I told you not to take a lantern into the barn?"

The tears increased and dripped off his quivering chin. Big brandy-colored eyes met her gaze. Fear filled them. Was it fear of her, or the fact that he could have died in the fire? "I'm sorry, Ma." His voiced choked; he threw his arms around her waist and buried his head against her.

Rebecca ran her hands down his thin arms then embraced him tightly, unmindful of the black soot being smeared against the white of her apron.

Her gaze moved from one to the other of the six young men who stood in the yard. Her other adopted sons. Rebecca barely held back the tears, her heart winging a prayer of thanks that none of them were hurt putting out the flames.

Her oldest son, twenty-year-old Jacob, stared morosely at what used to be their barn.

The second oldest son, nineteen-year-old Andrew, kneeled on one knee at the edge of the clearing. He most likely desired privacy when he prayed, but that was a luxury big families couldn't afford. How she'd love to join him and thank the Lord for His protection. Each of the boys had learned early on from her deceased husband, John, to pray about everything. She couldn't help but be proud of Andrew for knowing where their help came from. Clayton, who'd just had his nineteenth birthday, dropped his water bucket, pure frustration lining his young face, and stomped back to the house. Rebecca knew he tried hard to hold in the pent-up fear and hopelessness that the burning barn

caused and made a mental note to go to him as soon
as she could.

Eighteen-year-old Thomas and eighteen-year-old
Philip stood side by side, eyes darting back and forth,
watching everything as it unfolded. The boys were best
friends and had vowed to always stick together even
before she and John adopted them.

Twelve-year-old Noah, the newest member of her
family, looked ready to bolt. He stood frozen, motion-
less, waiting for what she would say or do next. He'd
only been with her a couple of months and wasn't sure
about anything yet. He reminded her of a hungry dog—
ready to fight if needed, but hoping for love and a little
food to fill his belly.

The morning sun shone brightly over all of them
now. But when the fire had first been detected, it had
still been dark. Her boys had rushed to put out the
flames, but they'd been no match for the heat radiating
from the inferno. A heap of smoking, blackened tim-
ber filled the spot where the barn once stood. Thankfully, her five-year-old daughter, Joy, hadn't come out
to assist.

If John had been here, this never would have happened. Once more the loss of her husband struck home.
How often in the past eight months had she wished that
he was still alive? Too often.

After twelve years of marriage it was hard to believe he was gone. The boy sobbing into her apron drew
her thoughts away from the past and her sorrow. She
stroked Benjamin's light brown hair.

An unfamiliar cough sounded and then a man
cleared his throat. "I hate to disturb you, ma'am."

She had all but forgotten the stranger who had raced

into the yard and jumped in to help put out the blaze. Rebecca released Benjamin and turned toward the man. "I'm sorry, Mr...." She waited for him to fill in his name.

"Seth Armstrong."

Rebecca wiped her hands on her apron. "Thank you, Mr. Armstrong, for stopping by to help put out the fire." Thanks to his help, the fire had been subdued faster than it normally would have taken, but not before they'd lost the barn and everything in it.

"I was happy to help, Mrs. Young," Seth answered, pulling her from her musings.

How did he know her name?

Before she could ask, Jacob barked out orders to the other boys. "Andrew, you and Philip go gather up the horses that arrived yesterday, put them in the training corral and feed them. Thomas, milk the cow and go get Clayton, tell him I said to find Brownie and Snowball and hitch up the wagon. We're going to town for lumber." He watched as the boys scrambled to do as he said.

"What do you want me to do?" Noah asked quietly.

Jacob walked over to the twelve-year-old and bent down to eye level. In a softer voice he asked, "Would you take Beni into the house and give him a good washing?"

Noah nodded. He walked over to Benjamin. "Come on, Beni. Jacob says we have to get you cleaned up." The two boys left the yard and Noah had planted his hand firmly on Benjamin's shoulder.

Jacob stood once more and came to stand beside Rebecca. She was very proud of her oldest son. John's death had hit him the hardest and he'd taken to heart her husband's last words—to take care of the family.

Her gaze returned to Seth Armstrong. He was a big man with deep green eyes and black hair. His shoulders were wide. And his hair touched his collar. Rebecca wondered if she was in some sort of shock. What did it matter what the stranger looked like? More important, how did he know her? Did her deceased husband owe him money? She prayed not. Even though John had left her secure, she didn't have room in her budget to pay out extra money.

As if sensing her confusion, Jacob asked, "What can we do for you, Mr. Armstrong?"

His green eyes met Jacob's. "Well, I suppose you could show me to my room." He turned his attention back on Rebecca. "I'm the Pony Express station keeper that Mr. Bromley told you would be arriving." He walked back to his horse and pulled down a carpetbag from the back of his saddle.

If John hadn't already signed the contract to use their farm as a home station, Rebecca would have been tempted to call the whole thing off. But the boys needed the extra income and she didn't want them to be forced to leave the farm to find other jobs. If it was in her power she'd keep them together as a family for as long as possible. Now she simply had to trust in the Lord and pray that everything worked out.

When John had told Rebecca of the Pony Express and how Mr. Bromley, the Pony Express ramrod, would be by to tell them more about what their part in it entailed, Rebecca never dreamed she'd be singlehandedly dealing with this many changes. Now that Seth Armstrong was here, she felt even more alone. Her farm was to be the home station and her boys Pony Express riders.

The original plan had been for John to be the one running the station, not a stranger. But once Mr. Bromley learned of John's death, he had told her he'd be sending a station keeper to replace him. She'd suggested Jacob, but the route superintendent feared Jacob's brothers wouldn't listen and obey him like they would someone else, so he'd sent this new man.

"Mr. Bromley sent you?" Jacob's question was for Seth, but he looked to Rebecca for answers, not the man who had just claimed to be the new boss on the farm. Confusion and hurt laced the depths of his eyes.

Rebecca's heart sank knowing he wondered why she hadn't told him of this latest development. She nodded. "Yes. Mr. Bromley came out last week when you and the others were fixing fences in the back pasture. When he found out that John had passed, he insisted we needed a station keeper. I planned to tell you and the other boys soon." She hadn't expected the replacement to arrive a week later and had thought she'd have more time to break it gently to Jacob.

Jacob nodded, but a thin veil of hardness covered his eyes. He turned his gaze back to Seth. "I'll show you where you can put your things."

Rebecca watched them head to the bunkhouse. She heard Jacob ask, "You got any papers on you? Proving you are who you say you are?" His young voice held strength, a strength she'd leaned on too heavily in the past few months.

Seth Armstrong chuckled. "Sure have. Right here in my bag. I'll show them to you and Mrs. Young, once I get settled in." He pulled his horse behind him as Jacob led the way to the bunkhouse.

She turned and looked at the smoldering pile of embers that used to be her barn. Gone. In just a few minutes the barn had burned to the ground. What had Benjamin been doing out here? Especially in the early hours of the morning?

Rebecca stepped closer to the rubble. She sighed. It looked as if she would have to dip into her funds to re-build the barn. Jacob would have to ask for credit from the lumber mill and she'd add the nails to her growing tab at the general store. Once they had the total cost of the barn and all the supplies they'd need, she'd get the money from the bank and pay both men. She'd learned shortly after John's death that if she didn't deal with the men in this manner, they'd take advantage of her and she ended up paying more than what she'd actually owed. That wasn't going to happen again.

As she walked back to the house, Rebecca called to the new Pony Express station keeper and Jacob. "Breakfast will be ready in half an hour. Don't make me wait."

The desire to call out to Mr. Armstrong to return to where he came from pulled at her vocal cords. She would like nothing more than to have the peace and quiet of her farm restored. But Rebecca knew that wasn't possible. If she wanted to keep her family to-gether, then the Pony Express would have to be a big part of it, and that included Seth Armstrong.

Seth laid his bag on the bed. Jacob had taken him to the small room off to the left-hand side of the bunk-house. It contained a bed, a side table and a chest with a washbasin on the top. A wooden box hung above the trunk and held a razor and hand mirror. An adjoining door led to the remainder of the bunkhouse, giving him two methods of entry.

"I'll get my things out of here after breakfast." Jacob stood with his hand on the doorknob.

Seth hoped his words rang true as he said, "I hate to put you out."

Jacob shook his head. "The other boys will be more comfortable with me than you in the other room with them."

"I'm sure they will." Seth took his Bible out of the bag and laid it down on the table.

Jacob studied the book as if it was a snake. "You read that often?"

"Every night."

The boy nodded. "I'll leave you to settle in and go check on the others." He didn't wait for an answer, but simply walked out the door.

Seth looked down at the worn brown leather of his Bible. It was the same one that his father had preached from and studied over for many hours. Jacob had acted as if it was poisonous, or might inflict harm, instead of being a balm that offered soothing words to a troubled soul. Had he been placed here to help the boy find his way to God? He doubted Jacob would welcome him in that area of his life any more than he welcomed him now as the new Pony Express station keeper.

He moved to the only window in the bunkhouse and looked out at the burned barn. Smoke still spiraled upward to the sky. Building a new barn would help him get to know the young men who were now his charges. Seth planned on staying just long enough to teach them how to survive the trail they were soon to be riding and then he'd continue on to search for Charlotte, his lost mail-order bride.

His thoughts went to the woman who had promised to be his bride. The last letter he'd received from her said she was taking the first stage out of California and should arrive in a few weeks, only she'd never showed. After his grandmother's death, Seth had left his home in St. Joseph, Missouri, and begun searching for Charlotte. He was a man of his word and he intended to keep his promise to his grandmother. He'd find Charlotte and marry her. He knew he wouldn't fall in love. His mother had taught him that to love someone meant getting hurt and he'd never go through what his father had. Never.

He doubted Charlotte had come to any harm. Her letters had indicated she didn't want to get married any more than he did, but the girl had no other choices at the time. She'd been up-front in her reasons for answering his advertisement—lack of money and nowhere else to turn. He'd been honest, too, telling her he was trying to keep his last promise to his now-deceased grandmother. He'd also told her he didn't believe in falling in love, as it only led to heartbreak and death. His own mother had deserted him and his father when he was a child. No, he wouldn't open himself up to that kind of hurt again. He'd keep his promise to get married. He'd assured his grandmother he wouldn't be alone after she died and he'd keep that promise, one way or another.

Unfortunately, shortly after leaving St. Joseph, a couple of road bandits had relieved him of his money. Thankfully, with some quick thinking and the fact that

Sam, his horse, had been faster than the men, he'd gotten away.

Needing money, he'd returned to St. Joseph and signed on with the Pony Express. As the station keeper it was his job to swear in the boys and get them ready for the job ahead of them. But once he earned enough money, Seth planned on continuing his search for Charlotte. Taking a deep breath, he left the confines of his new room and walked outside just as Mrs. Young began to ring the dinner bell.

Its loud clang filled the yard and got the attention of all the boys. She looked to him and nodded. He returned the nod and headed toward the house. Rebecca Young looked as if she was in her early twenties, and from what he'd seen this morning, she seemed to rely on her oldest child to run the farm.

The boys were older than he'd thought they'd be. But from the looks of them, they would all make good riders. Mr. Bromley had told him they were just a bunch of farm boys and would need a lot of training. That was why Seth had arrived at the farm in early February instead of closer to his scheduled date of April third. He was happy to see the Pony Express horses had arrived safely. One of the boys closed the corral gate and headed up to the house.

Was he ready for all this responsibility? His gaze moved to the young men as they hurried to the house for breakfast. Mrs. Young stood on the porch hugging each of them before they went inside. She was a pretty little thing with a lot on her slender shoulders. He silently reminded himself not to get attached to any of the Young family, especially Rebecca Young.

He had to find Charlotte. Even though he had never

met her, he still felt responsible for her and he wouldn't break his promise to his grandmother.

Rebecca wasn't sure she was up to the changes about to take place on her farm and in her home. Already things were different. Breakfast proved to be a quiet affair. Everyone seemed lost in their own thoughts or afraid to speak lest something worse occurred. Seth Armstrong made several attempts at polite conversation, but finally lapsed into an awkward silence when no one seemed inclined to answer with more than one word. Finally they each took their plates to the kitchen and then left single file. Rebecca cleared the rest of the table and washed the dishes. She wiped up the countertops and table, then poured the dishwater into the hog slop bucket.

Wagon wheels crunched near the front porch, reminding her that they were going to town for supplies. "Joy!" she called up the stairs. "Time to go!"

A smile parted Rebecca's lips as she watched her five-year-old daughter cross the room. Joy had changed from her nightgown into a simple brown dress and had pulled her fine blond hair into a blue ribbon. "I got myself ready," she said, twirling in a circle.

"I can see that. You look very pretty." Rebecca grabbed her pale blue cloak and bonnet from the peg by the front door, then helped Joy into hers.

They stepped out onto the porch and Clayton jumped down from the driver's seat to help them up. Benjamin, Philip and Thomas ran from the bunkhouse and landed in the back of the wagon with loud thuds.

"Where are Andrew, Noah and Jacob?" Rebecca asked, looking back at her sons.

"Mr. Armstrong says Andrew and Noah need to stay here and take care of the place," Thomas answered, giving Philip a shove.

That accounted for Andrew and Noah, but not for Jacob and Seth. Rebecca looked toward the bunkhouse. "Where are Mr. Armstrong and Jacob?"

"Mr. Armstrong said we can call him Seth," Benjamin answered with a grin.

"That doesn't answer her question, Beni," Philip said. He turned to look at Rebecca. "They are inside talking about why Jacob thinks we should all go to town."

Thomas snickered. "If you call that talking."

Rebecca lowered herself from the wagon. It was bad enough that Seth Armstrong had announced he was their new boss, but to cause strife this soon…well that was unacceptable.

"Ma, I wouldn't interfere if I was you," Clayton warned from his seat. "Jacob is in kind of a foul mood."

"I can imagine." Rebecca turned to the bunkhouse. "You boys stay put. We'll be ready to go in a minute."

She heard raised voices before she got to the door. Rebecca pushed the heavy wooden door open and walked inside. Her sons turned expectantly. "What's the ruckus?" she asked, placing both hands on her hips and giving her children the "mother" look.

Jacob and Andrew each clamped their lips together. Noah studied the end of his muddy boot. It was obvious her boys had no intention of answering her.

Seth crossed his arms and met her gaze full-on. "We men are having a discussion."

"From what I heard—" she didn't bother telling him she heard it from Philip and Thomas "—you expect

Andrew and Noah to stay here while the rest of us head to town." Rebecca held up a hand to stop him from answering. "And if I know Jacob, he's not happy with the arrangement and intends to stay with Andrew himself." Her gaze moved from her oldest son to Seth. "Do I have it right so far?" Her eyes locked with the station keeper's.

"I'd say that about sums it up," Seth responded.

"Mr. Armstrong, may I ask why you want the two boys to stay behind? We've always gone to town as a family before." His eyes were the prettiest shade of blue-green that she'd ever saw. Did they turn that color when he was angry? She mentally shook the thought away and focused on the problem at hand.

Seth sighed. "With the horses loose, Indians or bandits could come and steal them while we are gone."

"That's why I should stay," Jacob growled between clenched teeth.

Seth turned to Jacob. "I need you to help me bargain for supplies. The men in town don't know or trust me just yet. And since I don't know them, either, I need you to make sure the Pony Express doesn't get cheated."

Rebecca realized that what he said was true. She knew that even though the men in town knew her, they didn't want to bargain with a woman. They'd made that very clear shortly after John's death. Jacob had a wonderful working relationship with them and the chances of them accepting Seth Armstrong from the get-go were slim to none.

"I have funds that we can use to rebuild the barn," Seth said. "I'm sure Mr. Russell and Mr. Bromley will approve, considering they need the barn to house the Pony Express horses."

Rebecca looked to Noah. The boy hadn't looked up from his boots. He was so young. She didn't like the idea of leaving him and Andrew alone on the ranch any more than Jacob. "Why leave Noah? He's only twelve years old."

"Because Jacob says that Noah is the best at using a rifle." Seth's gaze never left Jacob's face, daring him to deny it.

That was true, too. Over the past few weeks, Noah had proven he could shoot the antennae off a grasshopper, if he had to. Rebecca walked between the men and looked her oldest son in the eyes. "Jacob, what he's asking isn't unreasonable. I'm sure that Andrew will see that Noah is kept safe."

Jacob's eyes held warmth and sadness in their depths. He nodded. "I'm sure he can, but it is my job to take care of this farm and my family."

Unaware of the sorrow and weight of the promise Jacob had made to John, Seth interrupted, "Not anymore—it's mine. Be in the wagon in five minutes." He turned on his boot heels and left them standing looking at each other.

Rebecca concealed her anger toward Seth. Who did he think he was, coming in here and demanding that these boys follow him blindly? He didn't know them. Or what they'd been through since John's death.

She thought about staying home with Andrew and Noah, but she needed to get supplies for the house, and if she stayed behind, who would keep Seth and Jacob from coming to blows? She sighed. "Come along, Jacob. We'll do as he asks today." But as soon as they returned from town, she thought to herself, she'd be having a word with Seth Armstrong.

Chapter Two

The trip into town was frosty to say the least. Seth could feel the anger boiling over from both Rebecca and Jacob. He'd known coming into this job that it would be difficult. But he'd also thought that Rebecca and her boys knew what they were getting into.

As Dove Creek came into view, Seth stopped the wagon. After coming off the farm, the landscape had become flat and dusty. There were a few trees scattered about the town, but it didn't offer the peace and greenery of the Young farm.

"Is this the first time you've been to town?" Rebecca's soft voice drew him like bees to honey.

He nodded. "Yes. It's not quite what I expected. Dove Creek sounds so pretty."

A soft chuckle came from deep in her throat.

"Ma says that all the time," Benjamin said from the back of the wagon.

Seth glanced over his shoulder at the little boy. He was sitting beside Joy and they'd been looking at a picture book most of the way to town. "She's right."

Benjamin nodded as if they'd come to a profound

agreement and then turned his attention back to his sister and the book. Of all the siblings, those two looked most like brother and sister.

Bromley hadn't told him anything about the family, other than their pa had died and that Mr. Russell and Mr. Young had made an agreement before the Pony Express had even been constructed. Seth's orders were to swear in the boys by having them say the Pony Express rider's oath and teach them what would be expected from them as Pony Express riders.

He flipped the reins over the horse's backs and continued down the hill. The sooner they got to town, the sooner they could get home. He didn't like leaving the other two boys at the house any more than Jacob did, but without a bar, the animals were out in the open and needed protection from not only Indians and bandits, but also other wild animals.

Seth felt the restrained movement as Rebecca shifted on the seat beside him. His gaze moved in her direction and caught the profile of Jacob, who sat beside his mother. The boy's jaw was clenched and his eyes directed straight ahead. Rebecca had rested a slender hand on her son's leg in silent comfort.

Returning his attention back to driving, Seth inwardly sighed. He and Jacob would have to sit down and talk about the boy's attitude. Seth was sure there was more to it than just not wanting to leave his brothers behind.

"Would you drop Joy and me off at the general store?" Rebecca asked.

His gaze moved over the town. There was just a dirt road, and plain wooden-faced stores lined the streets. Smoke billowed from the top of each one and the smell of pine teased the air around them. At least they could warm up a bit before they started the long trek back. The church sat on the hill to the right side of them and he could tell by the children playing in the yard that it also served as the town school. Why weren't the smaller Young children in attendance?

Since it really wasn't any of his business, Seth chose to answer Rebecca's question instead of asking one of his own. "We can do that." He directed the horses down Main Street and continued to study the dusty town.

A saloon stood tall at the far end of the settlement. Not that he'd ever go there, but he knew the boys were of an age that they might be tempted. Seth mentally made a note to talk to the boys about such places, after they repeated the oath. As their boss he didn't want them coming to town and getting drunk. Best to nip that sort of behavior in the bud. It would not be allowed.

He pulled the wagon up in front of the general store and hopped down. Seth turned to help Rebecca down but Jacob assisted her, his gentleness evident in the way he held her hand until she got her balance. Clayton had climbed out of the wagon and helped Joy down, as well. Benjamin scrambled over the side.

"Whoa! Where do you think you're going?" Seth asked, moving to block the boy's descent.

Benjamin jerked away from him. "To help Ma."

"Not today. I need every man's help to load lumber and nails."

Benjamin's little chest puffed out. "I get to help?"

"You're one of the men," Seth said, walking back to the front of the wagon.

He grinned as Benjamin whispered, "Did ya hear that, Ma? I'm one of the men."

At least he'd made good points with one of the Young men.

* * *

Rebecca took Joy's small hand within hers and entered the general store. A bell rang out announcing their arrival. She inhaled the onslaught of scents that greeted her. Spices and leather fought the strongest for her attention. Colorful burlap flour bags lined the middle shelf, right at eye level, and she ran a hand over them, her mind zipping along with plans for Joy's next dress. The material proved soft to the touch and Joy loved to spin around, showing off the big flower design.

Joy's hand tightened on hers as if giving a warning and she looked up. The owner of the general store, a mountain of a man, approached them. She glanced down at her daughter, wondering if Joy felt the same sense of unease she herself did around him.

"Hello, Mrs. Young. What can I help you find today?" He kneeled down in front of Joy. "How are you today, Miss Joy."

As was her custom, Joy hid her face in Rebecca's skirt. She mumbled, "Good."

He held out his large hand. On top of his palm rested a lemon drop. "I'm glad to hear that." His big brown eyes looked up at Rebecca. "Cat got your tongue today?"

Rebecca felt her ire rising. The man never did or said anything out of place; but he constantly made her feel uneasy. She handed him her list. "Hello, Mr. Edwards." She patted Joy's back. "Go ahead and take the candy, Joy."

Joy tentatively took the candy and popped it into her mouth. Around the sweet she said, "Thank you."

Mr. Edwards laughed loudly and stood. "See, that wasn't so hard." His gaze moved to the list and he whistled. "I see the men running the Pony Express pay you well."

The list was longer than usual but Rebecca didn't really understand why he assumed that Mr. Russell gave her the money for the items. Still, she didn't correct him. She'd let him think what he wanted.

John had left his family in good financial stability. Thanks to his wisdom with money matters and his inheritance, she and Joy would never have to work a day of their lives. But it wasn't enough to give the boys money to start their lives. John had said the Pony Express would give them the money they needed and open doors for each of them. She prayed it would be so.

Once more Rebecca felt the store owner's brown eyes focused on her. "The church picnic is this Sunday. Would you like me to come out to the farm and escort you and the children to it?"

He'd never been so bold before. Rebecca's hand fluttered to her chest. What would her older boys think of Mr. Edwards calling them *children*? She focused on the best way to reject him. "Thank you, Mr. Edwards, but that won't be necessary."

Something flashed in his eyes before he turned away from her. "You might reconsider—I hear the road bandits are becoming bolder. I'm sure they wouldn't have a problem taking a single woman's wagon and any cash she carried from her and a passel of kids."

Did he think she and the boys were helpless? Heat filled her face and boiled through her blood. If so, was he threatening her?

She took a deep breath to calm herself. Experience had taught her to carefully consider her words before speaking. Her father-in-law, on the other hand, had often said plain talk was easily understood and that was just what the man in front of her would get.

"I don't need a man to take care of me, Mr. Edwards. The good Lord has protected us through many dangerous situations and I have no doubt He will continue to do so. I don't know if you've noticed, but my boys are no longer little boys, but men." As an afterthought she added, "But thanks so very much for your concern and for the invite."

Joy poked her head out. Her sweet young voice broke the awkward silence between the adults. Worry lined her words. "Mr. Armstrong and Jacob will be with us, won't they, Ma?"

She stroked her daughter's silky hair, wishing Joy hadn't broken her silence. "Yes, sweetie. There is nothing to fear."

The bell over the door jingled again. Rebecca turned to see Mrs. Little and her eldest daughter enter the store. She wondered if all the women in the area brought someone with them when they came to visit the general store.

Mr. Edwards paid no heed to the other two women. "Mr. Armstrong?" His eyes bore into Joy's as he waited for an answer. "Who is this Mr. Armstrong?"

Joy tucked her head behind Rebecca's skirt again. Rebecca stepped in front of her daughter, protecting her from questions she had no knowledge how to answer. "I'd like to get our supplies as soon as possible, Mr. Edwards. The men will be back shortly to pick us up."

Mrs. Little waited until the storekeeper went to retrieve the items on Rebecca's list. "So you have a new man working for you?" she asked.

Well, it sure hadn't taken long for that little tidbit to

make its way around the gossip mill. She had learned one thing living in Dove Creek and that was people had very little to occupy their minds, so interest in the people around them bordered on harassment. However, Rebecca couldn't dismiss the older woman as easily as she had Mr. Edwards. She'd been raised to respect her elders, and Mrs. Little could easily have been her mother. "He doesn't exactly work for me."

Mr. Edwards moved closer to them. He continued to add items to the box he'd begun to fill, but seemed to linger ever so near.

"I see." The condemning sound in Mrs. Little's voice had Rebecca quickly explaining.

"Mr. Armstrong works for the Pony Express. He's been hired to be the station keeper by Mr. Bromley." Rebecca moved to the fabric, where she knew Mr. Edwards couldn't pretend to be gathering her supplies, since she hadn't added any sewing notions to her list.

Mrs. Little followed. "Is this a young man, dear?"

Joy followed her mother about the fabric table. She picked up an edge to a pink print and said, "This is pretty."

Rebecca touched the material. "I'm not sure his age, Mrs. Little. I only just met him this morning."

The daughter snorted, drawing a frown from her mother's face. "Catherine, that is very rude."

Catherine was a newly married woman, but still had enough respect for her parent to look contrite and say "Sorry, Ma."

Mrs. Little patted her daughter's hand and turned her attention back to Rebecca. "Is he older than your pa?"

Rebecca hated this line of questioning. She knew

where the older woman was going and didn't like it. "No, but I don't know how much younger than Pa he is."

"Is he married?" Catherine asked, admiring a blue print.

Rebecca frowned. "I don't know that, either."

"Then what do you know?" Mr. Edwards asked.

"I know he showed up this morning, helped us put the fire out that burned our barn and announced that he is the new station keeper. That's all I know." Rebecca waved at the box in Mr. Edwards's hands. "One of the boys will be back shortly to get our supplies. Please add the total to my tab, Mr. Edwards. I will be in on the first of the month to settle up." She turned on her heels. "Come, Joy."

The sound of Joy's shoes tapping against the hard-wood floor assured Rebecca that her daughter had followed her outside the store. Rebecca wasn't sure if she was angry with Mrs. Little and Mr. Edwards, or at herself.

She didn't know a thing about Mr. Armstrong other than what she'd told them. Why had she been so quick to accept him at face value? He'd waltzed in, said he was the station keeper and proceeded to boss them all around.

"Ma! Slow down," Joy called behind her.

Rebecca stopped and looked at her daughter. "I'm sorry, Joy." She waited for the little girl to catch up with her, then continued on.

Her boys were with a virtual stranger. How had she been so careless? Rebecca planned on finding out just who Seth Armstrong was and she planned to do it now.

After all, once Mrs. Little realized that he was a

nice young man, she'd have the whole town in an up-roar. They'd be wondering what went on out at the Young farm. How could Mr. Bromley have put her in this situation? Could she continue with this business arrangement?

Seth handed Mr. Kaziah the remainder of the pay-ment for the wood and nails. He knew it would be pricey, but hadn't expected it to be quite this expen-sive and wondered if the lumberman had overcharged him and the boys. Thankfully, Mr. Russell, one of the Pony Express founders, had supplied him with a hefty budget for turning the farm into a Pony Express sta-tion. Seth had been told by Mr. Bromley that since the buildings were already there, they hadn't done much work to the place and to spend what he needed to on the repairs. He'd have to send a full report to the older gentleman, explaining this added expense.

"Here comes Ma and Joy," Benjamin announced from his perch on the bench of the wagon.

He turned to see the boy's mother heading toward them. Her face was set, but it was her eyes that caught and held his attention. She glowered at him, the blue orbs piercing the distance between them.

"She looks mad." Benjamin turned to face his brother, confirming Seth's earlier thought. "I wonder why."

Philip answered, "Beni, mas don't get mad. Dogs get mad. Mas get angry." A teasing grin touched the young boy's lips but his eyes seemed weary.

Thomas slapped his brother on the back. "Good one, Phil."

"Jacob, Mr. Armstrong. I need to speak to you both,

now please," Rebecca announced as she walked toward the lumberyard.

Seth turned back to Mr. Kaziah. "Thank you for helping us load the wagon. You'll be sending the rest out later today, right?"

The older man nodded and then leaned toward him. In a low, gruff voice he whispered, "I don't envy you. Taking on a passel of kids and that woman. She's a bit of a feisty one." He turned away and hurried back inside the lumber mill before Seth could answer.

What did he mean *take on*? Surely, Mr. Kaziah hadn't assumed that he and Mrs. Young were courting. He shook his head and then turned to face Rebecca. Jacob already stood by her side and was now holding Joy in his arms. The little girl rested her head in the neck of her big brother.

When he was within talking range, Seth asked, "What happened, Mrs. Young?"

She stopped as if his question took her by surprise. "I just realized that I never got a look at that paper you said you carried from Mr. Bromley." She placed both hands on her hips and waited for him to speak.

Seth frowned and tilted his head to the side. "That's important now?" he asked. What had happened at the store to cause her to demand to see it now? Was that a speck of fear he saw in her eyes?

She nodded, brought up her arms and crossed them over her chest. Her eyes bore into Seth's.

Jacob set down Joy. "Everything is all right, Ma. I saw it. Mr. Armstrong is who he says he is." He tilted up the little girl's face and smiled down at her. "Joy, go ask Thomas to help you into the wagon."

The little girl nodded. "All right, Jacob." She turned and ran to her other brothers.

So that was it. Rebecca had been afraid she'd left her children's care in the hands of a dangerous stranger. Even though they were grown men, Rebecca still saw them as her babies. He softened his voice and offered her a smile. "I will be happy to show them to you, too, Mrs. Young, when we get back to the farm." Seth waited for her nod then turned back toward the wagon. Over his shoulder he asked, "Do we need to return to the store to pick up your purchases?" He was aware that she hadn't brought anything with her except Joy and her handbag.

"Yes, please." Her voice sounded tired, almost sad.

Seth turned to look at her. Her shoulders slumped and her eyes had changed from angry to simply drained. Was the excitement of the day turning out to be too much for the woman? One would think she'd be used to busy days with seven boys and a little girl to take care of. He noted that both Benjamin and Joy were seated on the wagon bench. In a loud voice, he said, "We're done here. Let's go."

Without hesitation the young men climbed in on top of the wood.

Jacob walked with his mother, but as soon as he'd helped her up onto the wagon, he shook his head at his brothers. "Off, guys. The horses have enough to pull without adding our weight to their load."

Just as quickly, the young men all climbed back down.

Seth nodded. Jacob was right. "Beni, do you know how to drive a wagon?" he asked.

The youngest Young boy grinned from ear to ear

and nodded. He quickly picked up the reins. "Sure do, Seth. Want me to drive us home?"

Rebecca stood to disembark from the wagon also.

"Mrs. Young, why don't you stay seated?" He indicated with a tilt of his head that Benjamin needed a supervisor sitting beside him. The boy held the reins tightly, waiting for his reply.

She nodded her understanding and returned to her seat.

Seth answered the little boy. "I'd appreciate it if you would drive the wagon, Benjamin. Your brothers and I will follow behind making sure that the wood stays in place."

Seth looked down at his new brown boots. He had a sneaking suspicion that he would soon be wishing he had brought his horse to town before they got back to the farm. In his rush to prove his leadership, he'd decided to drive the wagon to town, never once considering that he'd more than likely end up walking back. *Lesson learned, Armstrong*, he thought as he followed the wagon toward the general store.

Other than the Pony Express horses and the two old mares, Brownie and Snow, Seth realized that the boys didn't have mounts of their own. Once they got back to the farm, he'd remedy that and give the boys each a Pony Express horse to take care of and bond with.

Jacob strolled along beside him. In a low voice he said, "We should have thought ahead and brought more horses."

Seth jerked his head around and looked at the young man. The twinkle in Jacob's eyes attested to the fact that he, too, saw the folly of their earlier disagreement. "Yep, won't let that happen again."

"Nope, I don't reckon we will," Jacob agreed.

A cold breeze stirred the hair on his neck. "I was thinking all you boys need a mount of your own to train with. What do you think?" Seth waited to see if the boy realized that he was being offered respect by his inclusion in the decision.

Jacob nodded. "We all know how to ride, you don't have to worry about that, but I'm a little concerned about the younger boys riding unfamiliar horses. All except Noah, who seems to be very talented with a horse as well as his gun."

Seth nodded and listened as the other boys joked and chatted behind them. "Well, that's one of the first things we'll do, then, as well as we rebuild the barn. I don't like that the animals are out in the open."

"Neither do I."

The wagon stopped in front of the general store. Rebecca turned on the seat. "Jacob, would you go in and get our supplies, please?"

"Yes, ma'am." Jacob stepped up on the boardwalk and entered the store. Rebecca turned back to her younger children.

Two women stood across the street and talked behind their fans, while a couple of well-dressed businessmen stood with their hands in their front pockets and Seth noticed that the sheriff leaned on the post in front of the jail. All eyes seemed to be trained on them.

Seth looked to the other boys. He wondered what the town must think of them all standing behind the wagon like a bunch of stray dogs. In two long strides he stood with the boys. "When we get back to the farm I'd like for you boys to go to the corral and pick out a mount. This is the last time we are leaving town on foot."

Excitement coursed through the boys at his words. The discussion of colors and gender filled the air. He grinned. So far his relationship with the Young family had been tense, but maybe now it would get smoother.

Seth turned back to the wagon in time to see Jacob exit the store. The young man's clenched jaw and burning eyes spoke volumes as to his anger. So whatever had set off Mrs. Young had just happened to Jacob.

His gaze moved to the store, where a big man now stood in the doorway. The man wore a shopkeeper's apron but something about him screamed he wasn't your typical salesman. No, this man meant trouble for the Young family and now with his eyes boring into Seth, Seth knew he meant trouble for him, too.

"Here you go, Ma." Jacob set the box on top of the lumber and then looked to Benjamin. "Lead the way home, Beni." He offered the boy a smile that didn't quite meet his eyes.

When Jacob fell into step beside Seth, Seth asked, "Want to talk about it?"

"Nope."

That was answer enough for Seth. "Fair 'nough, but if you change your mind…" He let the rest hang between them.

Jacob nodded his understanding. Glancing over his shoulder, he saw that his brothers were excited about something and asked, "What has them all in a dither?"

Seth grinned. "Just told them they can choose a horse when we get back."

Again Jacob nodded and then fell silent. His brow furrowed between his eyes. Seth realized that in a day, the Young family's lives had been changed.

He could relate to change; his life had also been

altered in the past few months. On her deathbed, his grandmother had made him promise to marry. He'd ordered a mail-order bride and then his grandmother had died. His mail-order bride, Charlotte, had disappeared. He'd quit his job at the St. Joseph railroad and begun his mission to locate her. He'd been robbed by outlaws and it had been necessary to find a job. Thus the reason he now found himself an employee of the Pony Express as the station keeper on the Young farm. He would work and save his money so he could continue the search for Charlotte because he had to fulfill his promise to his grandmother.

The air seemed to match Jacob's mood and turned frosty. Seth sighed inwardly. He had a job to do and knew he couldn't do it alone, so silently he turned to his Maker. *Lord, this family's emotions are all over the place. Please, help me to bring some kind of peace to them while I'm here.*

Chapter Three

Anger radiated from her oldest son. She'd felt it all the way from town. As she climbed down from the wagon, Rebecca called to him, "Jacob, will you help me carry the supplies into the house?" Rebecca had a feeling she knew what was wrong with Jacob.

"Sure, Ma." Jacob took the box from the wagon and followed her up the porch steps.

"Boys, let's unload this wood," Seth ordered. His strong voice had her other sons hurrying to do his bidding.

Rebecca held the door open for Joy and Jacob. Once inside she said, "Joy, go change into your work clothes." Then she headed for the kitchen, where the real work awaited her.

She allowed Jacob to place the box on the kitchen counter and then asked, "What happened in the general store that upset you so?"

Jacob met her gaze. "Do you have any idea what they are saying about you and Seth?" He lowered his eyes as if realizing for the first time how personal this situation was for his mother.

"I have a good idea of what Mr. Edwards says." She began to unload the box.

Anguish filled the young boy's voice. "It isn't right."

Rebecca sighed. "No, son, it isn't, but I can't stop people from talking." She met his gaze. "We need the money the Pony Express pays to provide a future for you boys and the experience it offers could be useful later in life. You're going to make history, I just know it. Papa John thought so, too."

"Well, we may not be able to stop them from talking but I made the decision to move back into the house on the way home. You and the little kids need a grown man to watch over things." He put both hands on the back of the chair and leaned into it.

She turned her back on him to hide her grin. Her oldest son planned to protect her reputation. Rebecca nodded. "I like that idea. Why don't you take the room across from mine?"

His sigh warmed her heart. Day after day, Jacob proved to be a good man and, God willing, would make a good husband someday, too. "I'll go help unload the wood and then bring my things inside."

Rebecca turned from the spices she'd just taken from the box. "Jacob, wait."

He stopped and looked at her, his eyes sad. Things had changed a lot for the young man in just a matter of hours. Rebecca walked over to him and wrapped her arms around his narrow waist.

Jacob hugged her back. "It will be all right, Ma. Seth seems like a good man. I'm sure he'll set folks straight soon enough."

Rebecca grinned. Once more the boy thought only of her. She pulled away. "I'm sure he will, son." She released him. "You better go on out and help with the lumber."

Jacob patted her shoulder, then turned to do as she said. Rebecca wanted to pull him back, offer him comfort, but Jacob wasn't twelve years old anymore. He'd work through whatever bothered him in his own time. She just prayed he'd share his troubles with her should they get too great for him to carry alone.

Seth looked around the barnyard. The lumber had been delivered from the general store. Each of the boys had chosen a mount to care for and Jacob had shared his concerns about his ma and younger siblings being in the house alone at night.

The horses moved quietly in the corral as the sun sank in the western sky. Weariness hung about Seth's shoulders like a dark thundercloud.

Rebecca stepped out on the front porch. He waved to her and watched as she walked across the yard to join him. A light blue shawl hung over her shoulders, and her hair, which he'd only seen up in a bun, now hung down her back in a braid that reminded him of a golden lasso.

When she got within speaking distance he said, "I'm about to swear the boys in as Pony Express men. Would you like to join us?"

"Yes, John and I had planned on doing that as a family, so I should be there, even if he can't be." Rebecca pulled the edges of her shawl tighter around her shoulders. Sorrow filled her pretty blue eyes. "Is it a ceremony-type swearing in or a simple handshake and 'welcome to the Pony Express'?"

"It's a solemn formality, so, yes, I guess it's a ceremony."

"Would you like to use the house? I could put on the tablecloth we use for special occasions. It's late but shouldn't take but a few minutes."

"No, that won't be necessary. In front of the fireplace will be fine. That way, Benjamin will see how we do things and learn what's ahead for him and perhaps even look forward to it."

Seth had thought about having her come to the bunkhouse, but at her suggestion he decided it might be better to have the boys go to her. Plus, she'd have to bundle up Joy and Beni, so it would be easier on her if he brought the boys to the house. "I'll get the boys and we'll be right in," he offered.

"Thank you." She turned and walked back to the house.

Ten minutes later, they assembled in the living room, Joy propped against Rebecca's legs, her cornsilk doll in her lap. There was an air of expectancy among them, an excitement about the unknown.

Seth cleared his throat. "This is an important day as you boys take your first step into manhood. When a boy can handle responsibility, can be depended on to carry out a job, then he is thought to be a man. I trust that each of you will with honesty and pride uphold your position in the United States Postal Service." He reached to pick up his Bible from the table. "If you young men will step forward we will commence with the swearing in." They walked forward, shyness preventing them from showing how eager and proud they were to be involved in something bigger than themselves.

When they stood in front of him, he paused a moment, his gaze moving from one to the other. "Lift your right hand and repeat after me. 'I—'" he waited until each boy had voiced his name, then continued "'—do hereby swear, before the Great and Living God, that during my engagement, and while I am an employee of Russell, Majors and Waddell, I will, under no circumstances, use profane language, that I will drink no intoxicating liquors, that I will not quarrel or fight with any other employee of the firm, and that in every respect I will conduct myself honestly, be faithful to my duties, and so direct all my acts as to win the confidence of my employers, so help me God.'"

The boys repeated the words with force and pride. Seth glanced at Rebecca and noticed Benjamin standing beside her, holding the same pose as the other boys. He walked over to him. "Benjamin, did you say the oath, also?"

Benjamin nodded his small head, his eyes down.

Rebecca dropped a hand onto the little boy's shoulder and gave it a gentle squeeze. Her eyes begged Seth to let the boy pretend to be a Pony Express rider.

Seth kneeled down in front of him. "Do you understand what you've agreed to?" he asked.

Benjamin bravely met his gaze. "Yes, sir."

Seth nodded. "Well, in that case, go get in line with the other men. You've pledged to be a Pony Express man." He stood and met Rebecca's gaze as the little boy darted around him and went to stand beside Jacob. Gratitude and moisture filled her eyes.

For a moment, Seth understood her burden. She had a houseful of children to care for and she did it on her own. His respect for her inched up a degree. Seth nodded at her then returned his attention to the young men now fully in his charge.

Seth picked up the stack of Bibles that he'd carried with him to the farm, now a full-fledged Pony Express station. He handed one to each of them. "You are now employees of the Pony Express. Jacob, I have decided that you will be the station's stock tender. Your job is to take care of all the horses and make sure that a horse is ready to ride at all times. Andrew, Clayton, Thomas, Philip and Noah, you will all be riders. Your job is to make sure that the mail goes through." Each young man nodded in turn.

Benjamin studied the tip of his brown boots. Seth knew the boy felt left out. He ran his small hand over the engraving on the front of his new Bible.

Seth fought the grin that threatened to break across his face. He steeled himself and then said, "Benjamin, you are too young to be a Pony Express rider, so I am making you the stock tender's assistant. It will be your job to help Jacob take care of the horses and barn. Whatever Jacob or I ask you to do, you will do it."

A smile split Benjamin's lips. "I'll be the best stock tender's 'sistant that anyone has ever met."

Seth wasn't sure there were other stock tender assistants in the Pony Express, but he nodded just the same. "I'm sure you will." He motioned for everyone to sit down, then pulled up a stool for himself and faced them. "I'm not sure what Mr. Bromley told you about your jobs, but let me assure you they are dangerous. You will face bad weather, robbers, outlaws and Indians. None of these should be taken lightly. You'll have to think on your feet, learn to outrun, outsmart, and you need to trust your gut. The main point is, stay alive but get the mail through. Do you have any questions?" Seth immediately looked to Benjamin, but the boy remained silent along with his brothers. "Since there are no questions, let me explain to you exactly what my job entails. I am called a station keeper for a home station—that's what the farm is called. I make sure that you men are ready to ride. That the station runs smoothly and that the horses are tended well. I also make sure that during your stay at the home station you aren't idle. You will follow my orders. If I say build a fence, you build a fence. If I say ride on out, you ride on out. Is that understood?"

"What about Ma?" Benjamin asked.

Seth looked at the boy. "What about your mother?"

"Does she have to take orders, too?" His eyes challenged Seth, something Seth hadn't expected. He smiled at the boy.

"No, your mother isn't a Pony Express employee."

"Oh."

Clayton asked, "What if Ma says to chop wood and you say to ride out, then what?"

"You ride out," Seth answered, aware they walked a tight line here. "But if you aren't working for me and your Ma says chop wood, you best chop wood."

Rebecca spoke for the first time since they'd all arrived in her living room. "Mr. Armstrong, I can understand the boys' confusion." She pushed a strand of hair behind her ear. "They simply want to know who has the most authority, you or me?"

Seth knew that. How many other station managers had to answer questions like these? He doubted any of them did. "It's really very simple. They work for me.

Each boy will have time off and that is when they can do whatever you need or want them to."

Her eyes flashed but she simply nodded. He noted her growing quietness as he outlined the job. First the barn had to be rebuilt and second they'd need to work on their riding skills.

Did she disagree with him on what her sons would be doing? Or did she just not like the way he'd come in and replaced her deceased husband? Confrontation wasn't his strong suit when it came to women, but Seth had known from the start that he and Rebecca Young must have a heart-to-heart discussion about what might and would happen to her farm and children.

Rebecca finished making Jacob's bed then headed to the living room to wait for Seth and Jacob to return to the house. Joy and Benjamin were both tucked in for the night and the house seemed very quiet. Normally she relished this time, but tonight the stillness seemed to grate on her frayed nerves.

Earlier, as the boys had filed out to return to the bunkhouse, Seth had stood beside her and quietly asked if he could speak to her in private. She'd agreed. Not because he'd asked for the meeting, but because there were things she needed to say to him.

She'd have to be both blunt and gentle in her words to the man. Rebecca knew without him having to say so that he wasn't going to agree with her thoughts, but she had to speak them.

Would he fire the boys? Tell Mr. Bromley that the Young farm wouldn't make a good home station after all? What would she do if he did that? What would become of her boys?

If they worked for the Pony Express, each one of them could potentially earn enough to buy a parcel of land, or go to a college back east. They would have a foot up to a better life. John had left her well-off, financially, but the boys would need to earn their own way.

But at what cost? Their lives?

Chapter Four

Rebecca heard them come through the door and stopped pacing. Jacob carried a box with his things in it. Cold air whipped about the room as Seth closed the door behind them. He, too, carried a box of Jacob's things.

"I'll take these to Jacob's room and then be back for our talk," he told her as he passed.

She had to get her thoughts together. How should she approach her concerns with him? Calmly and quietly. That was the way she always approached John—Seth would be no different.

He reentered the room alone. Rebecca sat down on the couch and motioned for him to take the chair across from her. She decided that since he asked to speak to her, she'd let him go first.

Seth sat down but leaned forward on the edge of the seat, placing his brown hat on his knee. "Mrs. Young, I get the impression that you don't care for the way I'm running things around here." He lifted his right eyebrow as if to accent his statement.

Rebecca chose her words carefully. "I have my concerns. You've been here one day and I can't say what you are doing is good or bad."

"But?"

She took a deep breath. "But I didn't think my two youngest boys would be working with the Pony Express."

He sat back. "So you are objecting to me swearing Noah and Benjamin in as employees of the Pony Express?"

"Yes." She knitted her fingers together and laid them in her lap. "Well, no." She shrugged to hide her confusion. "I know you included Beni so he could feel important. I'm grateful." To her annoyance she heard herself start to stammer. She forced her voice to steady and reined in her thoughts. "I just feel Noah is too young and small to be a rider and Beni shouldn't be burdened with such a heavy workload." She searched his eyes, looking for signs of anger.

Seth offered her a grin. "Benjamin is too young to ride. That's why I made him Jacob's assistant. The boy wants to prove himself and who would be a better teacher than his oldest brother?"

Rebecca recognized a spark of amusement in his gaze and relaxed a little. "Yes, Beni wants to do what his big brothers do."

"As for Noah, Jacob seems to think Noah is the best horseman on the farm and stated that he is good with his gun. Both are important skills I need in riders."

She clutched her hands tightly in her lap. "But he's twelve and I've only had him a few months. I don't know if he's ready for this responsibility." Rebecca searched Seth's face. Did he understand what she was saying?

Seth leaned forward again. "What do you mean you've only had him a few months?" His eyes searched hers, looking for what she could only assume was both confusion and truth.

"Noah is adopted, Mr. Armstrong. All of the boys are. I thought Mr. Bromley would have told you that." From the look on his face it was obvious Seth hadn't known.

"No, he didn't," Seth said. "I thought it odd that none of them look like you or each other. Well—" his voice broke in midsentence "—except Joy, she looks like you." He offered her a smile.

Rebecca couldn't help but smile. "Joy is my daughter by birth. She is the only child John and I have. But that doesn't change the fact that I love the boys just as much as I do Joy and I don't want to see them get hurt...or die."

Seth met her gaze and held it. Sincerity rang through his voice as he vowed, "I promise as long as I am the station keeper here, I will do everything in my power to keep the boys safe and alive. Safety is the reason I will teach them how to ride, shoot and avoid trouble while out on the trail."

She understood that the boys would be in danger and that she didn't consider them to really be men. The orphanage had called them men at the age of twelve, the same age as Noah, but to her they were still her little boys.

"I know you are still concerned and I can't blame you. Being a Pony Express employee is dangerous. The only thing I can do is teach them how to survive and pray that God keeps them safe. It's either that or I fire them all and have Mr. Bromley send me a new set of men." He shook his head. "I really don't want to do that, Mrs. Young. I truly believe these young men have what it takes to be riders. I'll leave that decision up to you."

Rebecca didn't want him to fire the boys. She'd promised John that she wouldn't interfere when this time came. John had wanted his sons to become honorable, strong individuals who could take care of themselves and their families, should the Lord one day bless them with such. He firmly believed the Pony Express would provide the training that life had cheated these boys out of. "No, they would never forgive me if I asked you to fire them." She didn't tell him that the money the boys made would provide for their future well-being, establishing them in whatever careers they chose.

He exhaled as if he'd been holding his breath. "Thank you. I know this is hard for you and I want to make it easier on both of us. How about we have a nightly meeting? I can fill you in on what I'm doing with the boys in regard to their duties as Pony Express riders and you can tell me if you need them to assist you with something specific around the farm."

It was a reasonable request and far more than some men would have offered her if they had been in Seth's position. Rebecca nodded. "That would be nice, thank you."

They sat still for several moments. The sound of boots retreating down the hallway alerted Rebecca that one or more of her children had listened in on their conversation. A grin crossed Seth's lips. He'd heard it, too.

"Mr. Armstrong, I'd like to suggest that we have our conversations out on the porch if the weather permits. I'm sure there will be times when we don't want others hearing your reports." Rebecca unclasped her hands and then stood.

"That sounds like a good idea to me. If the boys think you need a chaperone, they can watch us through the window of the bunkhouse." He picked up his hat from his knee and stood also. He pulled a piece of paper from his hip pocket and handed it to her.

Rebecca looked down at the paper. "What's this?"

"The letter from Mr. Bromley. I should have shared it with you sooner. You can return it to me in the morning." Seth walked to the door and left.

She sank down onto the couch. Was she doing the right thing letting the boys continue working for the Pony Express? Sure, they each would need the money they'd make, but... Rebecca warred with her conscience—did they need the money so badly that she'd allow them to put their lives in danger? Wasn't her job as the adult and their mother to protect them until they were old enough to know what they were doing?

Not wanting to answer that question, Rebecca pressed on with her thoughts as she looked down at the letter. Without the money, the older boys would have to leave home and seek out work. Her family would swiftly break up.

So soon after losing John, Rebecca knew she wouldn't be able to cope with losing any of the boys. And there was always the likelihood that they'd find other work, maybe even more dangerous work. She shuddered at that thought.

She couldn't allow that to happen to her precious boys. No, to keep her family together Rebecca would allow the boys to continue working for the Pony Express.

* * *

Seth looked up at the framework of the barn. He stood amazed at how quickly he and the boys had gotten the structure up. Sawdust floated in the sun's rays and the pleasant smell of pine mingled with their sweat and filled the air around him.

He placed a hand on the pole closest to him and gave a shove. It didn't budge. Solid and stable. His smile broadened in approval. They'd worked hard and accomplished a lot in one morning. Could be that this little group of misfits would accomplish much more than he had hoped for. But one thing had been proven to him as they worked. The boys needed a firm hand to stay at the job; they worked as long as you kept your eye on them, but fun was uppermost in their minds.

His gaze moved to the boys now washing up for lunch. It wasn't hot outside, but all of them had cast off their coats while they worked. Even little Benjamin had worked hard alongside his brothers.

Seth had been aware of Rebecca watching them all morning. She'd frowned when he'd yelled at Philip for playing around instead of doing his work. It wasn't hard to figure out that the boys worked on their own time schedule. Seth wondered how long their adoptive father had been dead. Had he allowed them to play when they were supposed to do chores?

A good while later, Seth left the bunkhouse feeling refreshed. Thanks to his time alone with the Lord, he now had more direction. Clayton carried a sandwich and a glass of milk out to him. The rest of the boys followed.

"Ma said you need to eat something." The young man handed him the sandwich and milk.

He grinned his thanks and took a big bite. Thick ham and cheese coated his taste buds. The butter-flavored bread that surrounded them tasted wonderful. His stomach growled its appreciation. Seth swallowed. "Let's head to the corral." He waved the sandwich.

Feeling as if someone was watching them, Seth turned to the house and found Rebecca standing in the doorway. He waved to her and once more smiled his thanks before turning back to the corral, where the boys waited.

"I thought we were going to work on the barn," Jacob said as Seth approached.

"We are, but first I wanted to spend some time with the horses." He looked out at the ten horses. "Have you each chosen the horse you want to train with?" He knew they had but wanted to make sure that one of them hadn't changed his mind.

The six older boys nodded. Benjamin climbed up on the fence. He looked longingly out at the horses.

"Benjamin?"

The eight-year-old turned to look at him. "Yes, sir?"

"Sir?" Seth allowed a surprised, questioning note to enter his voice.

Benjamin nodded.

"Benjamin, looks like you and I need to get a few things straight." Seth walked over and leaned against the fence beside the little boy. "The rest of you, go find some rope and then round up your horses."

The boys pushed and shoved as they went in search of rope. Jacob and Andrew followed at a slower pace, shaking their heads. When they were all out of earshot, Seth told Benjamin, "First, let's get this straight. I'm not sir, I'm Seth."

The boy nodded still, looking sad. Seth reached over and tousled his hair.

"Good. Now, how come you didn't pick a horse?"

Benjamin sighed and climbed a rung higher on the fence, watching the boys exit the stable and enter the corral. "I'm not going to be a rider. I heard you tell Ma last night."

Seth rubbed his chin. So it had been Benjamin eavesdropping the night before. "Yes, I did say that, but I think you should have a mount." He watched closely as Jacob returned and quietly singled out a rum-colored pinto, gently rubbing its mane, talking in a low voice. Thomas and Philip followed suit. For all their pushing and shoving, once they were within the corral, they became serious.

"You do?" Hope filled the little boy's voice.

"Yep, seems to me you'll need one if we all ride into town or if I need you to go out to the back pasture and get one of the other boys. There are all kinds of reasons a boy needs a horse." Seth lifted a brow in question, holding the boy's gaze. "Don't you think so?"

Benjamin nodded. His hair flopped down into his eyes. "Can I pick out one now?" he asked, already preparing to climb down from the fence.

"Yes, but go see if one of the older boys will help you find some rope."

"Yippee!" Benjamin ran to the barn, where Andrew and Noah stood cutting lengths of rope.

Each boy returned to the corral and began trying to catch the horses. They weren't all bad at roping. Jacob, Andrew and Noah were the best and as soon as each caught their own horse, they helped the four brothers. Seth coached from the sidelines.

"I want a horse, too, Ma." Joy's young voice sounded behind him.

He turned to face the little girl and Rebecca. Seth finished the milk in his glass and handed it to Rebecca.

"You don't need a horse, Joy," she answered her daughter, taking his glass but looking down at her little girl.

"Thanks for lunch," Seth said, even though he could tell her attention wasn't on him.

"What if I need to go get one of them out of the pasture? I'll need a horse then," Joy argued. Her lip protruded as she looked up at her mother.

Seth was no child expert but he could read the defiance on the cute little face. Her blue-green eyes demanded answers. He had to turn his head to hide his grin, but just as quickly he returned his attention to them. What would Rebecca's argument be with the child?

She shook her pretty head. "You won't be going to the pasture to get the boys. Now stop sassing." Rebecca looked back to Seth. "Are you sure it's wise to give Benjamin one of the horses?" She tugged her shawl tighter around her shoulders.

"I wouldn't do it if I didn't think so," Seth answered. "He needs to learn to ride just like the others." He called to the young men behind him, "Boys, bring the horses out here."

"Come along, Joy. We need to get back to the house and let the men work." Rebecca's voice seemed to hold frost. She took the little girl's hand and headed back to the house.

Seth sighed. He'd warned her that the boys would all have horses. Clayton opened the gate to the corral and waited until all his brothers had passed through before closing it again.

The animals tossed their heads in obvious dislike of the ropes. "Since we lost all our tack in the fire, we'll need to buy new harnesses and saddles next time we're in town," Seth told them as he walked about, inspecting each horse.

"Until then, I suppose we can use my horse's saddle and bridle. Wait here and get to know your horse." Seth walked back to the bunkhouse and retrieved his bridle and saddle.

"Since we only have one, you will have to take turns. Starting with the oldest. The rest of you will walk about the farm with your horse. Talk to it, sing to it, do whatever it takes for it to learn the sound of your voice." Seth carried the bridle and saddle over to Jacob.

Jacob grinned. "Seth, I've been saddling a horse since I was twelve."

"Not this horse," Seth pointed out. "I want you to saddle and ride him for about thirty minutes and then come back." He turned to address all the boys. "These horses will become your best friends. It is up to each of you to take care of these animals as if they were family. They will most likely save your life out there, so give them the respect they deserve."

Each of the boys nodded and petted their horse.

Seth grinned. "Now, I know this is going to sound silly, but if you have a girl horse, talk to her like she's your sweetheart. If you have a boy, talk to him as if he were your best friend. Animals can sense when they are liked and respected."

Benjamin kneeled down and looked under his horse. When he turned to Seth he announced, "I have a boy.

Good thing, too, 'cause I don't know how to talk to a sweetheart."

Laughter and good-natured bantering followed.

"Don't worry, little brother. You'll learn soon enough." Noah grinned across at Benjamin as if he already knew how to talk to a sweetheart. This created more teasing and joking among them all.

Seth shook his head and laughed with them. Working with the boys would be anything but boring. He felt, more than saw, Rebecca watching from the porch. Tonight he'd have to tell her more about how he planned to train with the boys. He hoped that would put her mind at ease. But from the way she paced on the porch, he somehow doubted it would.

Chapter Five

Rebecca tucked her daughter into bed.

"Ma, I want a horse, too."

She put Joy's favorite doll under her arm, then smoothed the quilt over them both. "I know, dear. I heard you asking the Lord to change my mind."

A big smile split the little girl's mouth and brightened her eyes. "Did He?"

Rebecca chuckled. "No, He did not." She picked up her daughter's dress and hung it in the closet. "He hasn't said a word to me about it, but if the good Lord sees fit to tell me to change my mind, I will. Until then, you put the thought out of your head and get some sleep." She leaned over and kissed Joy's forehead.

"I love you, Ma." Joy's soft whisper touched Rebecca deeply.

"I love you, too, my Joy." Rebecca blew out the candle and carried it from the room.

Benjamin's room was beside his sister's. Rebecca opened the door a crack. "All tucked in, Benjamin?" she asked. A soft snore was her only answer. Rebecca tiptoed into his room and looked down at him. His hair fell over his small forehead. He was just a little boy.

Memories of earlier in the day caused her heart to quicken in her chest. She'd about swallowed her tongue when she'd seen him leading the big black gelding about the yard. Benjamin looked so much smaller than the other boys and his horse appeared twice as big.

She brushed the hair off his forehead and planted a soft kiss in its place. A smile twitched at his lips. Rebecca stood. Seth worked the little boy too hard—she'd have a word with him tonight. Rebecca blew the candle out beside Benjamin's bed and left the room.

Jacob leaned against the wall outside Benjamin's bedroom. "How's the little guy doing?"

Rebecca smiled at her oldest son. "He's plum tuckered out."

Pride filled his voice as he answered, "He put in a full day's work."

"I know. I'm going to have a word with Mr. Armstrong about pushing him too hard. He's just a little boy." Rebecca set both of the candles on the table in the hall.

"Ma, Seth didn't drive Beni to work hard. The little guy is trying to prove that he can do anything us older boys can do." Jacob pushed away from the wall. "Seth seems like a good man. I don't think he'd do anything to harm Beni or any of the boys."

Rebecca studied Jacob. "You like him?" she asked, a little surprised. So far, Jacob seemed to buck every decision or action the station keeper suggested, but here he stood now, defending him.

Jacob looked down at his boots. "He's not Papa John

but unless I've read him wrong, he is a good man." He turned to enter his room. "'Night, Ma."

"Good night, Jacob."

Rebecca walked down the hall and into the living room. Seth Armstrong might be a good man but she still thought he might be a bit too hard on the younger boys. After all, the man wasn't a parent, had never dealt with little legs that hurt in the night from cramps or muscle spasms.

She'd seen how he'd pushed Noah hard all day while they worked on the barn. Noah wasn't like the other boys. Building things and working with wood wasn't something he enjoyed. Now, give the boy a rifle or a fishing pole and he'd do anything you asked with either of them and he'd do it joyfully. She'd have to explain that to Seth so he'd ease up on the boy. After all, it seemed as if that should be something he'd want to know.

She walked to the kitchen and set the coffeepot onto the back warmer. Rebecca inhaled the hearty aroma and decided one more cup wouldn't hurt her.

Seth's voice stilled her hand as she poured hot liquid into her favorite mug. "I'd like a cup of that, if you have plenty."

Rebecca turned and handed him her mug. "Here you go." Then she reached for another cup.

"You might want to grab your coat—it's getting colder and colder out there," Seth said, leading the way to the front porch.

Rebecca grabbed her blue cloak off the hook by the front door and followed him. He walked to the porch swing and sat down.

"I hope you don't mind sharing the swing. I'm a mite tired." Seth yawned as if to prove his point.

Rebecca eased down beside him. "Not at all." Her gaze moved out to the horse corral. Several horses could be seen, their hooves clopping against the hard ground. She noticed that one of the boys stood by the fence, but she couldn't make out which of her sons it was.

As if he could read her mind, Seth offered, "That's Andrew—he pulled first watch."

She turned to look at him. "What do you mean 'pulled first watch'?"

"Until the barn is finished, the boys have to take turns keeping watch over the animals. Indians or bandits could attempt to steal them." He took a cautious sip of his coffee.

Rebecca frowned. "Why aren't you guarding them? You are the station keeper after all." She heard the accusation in her voice and flinched inwardly.

As expected, he came back with a bit of harshness of his own. "Because I've assigned Andrew to do it."

"But he's just a boy." Rebecca wished she could take the spoken thought back as soon as it hit the night air.

His voice softened. "No, he's a man." Seth blew into his cup to cool the coffee.

Rebecca didn't see him that way. She still remembered the day she and John had brought Andrew home with them. He was twelve and scared. Andrew had clung to John and didn't want to let him go, even though it was way past bedtime. Andrew had reminded her so much of her brother, Mark, that she'd begged John to sleep in the little boy's room. John had, leaving her to dwell on the past and her brother's fear and eventual death.

It was Mark's death from exposure to the weather when he'd been forced to leave the orphanage at the age of twelve that had prompted Rebecca and John to adopt the boys on their twelfth birthdays. Rebecca wanted to save as many of the boys as she could.

"Rebecca, you are going to have to let them grow up," Seth said quietly.

It was the first time he'd used her Christian name and she enjoyed the way it sounded. Rebecca looked at him. The light from the moon shone across his face. His eyes held hers. There was no anger in their depths and for that she was thankful.

"You don't know them like I do. They all have pasts, pasts that you will never understand," Rebecca told him.

Seth nodded. His eyes searched out Andrew as he said, "You are right there. But I do know he's willing to protect you from all harm and that's what he's doing right now. He's being a man and he's protecting what he believes is his to protect."

Rebecca turned her attention to the corral also. Was Andrew really protecting her and not just the horses? "I still don't know why he has to take the first watch."

"He asked for it," Seth answered.

"Why?" Rebecca turned her attention back to the station keeper.

Seth laughed. "He said he's less likely to fall asleep now than later in the night or early in the morning. Made sense to me, so I agreed."

"So all the boys have a time to watch?" she asked, not happy with the idea.

"Yep, even Benjamin."

Did his shoulders just straighten? Was he anticipating her negative reaction? Well, she wasn't about to disappoint him. "I won't have Benjamin sitting out there in the cold alone while the rest of us sleep." She turned on the seat to face him. "I can't believe even you would do that to an eight-year-old boy."

"Well, that's nice to know. And I didn't say the boy would be alone." Seth pushed up from the seat and went to stand by the porch rail.

Rebecca felt heat fill her cheeks. She'd misjudged him. "Oh, good. I'm glad you are going to be with him."

"I didn't say that, either." Seth watched her over the top of his cup.

"Then who will be with him?" Rebecca was beginning to feel exasperated with him.

"Jacob. They are taking the last hour of the morning," Seth answered. "Before you ask, I'm taking the midnight shift with Noah. If danger strikes, it will probably be then."

So he would be with Noah. Rebecca had to admit that knowing this made her feel a little better. "Look, I don't mean to be a pain, Mr. Armstrong, but these are my children. I have a right to know that they are safe. Or at least as safe as you can make them."

He nodded. "I agree you do have that right. But you have to trust me to keep them as safe as I possibly can."

Did she trust him? No, why should she? Rebecca told herself she didn't really know the man at all. Still, Mr. Bromley trusted him, so what other choice did she have? She'd have to try to trust Seth Armstrong to watch after her boys. How did a mother release that kind of trust to a stranger? She reminded herself that to keep her family together, she'd have to try.

Seth watched the emotions war across her delicate features. He knew what he asked wasn't easy for her. She'd irritated him as well as made him feel empathy for her all in the past few minutes.

He tossed the remainder of his coffee off the porch. "Look, Rebecca. Over the next few days the boys and I are going to finish the barn and work with the horses—"

"That's another thing," she interrupted. "I don't think Benjamin is old enough to work with the horses."

Exasperation filled him. Why couldn't she just accept that he knew what he was doing? "Benjamin is eight years old. By the time I was six, I was riding and caring for my own horse. He's more than old enough."

Rebecca studied his face. "Why do you want him to ride a horse?" Suspicion filled her voice. "He's too small and you know it. Why, his feet barely reach the stirrups."

"Because he may need to do so. Being a Pony Express station makes this farm vulnerable to all kinds of enemies. Benjamin is small, he can ride fast and get help should we need it." Seth took off his hat and rested it on the railing.

"It's dangerous."

He nodded. "Yes, you're right, it is. But it's also why we train them the proper way to act and treat horses. If you don't trust me, then at least trust Jacob. He's in charge of Benjamin's learning." Seth had seen how she relied on her oldest son. The boy seemed dependable and for that Seth was grateful.

"All right, but please don't put them in unnecessary danger." Rebecca stood and pulled her shawl closer around her slender body.

Seth handed her his coffee mug. "I better get some shut-eye. Tomorrow is going to be a long day." He paused to look at her. "Do you need anything from town?"

"I don't believe so. Why?" She stopped in front of the closed door.

Seth hurried to help her open it. "We need saddles and bridles for the horses. The ones we had burned in the fire."

She turned to face him. "Do you need me to go with you?"

Her eyes searched his face.

"No. I just figured if you needed anything you might like to go." Seth enjoyed the way her eyes sparkled in the evening light. The moon hung in such a way as to shine in her eyes.

"I see. I don't believe I need anything but if I change my mind I'll let you know over breakfast." Rebecca moved into the house. "Thank you for keeping me informed." She smiled a tired grin and then shut the wooden door behind her.

She really was a beautiful woman. Her weary grin had caused his heart to do a little dance. For the first time, he had noticed twin dimples in her cheeks. He'd always been a sucker for dimples. Seth shook his head to clear it of those unwanted thoughts and feelings. He had a fiancée out there somewhere and had no room for such thoughts.

He walked to where Andrew sat on a stump keeping watch over the horses. His eyes looked heavenward.

"Looks like we might get some cold weather soon," Andrew said in way of greeting.

Seth followed his line of vision. The moon now played hide-and-seek with the dark clouds. A soft ring circled the moon.

"Rain or snow?" he asked.

"Probably rain," Andrew answered, meeting Seth's gaze. "I don't think it is cold enough for snow, but I could be wrong." The young man shrugged.

A nippy breeze lifted the hair on Seth's neck. "I believe you are right, but it for sure is getting colder."

Andrew pulled up his collar. "Yep."

Seth leaned against the fence rail facing the horses. The night's silence offered comfort. The horses snorted from time to time and their feet shuffled against the hard-packed dirt. If he closed his eyes he could almost smell their musky scents.

"It's peaceful out here," Andrew said. He'd moved to stand beside Seth at the railing. He laid his rifle on the top bar and sighed. "Did Ma give you a hard time about Beni taking a watch?" he asked.

"Not after she learned that Jacob would be with him," Seth answered truthfully. He'd expected her to put up a better argument. He glanced in Andrew's direction.

Andrew seemed ever watchful. "That's good. Ma's very protective of Beni, and now Noah."

"How long has Noah been on the farm?" Seth asked, deliberately focusing his attention on the horses.

Andrew heaved a sigh. "About three months, give or take a day. Beni has been here since he was three. The rest of us arrived shortly after our twelfth birthdays."

Seth could understand Rebecca's concern. Beni

probably still seemed like a baby to her. Noah hadn't been here long and with the changes going on at the farm and in his life, Rebecca must be worried about his reactions to those changes.

"Are you an orphan, too?" Andrew stared at Seth.

"I guess that depends on how you look at it. I didn't grow up in an orphanage but I no longer have any family left." He held the boy's gaze, waiting for the next question that was sure to follow.

It didn't take long for Andrew. He asked, "Is that why you signed on with the Pony Express?"

"No, I signed on because I'd been robbed by bandits and needed the money." Seth didn't add that he'd been searching for his mail-order bride when he was attacked.

"What was that like?" Andrew picked up his gun and cradled it in his arms. Whether he was angling for company on his watch or was simply curious, Seth couldn't tell, but decided to answer him honestly.

"Well, I was traveling alone and had decided to bed down in a small grove of trees just outside of town. Normally, my horse lets me know if anyone is around, but on this night, the horse didn't alert me. Or if he did, I simply didn't hear him. Anyway, the next thing I knew three men surrounded me with guns."

"Did you try to fight them?" Andrew propped his leg on the fence and turned from looking at the horses. His face filled with excitement. Seth made a note of his lack of attention to what might be happening around them.

"No, I chose to live instead."

Andrew sighed in disappointment. "So you just gave

them your money." He turned away and studied the house.

"Yes, I gave them my money and all my supplies, too."

"Why didn't you fight them?" Andrew faced him once more. The accusation in his voice caused Seth to pause. It seemed there was more to the question than just curiosity.

"Andrew, there is a time to fight and a time to surrender. Knowing the difference can mean life or death."

"But they took all your money and supplies."

Seth nodded. "Yes, but they left me with my life. There is no shame in not fighting when the odds are against you." He laid a hand on the young man's shoulder. It was obvious that Andrew had either backed down from a fight or had fought and lost.

"Maybe, but I will never let a man take what is mine away." Andrew straightened his shoulders and stepped away from Seth.

It was obvious that the boy was hurting, but Seth didn't think now was the time to confront that hurt. He decided to pray about it instead. "Well, I think I'll turn in now. Do you need me to spot you for a few minutes? Or will you be all right until Philip relieves you?"

Andrew's shoulders drooped. "I'll be all right. I don't have much longer to wait now."

"Good night." Seth walked away, leaving the young man to his guard duty and his own thoughts. Each boy had a story to tell. He couldn't help but wonder about Andrew's.

In his room, Seth kneeled down beside his bed and prayed. "Lord, please help me as I work with these young men. I know Andrew is hurting. Please help him to overcome his past and look toward a bright new future. And, Lord, if I can be of service to You or him, please show me how. Amen." He pulled himself up on the side of the bed.

Working on the Young farm could possibly be more challenging than he'd expected. Seth couldn't deny that he found Rebecca Young attractive and that made him cautious to even explore thoughts on the matter. How could a man, in such a short time, feel so strong a connection to another person? He could almost guess her next words and he read the expressions on her face and in her eyes so easily. Yet, when it came to the workings of her mind, she seemed to guard herself carefully. And that made him want to keep himself separated from Rebecca and the rest of her family, but, on the other hand, he also felt as if he wanted to jump in with both feet and help them in any way he could. But in doing so, would he regret the outcome?

Chapter Six

Rebecca peered out the window, tongue-tied in surprise as the stage sloshed through the rain puddles in her front yard. What on earth was it doing here? The stage never passed this way. She stepped out onto the front porch.

Seth dashed from the bunkhouse, trying to avoid the tracks made from the wheels. He pulled off his hat and arched a brow at her as he bounded up onto the porch. "I didn't think the stage stopped here," he said in way of greeting.

"It doesn't," Rebecca answered, watching as the stage came to a complete stop.

The driver jumped from his seat up top. Water and mud splashed around his already soaked pant legs as he hurried to open the door in the pouring rain.

Rebecca watched as a tall, thin, mustached man with graying hair descended the coach steps. He carried a briefcase and his boots shone like oiled lanterns. Rebecca almost cringed as he stepped from the last rung directly into the mud. Mr. James Bromley, one of the

Pony Express division superintendents, had graced them with his presence.

She whispered to Seth, "Were you expecting him today?"

"No, I was not," he said with quiet emphasis. "I can only assume he's here to check on my progress with the boys."

Mr. Bromley stepped up onto the porch. "Mrs. Young, Seth."

Seth stepped forward and shook the older man's hand. "Mr. Bromley, you chose a dreary day to come for a visit."

The other man laughed. "It's pleasant here. In other places along the route they're still getting snow."

Rebecca stepped forward. "Please, come inside out of the rain. I've made a fresh pot of coffee and you can conduct your business out of the weather." She held the door open.

"Thank you, Mrs. Young, that would be most appreciated." Mr. Bromley wiped his feet on the rag rug she'd placed in front of the door and then swept past her. The smell of cigar smoke wafted from him to her sensitive nose.

Seth took the door and held it open for her. He offered an encouraging grin. She passed him in the doorway and immediately noted that Mr. Bromley had made himself at home.

Joy sat on the floor beside the window playing with blocks the boys had given her from the scraps they'd used in rebuilding the barn. She looked up in surprise to find a stranger sitting on her mother's couch.

"Joy, come with me to the kitchen. We'll leave the men to discuss their business in private." Rebecca didn't wait for the little girl to respond but turned toward her comfortable kitchen. The hearty scent of fresh-brewed coffee filled the sweet-smelling kitchen.

When they were out of earshot the men, Joy asked, "Ma, can we give Seth some of the cookies we made?"

The two of them had spent the morning making sugar cookies. "I'm sure he would like that. Why don't you get a plate and put some on it. Make sure the plate isn't chipped. We want to present our best to Mr. Bromley, don't we?"

"Yes, Ma." Joy hurried to the cupboard and reached for one of the special plates used for company. "I hope he likes them."

"Who? Mr. Bromley?" Rebecca asked. She suspected her daughter was talking about Seth. The little girl followed him around like a puppy. Thankfully, he didn't seem to mind.

"Yes, but also Seth." The little girl moved to the big platter of cookies that sat on the counter and picked out several bigger ones. "I think these are the prettiest, don't you?" she asked.

Rebecca glanced over her shoulder and looked at the cookies. "They sure are," she agreed.

The smile that graced her daughter's sweet face pushed away some of the concern Rebecca felt at Mr. Bromley's arrival. She prayed he'd approve of Seth's methods and progress with the boys. She told herself it had nothing to do with liking Seth, it had to do with the boys having to adjust to a new station keeper, if Mr. Bromley didn't approve of Seth and his methods.

A few minutes later, she and Joy were back in the sitting room passing out coffee and cookies. Seth smiled his thanks. He appeared relaxed so Rebecca assumed all had gone well in the men's discussion.

"I hope you like sugar cookies, Mr. Bromley," Rebecca said as she handed him his cup.

He selected a cookie from the plate Joy held out to him and smiled. "As a matter of fact, I do." Mr. Bromley took a bite, closed his eyes and sighed.

Joy smiled at Seth. "I made them. Do you like them, too, Seth?" she asked.

Seth met Rebecca's gaze over the little girl's head. He took a bite of the cookie and chewed slowly. A teasing glint entered his eyes as he asked Joy, "Did you dip your finger in the batter?"

Joy shook her head. "No. Ma says that's yucky and not to do it."

Seth laughed. "Well, these are the sweetest and best cookies I've ever tasted."

"Mrs. Young, have you considered selling your coffee and cookies?" Mr. Bromley asked in a serious voice.

She set down the coffee tray and frowned. "No. Besides, who would I sell them to?" Rebecca doubted she could sell them at the general store and she didn't want to deal with Mr. Edwards to try.

He sat forward. "I'm glad you asked. Part of the reason I'm here today is to tell you that we'd like to use your farm as a stagecoach stop as well as a Pony Express home station." The older man stopped speaking and let his words sink in.

Rebecca looked to Seth, who simply shrugged his shoulders. She turned her attention back to Mr. Bromley and asked, "Do you need my permission to have it stop here?" She wasn't sure if having her home become the stagecoach stop was a good idea. How would it affect the boys?

"Since the farm belongs to you, yes. We've discovered that the stage riders need a break and your place is in the middle of the two stops it already makes," he explained.

Rebecca nodded. She knew the stage passed about a mile away from the house. It made sense that if they were going to add an additional stop they make it at her farm. She hesitated, though. Would the benefits of allowing it to stop here outweigh the drawbacks?

"If you wanted to sell refreshments to the passengers, we would have no problem with that and I'm sure they would be most appreciative," he added, as if trying to persuade her to allow it. "The stop would only be for about thirty minutes—enough time to allow the tired travelers to stretch their legs, and the coach driver time to water and rest the horses before pressing on."

Rebecca picked up a cookie and nibbled its crispy edge. If she could sell food to the travelers it would mean a little extra income. It would also mean she could have supplies delivered right to her front door, not to mention get to see people more often. She liked the thought of that. Even with all the kids it became very lonesome during the winter when they didn't go to town but once every few months. "How often would it pass through?"

"A couple of times a week. I'll be able to give you a schedule as soon as I have your permission to use the farm," he answered, reaching in his pocket and pulling out a slip of paper.

Deciding to give it a try, Rebecca asked, "The refreshments wouldn't need to be large meals, would they?"

"No, something simple, like these cookies or a sandwich." He unfolded the paper and studied it. "It looks like the stage would run on Mondays from east to west and Thursdays from west to east—they should both arrive around ten thirty in the morning." Mr. Bromley looked up at her. "So what do you think? Can we make this a regular stop?"

Rebecca nodded. "I think that will be fine as long as the stage rider will take care of his horses himself."

"That he will, Mrs. Young." Mr. Bromley finished his coffee and stood. "Thank you for the cookies and coffee. Now I need to be on my way." He pulled his hat back on his head and walked to the door.

Rebecca followed him. "When will the stage start stopping here?" she asked as her mind began to do a mental inventory of her supplies.

"We'll need to check the route, make sure there are no ruts or trees down. Plan for next Monday to be the first time it stops." He smiled at her. "Thank you for agreeing."

She returned his smile. "You're welcome."

The driver of the stage hurried to open the door for the businessman. Mr. Bromley dashed out into the rain and Seth ran toward the bunkhouse, where the rest of the boys waited. The stage pulled away and Seth disappeared into the bunkhouse. Disappointment ate at her. She would have liked to talk to him about her new business venture. When had she started thinking of Seth as a sounding board? He'd only been there a week and she realized she'd begun to look forward to their chats in the evening. That was only natural, wasn't it?

* * *

Seth felt as if a weight had been taken off his shoulders. He hadn't expected Mr. Bromley today, but his encouraging words had come at a much-needed time. His boss seemed happy the boys were doing well in their preparations for the many rides they would be completing in the days to come. The fact that his boss had arrived by stage at first had puzzled him, since the stage normally passed about a mile to the north of the farm. As their conversation continued Mr. Bromley had asked a few pointed questions about Rebecca, and Seth became a little uncomfortable, wondering why his boss needed to know if Seth thought Rebecca had a good business head. When he asked if she cooperated with Seth with regard to his training of the boys, Seth took the bull by the horns and asked him why all the questions. Once satisfied that the questions were for her good, he answered with honesty and told his boss that over the past few days he'd come to admire Mrs. Young and her family.

Then, just before Rebecca and Joy had returned, Mr. Bromley had given Seth more money to buy needed supplies for the barn, such as bridles, saddles and feed. All in all it turned out to be a good visit.

Seth shook the water from his hat and then entered the bunkhouse. Philip and Thomas were playing checkers beside the black potbellied stove. Andrew lay on his bunk with a book resting over his face. Noah sat on his bunk sharpening his knife. Jacob patiently schooled Beni on the different types of knots. They held a rope between them and Jacob watched Benjamin closely, only guiding when necessary.

"Jacob, can I have a word with you?" Seth asked, opening the door to his room.

"Sure, Seth." Jacob nodded to Benjamin. "Keep practicing, I'll be right back to see how you're doing."

Seth waited for the young man to walk to him then proceeded into his bedroom. He sat down on his bed and indicated that Jacob should take the rocker that sat in the corner. Once Jacob was seated, Seth said, "Now that the barn is built, I'd like for you to move into the tack room."

Jacob studied the tips of his muddy boots. "I'd like to, Seth, but someone needs to stay with Ma in the house."

"Why? When I got here you were all staying out here in the bunkhouse," Seth reminded him, aware that this was important to Jacob.

Still looking down, Jacob answered, "Yes, but you weren't here then." He looked up with challenging eyes.

Seth sat up a little straighter. "Jacob, I know you are trying to tell me something, but for the life of me I can't figure out what. Why don't you just spit out whatever is bothering you?"

"Ma needs a chaperone."

"A chaperone?"

Jacob nodded. "Yep, people in town are talking."

"About your mother and me?"

"Yes, sir."

Seth breathed in deeply. "Was that what had you and your mother tied in knots when we all went to town together that first day?"

Jacob nodded.

He should have seen this coming. Seth exhaled and

said, "I see. But how do the townsfolk know you are staying in the house?"

Jacob rubbed the dark stubble on his chin. "I guess they don't."

"So, if we moved Andrew into the house, no one would know that you moved out?" Seth asked, easing into a more comfortable position.

"No, I suppose not," Jacob answered, looking as if he might argue further.

Seth spoke quickly, not giving him a chance. "As the stock tender you need to stay in the tack room so that you are closer to the horses. We will need the horses ready to go at a moment's notice. Riders will arrive in the middle of the night as well as during the day. You have to be prepared. Do you want to have to tiptoe out of the house every time you hear a rider come in?"

"I'm not sure Andrew will want to move into the house," Jacob answered. He stood slowly. "I'll ask him—if he's agreeable then I'll move out to the barn."

He watched Jacob shut the door behind him. The sound of thunder shook the house. The storm reminded Seth of the Youngs. Just when he thought things were going well and they were all working together, lightning seemed to strike and was always followed by thunder.

There was no doubt in his mind that if Andrew didn't want to move into the main house, Jacob wouldn't be moving into the tack room in the barn. He laid down on his bed and listened to the rain hit the tin roof.

And if that wasn't enough, now the townspeople were talking about Rebecca and him. As far as he knew, neither of them had given them reason to talk.

Seth sighed. Jacob felt as if he needed to protect his mother's reputation but really wasn't able to.

Frustration gnawed at his gut. If he didn't need the money to find Charlotte, Seth would move on. He didn't need this family's problems and he certainly never intended to cause them more. Drawing on the only source that had sustained him the past couple of years, Seth closed his eyes and prayed that God would provide a way to keep Rebecca's reputation free of harm and that God would help him find Charlotte so that he could return home to St. Joseph.

Chapter Seven

After dinner, Seth walked out to the front porch. The rain had stopped but it had brought a chilling wind. He wrapped his coat tighter around his body and sat down on the porch swing. The sound of kids laughing and talking loudly caused him to grin. Even though the Young kids weren't related, they behaved very much like brothers and sister.

Over the meal, Rebecca had told them all that not only was the farm a Pony Express station, but now it was also a stage stop. She explained that twice a week the stage would stop there and she and Joy would sell things like sandwiches, cookies and beverages to the passengers. The boys had asked questions and Rebecca had answered each of them with more patience than Seth thought he could ever exhibit. Joy excitedly told her brothers how much Mr. Bromley had enjoyed her cookies. Seth had to admit that he'd felt a bit like an outsider.

Even now, sitting on the porch, he longed to join in but felt he had nothing to contribute. After he found and married Charlotte, would he then feel like part of a family? With no brothers or sisters, Seth had grown up an only child. His mother had abandoned him and his father when he was very young. Grandmother always said his pa had died of a broken heart. Seth gleaned from the retelling that women couldn't be trusted and loving one would break your heart and kill you. As an adult, he didn't believe that his dad literally died of a broken heart, but Seth did know that women couldn't be trusted. If it wasn't for his grandmother, he'd not be on this wild-goose chase looking for a woman who'd probably simply changed her mind about marriage.

"So this is where you got off to," Rebecca said, coming through the front door. She wore a light brown dress and her blue cloak covered most of it.

The swing rocked gently under her slight weight as she sat. He grinned over at her. "Yes, it's a little quieter out here."

At that moment, Joy let out a loud squeal and Rebecca laughed. "Yes, they are a mite keyed up tonight. It's probably from being cooped up most of the day."

If she hadn't said it, he would have. "Joy is very excited about the stage stopping here," he said as the little girl's voice drifted through the window.

"Yes, she wants to make all the cookies we sell." Rebecca pulled her cloak tighter about her middle.

"She told me she'd read a recipe that had nuts in it that she wanted to try. I didn't know she could read," he said, looking over at his pretty companion.

"Oh, she can a little, but mostly she calls looking at pictures reading." Rebecca smiled proudly. "But she'll be reading real books in no time."

Seth cocked his head to one side and studied her profile. She pushed back a wayward strand of dark hair, her fingers strong and slim, her face a perfect oval. She had a strength that did not lessen her femininity one bit and she carried herself confidently. The wind lifted one of her curls and his eyes followed the movement, making it difficult to concentrate on her words. No woman had affected him like Rebecca seemed to.

She looked at him expectantly and he reined in his thoughts to their conversation. After a moment he said, "I'm sure she will be reading soon. Joy's a very bright child. She's old enough to go to school now, isn't she?" As casually as possible, he stood and walked to the porch rail.

The smile slipped from her face and sadness filled her voice. "John and I had talked about letting her start this fall." She sighed heavily. "I think I'll continue with our plans and let her attend. Even though I hate letting my baby go."

Seth didn't know what to say. He hadn't meant to make her sad.

As if she realized her mood had changed the atmosphere around them, Rebecca offered him a bright smile that didn't quite meet her eyes. "So, did you and Mr. Bromley have a nice visit this afternoon?"

"We did. He gave us extra money to buy the barn supplies and seemed pleased with the boys' progress. Not a bad visit at all." Seth knew his words echoed his thoughts from earlier in the day.

"I'm glad." She paused then asked, "What do you think about the stage stopping here? You didn't say a word during dinner about it." She worried her bottom lip with her pretty white teeth.

"I think it's a great idea," he answered. He'd had a

thought earlier and maybe now was the time to ask Rebecca for a favor. Before he could mention it, she spoke.

"If the offer still stands, I need to go into town tomorrow after all. I don't have enough ingredients to make cookies and I'd like to pick up some tea. Ladies seem to like tea more than coffee, I think."

Seth remembered Jacob's words about the townsfolk talking about them. He'd planned on going for the needed supplies but now thought he'd send Jacob instead. "The offer still stands. I'll ask Jacob to hitch up the wagon in the morning."

"Thank you." She started to get up.

"Before you go inside, I'd like to ask a favor of you," Seth blurted out, afraid she'd leave and he'd lose his nerve.

Rebecca eased back into the swing. "All right."

He took a deep breath. "I know you don't know me very well and I probably shouldn't even ask, but since the stage is coming through here, it might be a good opportunity." Why did he feel so breathless?

Caution filled her voice as she asked, "What might be a good opportunity?"

Seth rolled his shoulders and started again. "Let me start at the beginning. A few months ago my grandmother asked me to find a nice girl and get married." He saw the shock on her face and held up his hand. "Hold on, let me finish."

At her nod, he continued, "So I placed an ad for a mail-order bride." Seth watched her relax and pressed on. "My grandmother's dying wish was that I get married."

Rebecca asked, "Why would she ask you to get married, if she was dying?"

"She didn't want to leave me without anyone to take care of me…love me, I guess you could say. Anyway, now that my grandmother has passed on, I have no other relatives that I know of." Seth glanced at her face to see if she understood.

Rebecca nodded. "That makes sense. Did you get a mail-order bride?" she asked, looking up at him.

"Yes and no."

A frown creased the center of her brow. "I don't understand."

Seth grinned. "Maybe I should just tell you everything and then let you ask questions." He hoped she heard the teasing in his voice and didn't think him rude.

Rebecca smoothed out her skirt and nodded. "That might work best." A tiny smile tilted up one corner of her mouth and she shook her head. "Although, men are not always the best at storytelling."

"Agreed." He wondered if she knew how easy she was to talk to. He'd never told his story to anyone, yet here he stood eager for her input. "Yes, a young woman answered my ad. Her name is Charlotte Fisher. She wrote and said she'd be on the first stage to St. Joseph, only she never arrived. Grandmother died but not before she made me promise to find Charlotte." He stopped and inhaled the cold night air. "I have been looking for Charlotte ever since." His gaze searched Rebecca's. Sadness filled her sweet face, only this time he could see that she wasn't sad for herself, but for him and his loss.

He pressed on with his story. "A few weeks ago while traveling alone, three men held me up and took all my money. When I filed a report with the town sheriff, I told him I needed work that would let me travel and keep me close to the stage route at the same time. He mentioned the Pony Express that had just started up. I found Mr. Bromley and he hired me. The rest you know. That's why I work for the Pony Express—to make money so I can continue my search for Charlotte." He eased back against the porch rail. Seth couldn't remember the last time he'd talked this much.

"So, no honorable intentions to see that the mail gets through?"

He stiffened at the challenge in her voice, but boldly lifted his chin and met her gaze. Only to stare tongue-tied. She had a hand pressed to her mouth to stifle the giggles threatening to escape. In spite of himself he chuckled.

"If you could only have seen your face when I said that."

"I thought you were judging my intentions."

"How could I judge your intentions when I'm doing the same thing?"

He quirked a brow at her. "How so?"

"My reasons for accepting the stage stop have nothing to do with the mail. It serves several purposes and all of them are personal." Her expression stilled and grew serious. "So, how can I help you?"

Seth had difficulty pulling his gaze away from hers. "Well, the stage runs both east and west, which means that Charlotte is probably somewhere along the line. Last I heard from her she was coming from California. What I'd like to ask you to do is each time the stage stops here to inquire if anyone knows her and, if so, where I can find her?"

Rebecca nodded. "I'm not sure that will work but I'm more than happy to help you any way I can." She stood and stretched. "I'm tired and if we're going to town, I'd like to leave right after breakfast."

"Oh, and one more thing before you go." Seth pushed away from the porch railing. When she turned to face him, he asked, "Did Jacob tell you I want him to move into the barn's tack room?"

"No, but that's understandable," she offered.

Seth was pleased that Rebecca wasn't going to fight him on this move. "I'm glad you don't object."

"I'll talk to him. There really is no reason for him to stay in the house with me and the younger kids." She reached for the door and then stopped and turned to face him once more. "Is there anything else?"

He shook his head. "Not tonight. Thank you, Rebecca. For everything." Seth realized he'd used her Christian name and quickly bounded off the porch. What had possessed him to become so personal with her? He couldn't slip up like that again. Even though he did enjoy the way her name tripped off his lips, with ease and satisfaction. No, it wouldn't—or rather, it couldn't—happen again.

Rebecca hadn't slept well. She'd wrestled with the fact that Seth had used her given name and she certainly hadn't minded. If anything, she'd liked the way her name sounded when he said it. All night she'd fought with herself. Should she ask him not to use her Christian name? Or pretend it wasn't a big deal?

"Ma, is everything all right?" Jacob asked. He guided the horses over the muddy road, careful to avoid all potholes. Concern filled his face.

"Everything's fine. I was just thinking about my supply list," she answered, attempting to smile at him.

They rode in silence for a few moments. Then Jacob spoke. "Seth wants me to move into the barn's tack room. I planned on asking Andrew to move into the house with you and the little ones." He grinned over his shoulder at Benjamin and Joy.

She knew her son thought himself her chaperone, but regardless of what he said, the townsfolk would continue to talk. Silently she prayed that the Lord would send an answer to this problem. "That's not necessary, Jacob. I can take care of things in the house," Rebecca answered.

Jacob started to argue but then clamped his lips shut. He focused on the road ahead.

"If he's moving out, does that mean I get to move out, too?" Benjamin asked, pulling himself up on his knees and clutching the wooden seat Rebecca and Jacob sat upon.

Rebecca frowned. "No, you stay in the house. We need at least one man watching over us, don't you think?" she asked, eyeing her eight-year-old son, hoping that he'd not realize she stroked his ego to get him to do what she wanted.

Benjamin puffed out his chest. "Oh, I hadn't thought of that. I suppose you're right."

The rest of the trip passed quietly. Jacob and Rebecca were each lost in their own thoughts. Benjamin and Joy played school in the bed of the wagon. He took his role as big brother seriously as he read to her out of one of her picture books.

Their stops at the leather and lumberyard were pretty uneventful. Jacob had no trouble acquiring the needed bridles and saddles. He'd learned from the lumberman that one of his neighbors may have extra hay for sale, at least enough for them until the Pony Express supply wagon came out to the farm.

Rebecca dreaded stopping in at the general store. If there were any other stores in town that supplied household items, she would very easily switch her business to them. But there wasn't. She stood to climb down from the wagon but Jacob placed a hand on her arm. "Ma, I'll go get what you need." He jumped from the wagon and looked up at her expectantly.

She handed him her list. "You sure you don't mind, son?"

He took the list and grinned. "Nope, if these two behave I might use some of my Pony Express wages and get them each a penny candy."

Benjamin beamed at his little sister. "We'll be good, won't we, Joy?"

She bobbed her head and smiled back.

Jacob stepped onto the boardwalk and entered the store. Rebecca heard the bell announce her son's arrival. She really should have gone herself, but the thought of facing Mr. Edwards left her feeling cold. Her gaze moved to her younger children, who were once more absorbed in the picture book.

Maybe now with the extra income, she could order a few more books for them. When John died, she'd stopped the one-book-a-month shipment she'd intended to use for educating the kids. She alone was responsible for the money John left her and she'd had to learn over the past couple of months how to manage, and though it wasn't necessary to be frugal, John had taught them the Bible's teachings on being a good steward. She needed the money to last so she would never have to seek work and leave Joy alone with strangers.

The sound of the bell ringing over the door to the general store drew her attention away from the children. Fay Miller wiped at her eyes as she closed the door behind her. When she turned to face the street, Rebecca could see that tears ran down her chubby cheeks. Rebecca climbed down the wagon at a fast pace.

"Mrs. Miller, are you all right?" she asked, feeling foolish. If the woman was all right, she wouldn't be crying.

The older woman sniffed loudly and looked up at her. "Oh, hello, Rebecca dear."

Fay Miller always had a smile on her face and her sparkling gray eyes usually held a teasing glint, but not today. Something had to be terribly wrong to dissolve the sweet woman into tears. Rebecca hugged her about the shoulders. "What's wrong?"

"I'm old and useless, that's what's wrong," she wailed.

Rebecca's heart broke for the woman. "Nonsense, why would you say such a thing?" she asked, leading her toward the bench that sat outside the store.

Once seated, Mrs. Miller wiped her face with a big floral handkerchief. She sighed heavily and said, "Rebecca, I have outlived my usefulness."

"Why don't you start at the beginning and tell me what is going on," Rebecca suggested, patting the older woman's arm.

She nodded. "This morning Mr. Welsh, the man who owns my house, said he's going to sell it so that they can put up something called a telegraph pole and use my home for a telegraph office. He told me I had

twenty-four hours to move out. Twenty-four hours!"
Mrs. Miller cried.

Mrs. Miller was a widower. As far as Rebecca knew
she and Mr. Miller had never had any children. The
late Mr. Miller had been gone for ten years and Mrs.
Miller had lived in that house for as long as Rebecca
could remember. How could Mr. Welsh just kick her
out like that?

She moaned into her handkerchief. "What am I
going to do?"

Rebecca stared at her wagon for several long moments. Did everyone have problems? It would appear
so, even sweet Mrs. Miller. She silently prayed for an
answer to help her old friend. As Rebecca prayed, a
thought began to build in her mind. Maybe they could
help each other. Would the older woman be willing to
move out to the farm? Or would she balk and say she'd
rather stay in town?

Chapter Eight

Rebecca turned to face her. She took the older woman's hands away from her face and looked into her tear-filled eyes. "Mrs. Miller, how would you like to move out to the farm with me and my boys?"

Mrs. Miller sniffled. "What?"

"Well, it occurs to me that the Lord may be answering both our prayers. I need a chaperone and you need a new home."

The older woman pulled one of her trembling hands free and wiped at her face again. "You want me to chaperone you?" Her voice quivered.

Rebecca explained, "Yes. I'm not sure if you've heard but the Pony Express sent out a man to be the station keeper at the farm. He stays out in the bunkhouse with the boys but last time I was in town, Mr. Edwards found out and he acted as if I was doing something wrong by letting the station keeper stay out at my place." Rebecca shook her head in disgust. "He is a Pony Express employee. It's his job, he has to live there. If you came to live with me, you'd be supplying me with a chaperone and I'd supply you with a roof over your head for the rest of your days." She smiled brightly at the woman. "Which, by the looks of things, will be for many, many years."

For the first time since she'd left the store, Mrs. Miller's mouth wobbled into a smile. "Are you sure you wouldn't mind an old woman rattling around in your house?" she asked.

"The only thing I mind is that you keep referring to yourself as an old woman," Rebecca assured her.

"Then I'll do it. But I don't want you thinking it's forever. We don't even know if we'll enjoy living together," Mrs. Miller said, but her actions belied her words. She eagerly reached for Rebecca's hand. "Oh, thank you, thank you."

Rebecca gathered her into a close hug. "I'll send Jacob and the little ones back to the house to unload the wagon and they can return for us in the morning. We'll get you packed up tonight." Excitement coursed through her at the thought of Mrs. Miller living on the ranch. She hadn't realized how much she'd missed another woman's presence. Her mother-in-law had died shortly after Rebecca's eighteenth birthday. That had been several years ago.

"Mrs. Miller, I am excited." Rebecca clapped her hands in glee.

"Now, now, Rebecca. If we are going to live together, you must stop calling me Mrs. Miller. Fay will do nicely." Fay's words chided, but her voice simmered with barely checked relief and joy.

Jacob came out of the store with a large box full of supplies. He looked from his mother to the older woman, but respect for his elders kept him from asking the questions she felt sure were on the tip of his tongue.

"Jacob, Fay is moving in with us," Rebecca announced, sliding an arm around the older woman's shoulders.

To her son's credit he acted as if things like this were an everyday occurrence at their house. "Well, Mrs. Miller, all orphans are welcome at our place, even older ones."

Rebecca saw at once that Jacob could not have said anything that would please Fay more. She beamed with pride at her son.

The woman's eyes widened and she clasped her hands together and placed them over her heart. Her voice seemed to have lodged in her throat because all she said was "Aw."

"Jacob, I need you to take the supplies and the younger children back to the farm, while I help her pack."

He carried the box to the wagon. "Yes, Ma." He set it in the back with the little kids and then turned to face her once more. "Would you like a ride back to her house?"

"Did you get us candy?" Benjamin asked. The picture book had been forgotten.

"I think we'll walk," Fay answered, smiling happily. She turned to look at Rebecca. "If that's all right with you?"

Jacob answered Benjamin by handing each of them a peppermint stick. "Here you go, buddy."

"That is fine with me," Rebecca answered. She looped her arm inside the older woman's and started to walk toward Fay's house. "I can use the exercise."

Jacob pulled himself onto the wagon and then called after them, "Ma, what about supper?"

Rebecca stopped and grinned at him. "I guess it's a sandwich night for you all. There is ham in the larder and fresh bread. For dessert you can open a few jars of peaches. Joy will help you. Won't you, Joy?"

The little girl licked the sticky candy from her fingers and nodded.

"Oh, and Jacob, go ahead and move your things out to the barn. Mrs. Miller will be staying in your room."

"If this is too much trouble—" Fay began but Rebecca cut her off.

"Why, it's no trouble at all. We will be helping each other out of troublesome situations and as for my family...they will be fine for one day." She turned back to the wagon. "You all be good and mind Jacob."

Both of her youngest children answered, "Yes, Ma."

Jacob nodded. "I'll pick you up tomorrow at Mrs. Miller's."

Rebecca waved at them as he turned the horses around and then headed home. It had been a long time since she had been childless. And she'd never asked them to fend for their own dinner. For a moment Rebecca wondered if she was doing the right thing, then shook off the slight feeling of guilt. Mrs. Miller needed her and she needed the older woman. For the first time in a while, Rebecca felt as if she had a companion, maybe even someone she could confide in.

Seth looked up as the wagon rumbled into the yard. He immediately noticed that Rebecca wasn't with Jacob and the two youngest children. He hurried to the wagon. "Where is your mother?"

Jacob jumped down from the wagon and then helped Joy over the side. "She stayed in town to help Mrs.

Miller pack her things. I'm to go back for them tomorrow."

"Who is Mrs. Miller?" Seth asked.

Jacob picked up the box of kitchen supplies and handed them to Benjamin. "Beni, take these to the kitchen and set them on the table." He turned to face Seth. "Mrs. Miller is a widow woman from town. Her husband passed away a few years ago and she has no children. I heard while I was in the store that the man who owns her house kicked her out this morning. I imagine Ma felt sorry for her and invited her to live out here."

"That was mighty nice of her," Seth said thoughtfully. Had Rebecca seen Mrs. Miller as a chaperone of sorts? Would her presence keep the townsfolk from gossiping about them? He hoped it would.

Andrew and Clayton walked out of the barn. Clayton laid the pitchfork he'd had in his hands against the wall. "Where's Ma?" Andrew asked, looking around as if he thought something terrible had happened to their mother.

"In town," Jacob answered.

Seth motioned for the boys to come closer. "Grab a saddle and take it to the barn." He turned his attention back to Jacob. "There are only three saddles here."

Jacob nodded. "Yep, that's all Mr. Grey had that we could buy today. I figured three would do until we got supplies from the Pony Express."

Seth picked up a bridle and examined the leather. "They won't be sending saddles and bridles. I'll go pick up the women and stop by Mr. Grey's tomorrow. Hopefully, we'll be able to order a couple more of each. What did you find out about hay?"

Jacob sat down on the bed of the wagon. "Mr. Browning has extra hay he can sell to us."

Seth nodded. He tried to focus on what Jacob was saying about the hay, but couldn't take his mind off Rebecca. What was she doing? Was she packing up Mrs. Miller and laughing? He loved her laugh. Sometimes she laughed softly and brought her hand up to quiet the giggles. Other times she burst out laughing, the sound floating up from her throat, most often at something one of the kids said or did. But her joy was always infectious, bringing a ready smile to others. With the widow coming to live with Rebecca, would their nightly chats on the porch end? Deep down Seth hoped not; he hated to admit it, but he'd miss those chats if they did. Then again, he'd begun to care about Rebecca and that was dangerous.

The next morning, Seth hitched up the wagon. His stomach growled and he grinned. Joy had decided to make breakfast for everyone and had served burned eggs, bacon and toast. He'd tried not to hurt the little girl's feelings but couldn't quite eat what she served.

It had been fun, though, watching her brothers distract her. While one pretended to eat the breakfast, another would rake theirs onto a plate below the table and pass it to the next one.

Clayton had rustled the plate outside. Seth had no idea what the boy had done with the burned mess once he was out of the house, but was glad that he hadn't had to choke it down. Little Joy had been thrilled to see all their cleaned plates.

Jacob had scolded his sister for cooking without supervision all while trying not to grin. They really were a unique and fun family to be around.

Once the wagon was hitched, he checked in on the boys and Joy. Jacob had taken both Joy and Benjamin under his wing. He had Beni mucking out one of the stalls and Joy rubbing oil into the leather on one of the saddles. Jacob himself forked fresh straw into each of the stalls. The other five boys each had a chore and were busy doing them. Seth sniffed appreciatively. New wood and new leather. What a combination.

"Jacob, I need you to make sure everything runs smoothly while I'm gone." Seth leaned against the barn door and met the young man's eyes.

Jacob laughed. There was no anger or animosity in his voice when he said, "I was doing that before you came along. I think I can do it again for one day."

Seth chuckled. "See that you do."

An hour later, he arrived in town. The streets teemed with people coming and going. He pulled the wagon beside the livery yard. Seth leaped down and walked to the general store. In most towns the general store was the meeting place for everyone. Seth hoped to get a bite to eat and then find out where Mrs. Miller lived. He pushed the door open and the little bell sounded off, announcing his arrival.

The storekeeper came out from behind the counter. "How can I help you, stranger?" he asked.

The place was empty of customers, which surprised Seth. He walked over to the apple bin and pulled out a handful of dried apple. "I mainly came in for directions," he answered, taking a big bite from the fruit.

"As soon as you pay for the apples, I'll be happy to give you directions," the big man answered.

Seth looked at the marked price and pulled money from his pocket. "That should cover this handful." Seth handed it to the storekeeper. "Sorry about that. I forgot myself."

The big man took the money and walked back to his counter and the register. "Where do you need directions to?" he asked, dropping the coins in the drawer.

"Mrs. Miller's house," he answered, studying the man while he chewed. The store owner was tall and big-bellied, and his eyes were hard. Nothing about the man appealed to Seth. He seemed like a bully, which might explain why there were no customers in his store.

"Now, what business do you have with that sweet old woman?"

Seth could tell that the man didn't care about the woman but was simply being nosy. "It's a private matter and my own."

The man nodded. "I see." He stepped from around the counter and puffed up his chest, all the while tapping the side of his head and squinting as if he'd forgotten something. "You know, my memory isn't as good as it used to be."

"Then I won't waste any more of your time." Seth turned on his heels and left the store. He stood on the boardwalk and looked up and down Main Street. The last time he'd been in town he hadn't really taken the time to look around. He figured he had a few minutes and decided to do just that. His eyes scanned each building.

Dove Creek wasn't a very big town. Next to the general store was a small house—he assumed the general-store owner lived in it—and next to it was the doctor's home and office. On the next block sat the bank. It seemed to fill the whole block.

Seth walked toward the bank. Surely the banker would know where Mrs. Miller lived.

He entered the bank and looked about. Dark panel covered the walls and floor. A big desk sat in the middle of the room. He noted offices off to the sides and a staircase that led to the second floor.

Several people stood around the room. A line had formed in front of the bank-teller cage. He noticed that a checkerboard had been set up in one corner of the bank and two elderly gentlemen sat playing the game.

It dawned on Seth that this had become the meeting place of the townspeople instead of the general store. How odd, he thought.

"May I help you?" asked the man sitting at the desk.

Seth walked over to him. "Yes, I am looking for a Mrs. Miller."

"I'm sorry, no one works here by that name," the man said, looking down at the pile of papers in front of him.

He realized his mistake and tried again. "No, I don't expect she does. I was wondering if you could direct me to her house."

Once more the man looked up. "No, I'm not sure that I could and even if I could, I'm not sure that I would or should." His eyes moved up and down Seth as if assessing his appearance.

"Is there someone here that can tell me?" Seth asked, beginning to feel flustered and realizing that he was drawing quite a bit of attention from the others.

The man sighed and stood. "Wait right here."

Seth nodded. The man walked toward one of the offices. He knocked on the door and entered shortly afterward. Maybe the bank wasn't the best place to ask for directions, he thought as he waited.

It felt as if everyone watched him, but Seth knew that was ridiculous. The line continued to move where the two bank tellers were working. He looked down at the chair in front of the desk and thought about sitting down to wait, but at that moment the man reappeared.

When he was within hearing distance, he said. "I'm sorry, sir. Bank policy is to not give out personal information on our depositors."

Well, that was good to know. Seth nodded his understanding and then turned to leave. The man laid a hand on his arm. He looked at him. With a nod of his head toward the old-timers playing checkers, the man said in a low voice, "But there is nothing to stop you from asking around."

Seth grinned. "Thank you. I think I will see how the game is going."

The man nodded once and dropped his hand. "Thank you for coming in. If you ever need help opening an account, come on back in."

The two men looked up when Seth approached their table. "Good morning, gentlemen. I was wondering if either of you could tell me where Mrs. Miller lives. My name is Seth Armstrong and I'm supposed to pick up her and Mrs. Young this morning, but I forgot to get the address from Jacob."

One of the men held out his hand. "Nice to meet you, Mr. Armstrong. I'm Caleb Smith and this is my brother-in-law, Marcus Boyd." He returned to his game.

Seth leaned against the wall and waited. Sometimes older fellas wanted time to think about their next move both in life and while playing a game. Mr. Boyd jumped two of Mr. Smith's pieces.

With a grin, he looked up at Seth. "She lives behind the bank here. Her house is the one with the windows boarded up. I saw that landlord of her boarding them up this morning. Just go to the end of the block and turn left. You won't miss it." He returned his focus to the game.

"Much obliged." Seth walked out of the bank.

The bright sunshine felt good on his face. He hurried to the livery and climbed aboard the wagon. If all went well, he'd have the ladies out to the farm by dinnertime.

As the horses rounded the corner, he saw Rebecca carrying a box to the edge of the street. He waved at her as he set the brake.

"Good morning, Mr. Armstrong."

Mr. Armstrong? Seth didn't like that. "Good morning, Mrs. Young." He frowned, not liking how that sounded any better.

"We're just about done packing," she said as she turned to walk back to the house. "I thought Jacob or Andrew would be coming for us."

Seth jumped down from the wagon and caught up with her. "I had Pony Express business to take care of."

"Are you finished with your business?" she asked, turning to face him.

"No, I wanted to find you first." Seth looked down into her pretty blue eyes. He should have taken care of ordering the saddles and tack before searching for her. Confusion filled his mind as he questioned his own motives for coming to her first.

"Why?"

That was the question of the moment, wasn't it? His

gaze moved to the wagon. "I thought you might like to have the wagon to start loading up Mrs. Miller's things."

"Oh. Well. That was very sweet of you," she answered, though her expression made him think she doubted that was what he'd intended.

"I'll go take care of my business and then come back and help you finish loading," he offered.

Mrs. Miller came out of the kitchen. She smiled at Seth.

"Hello."

He nodded at her, tipping his hat. She was a plump little woman with graying brown hair and sparkling blue eyes. Seth fought the urge to stare. She reminded him of his grandmother. A lump the size of river bedrock clogged his throat and he quickly turned away from the women. "I'll be back shortly." He was surprised that his vocal chords worked at all. He hurried away and couldn't get away from them fast enough. His heart felt as if someone had plunged a knife through it. He'd thought he was done grieving for the woman who raised him, but he was wrong.

He walked to the livery with a heavy heart. Seeing Mrs. Miller made him realize that he needed to finish his job with the Pony Express so he could find the mail-order bride he'd promised his grandmother he'd marry. He had to get away from the family that made him long to be a part of them.

Chapter Nine

A few days later, Rebecca happily baked sugar cookies in the kitchen while Joy played on the rug in the living room. The little girl had helped to make the batter and shape the sweet treats, but for the actual baking process, Rebecca insisted that she do it alone.

Fay sat at the table reading her Bible. Every so often the older woman would say "Amen." Or "Yes, yes, Lord." Rebecca knew she wasn't talking to her, but to her Bible and God. It hadn't taken Rebecca long to learn that Fay had a true love for their Lord. She prayed that someday she'd have the same strong convictions as Fay. Oh, Rebecca loved the Lord, but knew she failed Him in many ways.

Having Fay around the house had turned into a wonderful blessing. The older woman pitched in with the chores and meal preparation. She helped the boys if they needed something done, such as mending a sock or washing a shirt. And could the woman ever cook! What a blessing that was to Rebecca. She thanked the Lord she no longer had to eat her own cooking all the time.

At first, she'd been worried about how the kids

would adapt to Fay moving in, but they all welcomed her with open arms. Fay said she enjoyed having them around and helping out around the house.

"What time will the stage arrive?" Fay asked, looking up from her Bible.

Rebecca glanced at the clock that sat beside the stove. "In about thirty minutes. Mr. Bromley sent a new schedule and it said around one." She looked at the plates of cookies and the sandwiches. "Do you think I should offer hot tea for the ladies?"

Fay shrugged. "If you have it, it can't hurt." A grin split her face. "I wouldn't mind having a cup myself."

"Then I'll make a pot." Rebecca pulled her other coffeepot from under the cabinet and poured fresh water into it. John had spoiled her years ago by purchasing the extra pot. Every day she found some way to remember him.

As she made the tea, Rebecca allowed her thoughts to linger on her deceased husband. When she'd taken the job here on the farm as his mother's helper, she'd never dreamed they'd end up married. John's father had wanted his son married before he passed on and since Rebecca was the only gal around who was close to his age, John had offered to marry her when his mother died. By doing so, he'd fulfilled his father's wish and made sure that Rebecca would always be cared for. They had been good friends, and even though they weren't in love, he'd made sure she was happy. Somewhere along the way she supposed it might have turned into a deep love, the valuable kind, because how could you not love someone that forever put your happiness above his own. And he'd done that with everyone connected to him—the boys, Rebecca and most certainly the child of his heart, Joy.

Coffee wasn't a beverage Rebecca enjoyed, but, tea? She could drink her weight in tea. As the water heated, Rebecca realized that somewhere in the past few months, she'd given up her favorite beverage. Was it because making it reminded her of all that she'd lost? Or was it simply that until now, she'd had precious little time to think about her own likes and desires? Raising seven boys and a little girl left no time for oneself. In fact, it took all her time and energy.

She turned her attention back to Fay. The older woman had gone back to reading the Bible. "What passage are you reading today?"

Fay looked up. "The Book of Job." Her eyes took on a faraway look as she stared out the kitchen window. "That man has always fascinated me. He lost everything but his faith." She looked to Rebecca once more. "Faith is the strongest thing we have in our possession. Man can take everything else, but he can never take our faith in God. Never lose faith, Rebecca, and God will restore what has been taken from you."

The sound of the stagecoach pulling up in front of the house had both women jumping to their feet.

"It's early," Rebecca gasped. Grabbing the platter of sandwiches and cookies, she hurried to the sitting room and placed them on the sideboard she'd arranged for just that purpose.

Fay joined her a moment later, with serving plates and several cups.

"Thank you, Fay," Rebecca said as she hurried back to the kitchen for the coffee and tea. Silently she prayed, *Lord, please let this go well.*

Joy stood on the rug now, wringing her little hands together. She looked at her mother with concern etched on her sweet features.

Rebecca stopped and reassured her daughter. "Joy, there is no reason you can't stay in here and play if that's what you want to do."

Joy smiled. "Thank you, Ma." She slipped back down onto the rug.

What had caused Joy to become so tense at the arrival of the stage? Rebecca picked up both the tea and the coffeepot and hurried back to the sitting room. She made a mental note that after things settled down, she would ask her daughter about her reaction.

"Would you like for me to open the door?" Fay asked.

Rebecca set down the pots. She glanced up at the sign she'd created earlier in the day that had the prices of the food and beverages posted—sandwiches, five cents; two cookies, one cent; a cup of coffee, two cents. Fay had assured her that the prices were reasonable.

She turned around and smoothed out her apron over her dress. "Yes, please." Rebecca held her breath as icy air entered the room.

"Please, come on inside and warm up," Fay called to the passengers.

Two women and a man hurried into the warm room. They stopped just inside the doorway.

"Come on inside." Rebecca motioned for them to come sit down on the sofa and chairs.

She looked around the room, trying to see it as they would for the first time. The fireplace had a hearty fire roaring in it. The plush couch and chairs sat on each side of the fire, creating a rectangle. In between them was a small table that sat upon a light-colored rug. To her it felt cozy; what did it feel and look like to them?

The women hurried into the room, each taking a spot on the couch. They pulled their cloaks tightly about their bodies. They looked as if they were mother and daughter. Both had light blond hair and blue eyes. They were thin with pinched lips. "Thank you," the eldest said.

The gentleman moved closer to the fireplace and stood beside it. "That coffee smells wonderful."

Rebecca wasn't sure how to say that it was for sale. She glanced at Fay, who seemed to understand.

"Mrs. Young makes the best coffee in the whole territory," Fay proclaimed. "And she offers the fairest prices for the cup, too." She walked over to the sideboard and pointed up to the sign.

After reading it, the gentleman moved forward. He dropped several coins into the tin cup she'd placed on the sideboard for money and picked up a plate. "What kind of sandwiches are these, Mrs. Young?" he asked, placing one on his plate and then taking a cup of freshly poured coffee from Fay.

"Egg salad. The dressing is fresh. I made it just this morning," she answered.

The eldest woman stood. She dug in her purse and pulled out several coins.

Rebecca smiled. "What can I get for you?" she asked as the woman dropped her money into the cup.

"I'd like a sandwich. I've never acquired a taste for coffee." She wrinkled her nose as if the smell displeased her.

"We also have hot tea," Fay said, waving her hand to indicate the second pot.

A smile broke out over the woman's face. "Now, tea I could drink all day." She dropped more coins into the cup.

Soon all three of the passengers were munching on sandwiches and drinking from Rebecca's best china. She felt a moment of pride that the ladies and gentleman were enjoying her small serving of food.

Cold air filled the room as the stagecoach driver entered the house. "I think the weather's getting worse, folks. We need to get back on the road."

He was a skinny man who didn't appear to be over five foot three inches tall. Did stagecoach drivers have to be of small stature, like Pony Express riders? She hurried toward him. "Why don't you come in for a quick cup of coffee and a sandwich?" she asked, directing him toward the sideboard.

A worried expression covered his face. Maybe he didn't have the extra money for such things. If she wanted him to linger, she'd have to make it worth his while. "For the coach drivers, the coffee and meal are on the house, Mr...."

"Alexander, ma'am." He hurried to the food and scooped up a sandwich.

Fay poured him a cup of the coffee.

In two bites the sandwich was gone and the coffee gulped down. "Thanks for the grub, ma'am." He motioned to the passengers. "Time to load up. We leave in two minutes." Mr. Alexander stomped across the floor and jerked open the door. Cold air rushed inside.

Fay chuckled. "Well, he's in a mighty big hurry."

The male passenger put his cup in the washtub that Rebecca had supplied and grinned. "I'd like to buy a couple of those cookies, Mrs. Young. If they are nearly as good as the sandwich, I'll be a very happy man."

Rebecca smiled her thanks, then quickly placed two of the biggest cookies into a cloth bag. She heard his coins hit the others in the cup.

He took the bag with a nod and then proceeded toward the door.

The two women, who had spoken quietly to each other during their short meal, hurriedly stood. The older one ordered, "Mr. James, wait just a moment and we'll go out with you. There is no reason to open that door more than we have to." She placed her dishes into the tub and also dropped money into the tin. "I'm sure Mrs. Young doesn't enjoy the cold air that comes in every time it's opened." She looked pointedly at the man then turned back to Rebecca. "I'd like two more sandwiches, to go. Me and my daughter still have a long journey ahead of us and I'm sure we'll find no better meals than the one you've provided today."

"Thank you." Rebecca reached for another bag and placed one sandwich inside. "Do you want them together or separate?" she asked, reaching for another bag.

"One bag is plenty."

She nodded, put the second sandwich with the first and handed the bag to the woman, who took it and then walked toward the other two passengers.

Just as the man started to open the door, Rebecca remembered her promise to Seth. "Oh!"

They all three turned and looked at her startled.

"I'm sorry, I just remembered I promised to ask if any of you ever met a woman named Charlotte Fisher," Rebecca blurted out.

The two women shook their heads and the man answered, "Can't say that I have."

"Well, thank you." Rebecca walked toward them and closed the door as they left.

She turned to find Fay standing behind her. "I'll have to say, that went well." Fay patted her on the arm.

As Rebecca cleared the sideboard, she had to agree with Fay. They'd sold four cookies, one cup of coffee, two teas and five sandwiches. She added the money up in her head—that was thirty-three cents.

Fay picked up the dirty dishpan and headed to the kitchen. "You did good, Rebecca. But you have to get braver in telling them your prices." A teasing glint filled the older woman's eyes just before she disappeared into the kitchen.

Rebecca decided to split the money with Fay. The woman had helped her make the food and created the prices. Plus, at this rate, Rebecca felt she could be generous.

She scooped up the two plates of leftovers and headed back to the kitchen. Rebecca dreaded telling Seth that the passengers hadn't heard of Charlotte. Would he be terribly disappointed? Earlier he'd reminded her to ask. She cared about Seth—what would his reaction be should a passenger know her or her whereabouts? Would he leave them quickly? Or would he hesitate? After all, he'd never met Charlotte. A part of Rebecca dreaded that day. She told herself it was because she liked Seth and didn't want to see him hurt. Not because she was getting used to having him around and would miss him when he left.

Seth pointed the rifle at Clayton as he passed on his horse. The boy leaned across the side of the horse as if dodging a bullet. "Pkew!" Seth made the sound of a shooting gun and lowered the weapon.

Rebecca yelled behind him, "Have you lost your mind?" She came running across the pasture looking madder than a hornet. Her blue eyes blazed and her cloak flew around her.

When she came even with him, Seth answered, "No." Then he turned his attention to the thundering hooves that were fast approaching.

Noah came across his path. Once more Seth raised the gun.

Rebecca screamed and made a grab for the rifle. "Seth, stop!"

He lowered the weapon and faced her. "Rebecca, we are training here."

"You could kill him."

He shook his head. Didn't she trust him yet? Each night for over two weeks he told her what he'd done during the day and what he was planning for the next day. Fay would listen at the window and every once in a while they'd hear the older lady chuckle at Rebecca's many questions. He'd been patient but she had to let him do his job.

Trying to conceal his aggravation, Seth answered, "Not likely, Rebecca. The gun's not loaded, but don't tell them that—they need to believe the threat is real. I am teaching them how to avoid getting shot using their horses as shields."

Rebecca turned on her heels and marched back toward the house. Seth watched her go. Would she ever trust him with her boys? He'd hoped she'd realized that he wouldn't intentionally allow harm to come to them. Maybe she needed more than a couple of weeks.

The thought came to him, could he ever fall in love? Would he ever trust a woman not to leave him? Seth shook his head. That was nonsense thinking. Or was it?

His fondness for Rebecca was like a wild plant that was growing every day. Leaving her and the boys would probably be the hardest thing he'd ever have to do but he'd do it. He had made a promise to his grandmother and no matter how badly he might want to stay with the Young family, he couldn't.

Chapter Ten

Seth watched as Noah and Clayton worked with their horses. He stood by the corral gate. It had been a couple of hours since Rebecca had come out and found him pretend shooting at her boys.

He'd since sent the boys off to do chores, except for Noah and Clayton. He pulled the two boys so that he could see where they were with their riding skills. Seth's plan was to spend a little time each day with separate boys so that he could assess their strengths and weaknesses.

Noah rode as if he'd been born on a horse. His body moved with the animal and he instinctively seemed to know what it would do next. He paid close attention to the horse and made sure to use his softest voice when speaking to her.

Clayton, on the other hand, acted as if he'd never seen a horse, let alone rode one. He mounted like a young girl, clung to the saddle horn and looked as skittish as a rat around a snake. He never spoke to his horse or directed it in any manner.

Seth called to Noah, "Noah, take your mount to the barn and cool her down. You've done a good job today."

"Thanks, Seth." The boy smiled broadly as he rode past.

He nodded to Noah and then called to Clayton, "Clayton, bring your horse here."

Clayton dismounted and then walked the horse to the railing, where Seth stood watching. "Yes, Seth?" Weariness filled the boy's voice.

"Why did you walk him over?" Seth asked, reaching out to pat the horse's velvety nose.

The boy shrugged. His head was down and his shoulders slumped under his coat.

"Do you like the horse?" Seth asked.

Clayton looked up and grinned. "It's a horse."

"Yes, but do you like him?" Seth ran his hand over the animal's neck.

"I suppose. Never been around horses before. The other guys like them, so I guess I'll grow to like them, too." Clayton twisted the lead rope in his gloved hands.

"How would you like to go out with me into the west pasture?" Seth asked, opening the gate and motioning for Clayton to lead the horse out.

"Sure. What are we going to do out there?" Clayton asked.

Seth fell into step beside him. He nudged the boy with his shoulder. "Honestly, I just want to take ol' Sam out for a ride."

"You named your horse ol' Sam?"

He chuckled at the boy's shock. "Well, just Sam. What have you named your mount?"

They entered the warmth of the barn, where Jacob and Benjamin sat playing a game of checkers on a bale of hay. Seth walked back to the stall that held Sam. He listened as the boys talked.

"You beating him, Beni?" Clayton asked.

"Nope. Second game and I still haven't won," Benjamin answered Clayton. "But I ain't gonna quit tryin'."

"What would Ma say if she heard you talking like that, Benjamin?" Jacob scolded.

"Like what?" The boy's voice sounded defensive.

Seth thoroughly cinched the saddle under Sam's belly, grinning.

"Ain't? Gonna? Tryin'?" Jacob repeated.

Clayton laughed. "He sounds like a hickabilly to me."

"Ma would say he's uneducated and probably make him come inside for grammar lessons if she heard," Jacob replied with seriousness.

Benjamin whined, "You aren't going to tell her, are you?"

Seth pulled Sam from the stall. He watched Jacob ruffle the little boy's hair and laugh. "Not this time, but you really should watch how you talk. If Ma hears you talking like that, she'll have you in the house instead of out here in this nice warm barn. And you wouldn't be playing checkers, either, but reading from that grammar book she's so fond of."

"What about you, Clayton? Gonna tell on me?" Benjamin asked, looking up at his older brother.

"Not me. Be my misfortunate she'd make me practice with you. You're safe." Clayton grinned down at Benjamin.

Benjamin and Clayton seemed to have a special relationship. The boys' closeness made Seth wish he had brothers. It was too bad he was an only child. He pulled his horse up beside Clayton's. "Ready?"

Clayton nodded. "Ready as I'll ever be." Most eighteen-year-old boys would be thrilled to go out riding, but Clayton's tone sounded anything but thrilled.

Seth looked to Jacob. "Clayton and I are going to go check the fence along the west side of the border. We should be back in time for supper."

"I'll have Ma keep a plate warm for you both if you're late." Jacob turned his focus back on the game.

Once out of the barn, Seth pulled himself up into the saddle. He watched as Clayton did the same. Then he proceeded toward the west pasture.

After a few minutes, Clayton said, "I'm not sure I'm going to be a very good Pony Express rider."

Seth slowed Sam down so that he could talk to the boy. "No?"

Clayton shook his head.

"Why not?" Seth tilted his head to look the boy in the eyes.

"Riding horses has never been of any interest to me," Clayton answered, hanging on to the saddle horn as if he feared falling off.

Seth couldn't hide his surprise at the boy's words. He let them go for several moments before asking, "Then what does interest you?"

Clayton swallowed hard. "You'll just laugh."

"Maybe, but I promise I won't laugh out of meanness."

"All right. I like to doctor stuff."

There was nothing funny about that. Why would the boy think he'd laugh? He'd never understand the workings of a young boy's mind. "Man or beast?"

"You aren't going to laugh?"

Seth frowned. "I don't understand why you would think I'd laugh. Doctoring is an honorable profession. There is nothing to laugh about." He led his horse down to the stream and dismounted.

Clayton followed. When he was on the ground, too, he answered, "All the guys laugh at me. Ma's the only one who doesn't. She's bought me a couple of books about doctoring people and told me I can do anything I put my mind to."

"She's right." Seth admired Rebecca for her wisdom in not discouraging the boy like his brothers had.

"You really believe that?" Clayton asked, rubbing his horse's shoulder as it drank from the cold stream water.

"Yes. I believe that you can do anything you put your mind to. I also believe that God gives us our dreams and desires. So, if you want to be a doctor, who am I to question that?"

Seth pulled his horse back up the stream's bank. When on solid ground, he swung up into the saddle.

Clayton followed. He seemed in deep thought.

Seth led the way to the west pasture. His gaze followed the fence line, checking to see if there were any holes in the fence. Not finding any, he glanced back at Clayton.

The boy sat tall in the saddle. His hand no longer rested on the saddle horn. His head was back and he looked up into the sky. He'd been quiet for at least half an hour.

Not sure what more to say to the boy, Seth turned Sam back in the direction of home. They rode another ten minutes and Clayton galloped up beside him.

"Seth?"

"Yes."

"Do you think Ma will let me keep a little of the money I make with the Pony Express?"

Answering honestly, Seth said, "I don't know. You'll have to ask her." He watched the boy study the workings of the horse's neck. "What do you want the money for?"

"Well, I been thinking about what you said down by the stream and I think you are right. God did give me this dream to doctor animals, but I need to learn more about how to do it. So if Ma will let me have some of the money, I can buy books and learn more about doctoring," he answered with a faraway look in his eyes.

Seth wondered if doctoring people and doctoring animals were similar. Would studying books on how to take care of people also help Clayton learn to take care of animals? They weren't exactly the same thing. He almost laughed at his line of thinking, but then decided that Clayton might think he was laughing at him. Instead he decided to bring the subject back around to the reason he'd brought Clayton out to the pasture.

He looked over at the boy, whose thoughts seemed miles away. "You know, Clayton, you need to learn how to take care of your horse and how to ride him really well so that you can earn the money you need from the Pony Express."

The boy nodded. "I'll work really hard, Seth."

"Have you thought up a name for your horse?" Seth asked, patting Sam on the neck.

"Bones."

"Bones?"

Clayton smiled broadly. "Yep, he's going to be a

doctor's horse. I once heard Papa John call the doctor in town Bones. He's going to help me earn the money to become a doctor. So I'm going to call him Bones."

Seth chuckled. "I like it."

They rode back to the farm with Seth giving Clayton pointers and teaching him how to control the horse with his knees. Seth couldn't help wondering what Rebecca would think when she learned from her son that Seth had encouraged him to become a doctor, an animal doctor at that. Would she be pleased? Or would it be another thing that he'd done she didn't approve of? Why did her approval matter to him? Seth didn't know why it mattered; he just realized that it did.

"Can you believe he was pretending to shoot them out of the saddle?" Rebecca asked Fay as she sewed a new button on one of the boy's shirts. She didn't give Fay a chance to answer. "He said he was teaching them how to use their horses as shields. Shields from what? Who would want to shoot at them?" She sighed in exasperation.

"Indians and robbers," Fay suggested, knotting off her thread. Using her teeth, she broke the thread from the sock she'd just mended.

Rebecca frowned. The thought of her boys being shot at frightened the daylights out of her. But in the world they lived in and with the talk of war in the air, it might become a reality. She shuddered at the thought of war and her boys forced to fight. "Yes, you're right. What Seth teaches them is important, but still I worry."

Fay stood up and stretched. "You wouldn't be much of a mother if you didn't worry," she told Rebecca, rubbing her back. "You know, I'm tempted to go take a nap like Joy."

"There is nothing stopping you from doing just that." Rebecca smiled up at her. "You've earned it. You've worked since sunup this morning."

"I'm not the only one who's worked hard today." Fay covered a yawn then continued, "I'm looking forward to having that beef stew you tossed together this morning."

Rebecca inhaled the aroma of thick beef-and-vegetable stew that filled the house. The wind blew against the house, making her shiver. "I hope it tastes as good as it smells," she said, picking up another shirt. This one had a tear in the sleeve.

"I'm sure it will taste even better."

Rebecca laughed and said, "Don't count on it. I've been known to make things that smelled wonderful but tasted like there might be skunk in it." She threaded her needle and began patching the shirt.

Fay stood by the fireplace for a moment, yawned once more and then said, "Yes, I believe I will lay down for a few minutes. If you are sure you don't mind."

"Not at all. I may close my eyes for a few, too," she said to make the older woman feel better about needing a rest.

Fay left the room. Rebecca heard the bedroom door shut. She leaned her head back and closed her eyes. How many times would the prayer come to her mind? *Lord, am I doing right by my boys?* Watching Seth point that rifle at Clayton had taken her breath away. What if he'd forgotten and had a bullet in the chamber? Then what?

Rebecca kept her eyes closed as she thought about

the days ahead. She knew now that the Pony Express wasn't safe. John had warned her that the boys would be alone on the trail. He'd told her he'd need to teach them how to survive while delivering the mail. It hadn't seemed real not that long ago. But now she had a better understanding of what the job entailed and the reality stated danger in more ways than one.

Since her husband was deceased, Rebecca knew that if the boys were to continue working for the Pony Express, she'd have to trust Seth. They seemed so young, but the orphanage had declared them men at the age of twelve.

Rebecca reminded herself that they were all just a few years younger than herself, except Noah and Beni. At the age of twenty-eight she felt very old. Weariness seeped from her in the form of a heavy sigh.

Seth Armstrong seemed to be doing all he could to teach the boys how to survive the Pony Express. Every evening, he reported to her the day's events and how well they were learning. Even Jacob seemed to be coming around. Her oldest son had told her that he trusted Seth's decisions.

Could she trust the Pony Express man? How far was he willing to go to make the boys into men? Had it entered his mind to start out with an unloaded gun and then move on to a loaded one? Rebecca's eyes snapped open. That was the first question she intended to ask him this evening. She'd most certainly not have him pointing loaded rifles at her boys. That was where she'd draw the line and dare him to cross it.

Chapter Eleven

Seth thought she was joking but the seriousness reflected in her eyes told him otherwise. "You think I'd point a loaded gun at them?"

She crossed her arms over her chest. "How should I know what to think? When I came out to check on them this afternoon, you sure enough had a rifle pointed at their heads. I had no clue at the moment whether it was loaded or not."

He inhaled deeply and slowly released the air in his lungs. "What do I have to do to get you to understand that I would never put your boys in unneeded danger?" He heard the creaking of Fay's rocker that sat across the room from them. Her Bible lay on her lap and she seemed to be absorbed in its words.

They'd moved their nightly discussion into the house. It was nice to have the older woman in the house. Seth felt thankful that Rebecca had another woman to talk to. Had she discussed her fears with Fay? Did Fay trust him to take care of the boys?

"I don't know how you can make me understand,

but I do know that I thought I'd faint when I saw you pointing the gun at them."

Seth turned to face her. "Would it have made you feel better if I'd told you last night exactly what my plans were in teaching them to avoid bullets?"

"Perhaps—at least I would have known you weren't going to shoot them. All you said last night was that you were going to teach them how to avoid bullets on horseback." Rebecca walked to the fireplace. "I know you think I'm being difficult but I'm the only parent these boys have."

Interfering parents was probably the biggest reason why the owners of the Pony Express had asked for orphans. Seth kept the thought to himself. "I understand your concerns and I'm willing to help you put them aside. I just need to know how."

"Maybe you could let me know what you plan to do with the boys the night before you actually do it," she suggested.

Half an hour later, Seth dashed across the yard to the bunkhouse. He was no closer to gaining Rebecca's trust than he'd been when he'd entered the house earlier. Hopefully, telling her his plans for the boys tomorrow had made her feel better.

Andrew looked up when Seth entered the bunkhouse. A quick glance around told Seth the other boys had gone off to their beds. He asked in a soft voice, "What are you still doing up, Andrew?"

The young man stood. "I was waiting for you."

Seth motioned for Andrew to follow him into his room. Once they were both inside, he shut the door. "What can I do for you?"

"Clayton told me that Ma wasn't happy with you earlier today."

Seth walked over to his bed and sat down. "He did, did he?"

"Yes, sir. I wanted to tell you not to get upset with Ma. She means well."

Seth motioned for Andrew to sit down. When the boy had done so he answered, "I know she does, but your Ma has to let me run the Pony Express the way I see fit."

"Yes, sir, but Ma is just afraid we'll get hurt or quit and she wouldn't be able to stand that." Andrew looked down at his hands.

"Andrew, I am not going to hurt any of you boys. Everything I try to teach you is because I want to keep you from harm." Seth felt as if he was having the same conversation with Andrew that he'd had with Rebecca moments earlier.

"Not physical hurt, Seth."

Seth sat up straighter. "What kind of hurt?"

Andrew licked his dry lips. "In an orphanage there are many ways a child can be hurt. We all came from the orphanage and most of us wear the scars inside, where no one will see them. Ma doesn't want us to be hurt like that ever again." Determination filled his eyes as he met Seth's. A harshness, whether from anger or bitterness, filled his voice. "Ma and I are those kinds of orphans and we will not allow the other boys or ourselves to ever be hurt like that again."

Seth reached for his Bible, which rested on his nightstand beside the lamp.

"Don't tell me what that Good Book says or that you are a Christian and will never hurt us. I've met

Christians before and I have scars to prove it." Andrew jerked to his feet. He walked to the door with his head held high and his shoulders back. Just before he opened the door he said, "Seth, I'll ask you again not to be upset with Ma. She means well."

The new information that Rebecca had been an orphan, too, explained why she was so protective of the boys and why she didn't trust him to keep his word, and also accounted for her need to have the boys close. Aware that Andrew waited for a reaction from him, Seth nodded.

It seemed to be what the young man was waiting for. Andrew gently shut the door behind him, leaving Seth to question God on how he could help this family. Especially since he had a promise to keep to his grandmother.

The next morning, Seth chose Thomas to spend time with. He wanted to know what the boy knew and understood about the Pony Express and he also wanted to know the boy better.

The mount Thomas had chosen was a spirited mustang. Thomas could only ride him a few minutes before he ended up on the ground.

A jagged scar marked the right side of his youthful face and Seth figured the eighteen-year-old had a story to tell. Blond hair seemed to constantly hang in the boy's laughing green eyes.

"Well, how am I doing?" Thomas asked. His dancing eyes looked up at Seth from where he sat on the ground.

Seth laughed. "Well, considering your horse just

threw you and you can still smile about it, I'd say pretty good." He reached down and offered the boy a hand up.

"Yeah, that's what I thought, too."

Thomas seemed to enjoy everything life tossed at him, from getting thrown off of his horse, to mucking out stalls. The boy really seemed to take life one event at a time. "I should have chosen a more agreeable horse, I suppose." He picked up his horse's reins and limped to the railing.

"Why did you choose this one?" Seth asked, following.

The boy looked over his shoulder at the compact black horse he'd chosen. "I suppose I liked his spirit. No matter how many times I get up on him to ride, he always proves that he might be little, but there is a lot of power in him."

Seth thought about the boy's words for a moment as Thomas dusted off his pants. He watched Thomas rub the horse's nose as if to tell him he was forgiven for throwing him to the ground. "So what you are telling me is that you like that he is small, but has lots of energy and you want to give him a chance to prove himself?"

Thomas nodded. "Everyone needs a chance to prove themselves, even horses." He reached up and rubbed the horse's velvety ears. "Isn't that right, boy?"

"You know, there is an easier way to let him get his energy out besides him flinging you to the ground like a sack of flour." Seth leaned against the fence and smiled.

"How's that?" Thomas asked, looking interested.

Seth pushed away from the rails. "You could start

by taking him on a fast ride. Wouldn't it be better to have wind in your hair instead of dirt in your drawers?"

Thomas laughed. "Sure would. I didn't think we were allowed to take them out without permission," he admitted.

"Spirit is yours to do with as you see fit, to make him a good Pony Express horse. Just be courteous and let one of us know when you are going out."

Thomas studied him. "You named him Spirit?"

Seth shrugged. "It seemed to fit at the moment, but he's your horse and you can name him whatever you want."

"I thought more on the name Diablo, but Spirit works better." Thomas grinned. "Can we take Spirit for a run now?"

"Let me get Sam and we'll go for a long hard ride." Seth walked toward the barn, his thoughts filled with Thomas and what he'd learned from the boy. If he related to a spirited horse that he felt only wanted to prove himself, did that mean Thomas felt he had to prove himself to everyone around him, too?

Once more Seth felt the need to pray for the Young boys. They were orphans. Even though they were adopted by Rebecca and her deceased husband, in their hearts and minds they still felt like orphans and had many hurts to get through.

A few moments later, he and Thomas raced across the pasture. "Watch out for gopher holes," Seth called to the rushing boy and horse.

Thomas nodded. His hat hung down his back, his blond hair waved in the wind. The scar down his face looked white against his tan skin.

How had Thomas obtained the scar? Had he been in

a knife fight? Fallen on something sharp? There were so many unanswered questions about each of the boys. Someday, when they were better acquainted, he might start asking. An unwelcome tension entered Seth, right between the shoulder blades. He stretched in the saddle, seeking relief. Bit by bit, this family wormed their way into his thoughts and heart.

They rode on for several minutes. Seth slowed and allowed Thomas to speed ahead. The weather wasn't as cold as it had been the day before. He looked up into the sky and saw dark clouds coming in from the west.

Thomas pulled up beside him. "Looks like the weather might take a turn for the worse. Would it be all right with you if we stopped by the family cemetery before heading back?"

Seth glanced over at the boy. "Of course." He followed Thomas across the meadow to a small wooded area.

They crossed the stream and continued through the woods to a quiet open area. Thomas stopped his horse and dismounted. "Papa John always said to walk in from here. He said it showed respect to those who have gone home before us."

Sam came to a halt and Seth dismounted also. Seth followed Thomas the rest of the way. It would seem that at least one of the Young boys had learned respect from their adoptive father.

As they continued a short piece through the trees, silence surrounded them, although an occasional bird-call interrupted the peace of the woods. They came out of the trees into a small meadow. Three graves rested under a grove of cottonwood trees on a hill.

When they reached the top of the knoll, Seth could

see the road that led to the farm. So this was where Rebecca's family had been laid to rest.

Thomas kneeled down on one knee beside the grave marked John Percival Young. He brushed sticks from the grave and sighed. "He was a great man."

"I'm sure he was," Seth replied, taking his hat off and holding it respectfully in his hands.

"In the five years I knew him, he never raised a hand to me or any of the boys." Thomas stood and brushed his hands against his pant legs. "Someday, I want to build a fence around the graves to keep wild animals out of here." He wiped the hair off his forehead.

Seth stood beside him and placed a hand on his shoulder. "I'd be happy to help you build it."

The two of them stood silently looking down on the graves. Seth read the names on the other two headstones and realized that these must be John's parents. They were older, the names and dates wearing off the wooden crosses. "We could also freshen up the crosses," he suggested.

"I think Ma would like that," Thomas agreed.

A big drop of water hit Seth on the bridge of his nose. "We better head back before the storm hits." He touched his forehead slightly in a salute then slapped his hat back on his head.

Thomas nodded and turned to walk his horse down to the road. Seth kept a shoulder beneath his horse's neck, sheltering as best he could, but more drops of rain hit them both. Within minutes they were soaked through. The wind had turned cold while they'd been out riding and right now Seth wished he was back in his room, where warmth and dry clothes waited for him.

Once they were at the road, Thomas mounted his horse. "I'll race you back," he challenged.

Seth climbed aboard Sam and nodded. "Ready."

Together the two of them raced toward the barn. The horses' hooves beat a rapid rhythm against the wet ground. Seth lay close to his mount's back, urging him on to the barn. Rain pelted them, soaking both man and beast. Seth couldn't remember ever being so wet. When they got to the barn, Jacob met them in the doorway.

Both Seth and Thomas slid from their horses' backs. Thomas had won and the grin on his face spoke volumes of the pride he felt. Seth slapped him on the back. "Keep riding like that and you'll be a top-notch Pony Express rider," he assured him.

Thomas's grin spread even farther across his scarred face. "Thanks."

"I'll take care of Sam for you," Jacob offered, reaching for the reins. "Ma would like to see you in the house."

"Did she say what she wanted to see me about?" Seth asked, handing the reins over.

Jacob shook his head. "Nope. Just said to ask you to come inside when you and Thomas got back."

Seth looked out into the pouring rain. Within the past few minutes, it had created what looked like a small river through the middle of the front yard. He didn't look forward to getting even wetter, but the sooner he spoke to Rebecca, the sooner he could go to his room and get dry.

He looked at Thomas, who already held a towel and was drying his mount. "Thomas, do that quickly and get into some dry clothes. I don't want you getting sick."

Send For
2 FREE BOOKS
Today!

I accept your offer!

Please send me two
free novels and two mystery
gifts (gifts worth about $10).
I understand that these books
are completely free—even
the shipping and handling will
be paid—and I am under no
obligation to purchase anything,
ever, as explained on the back
of this card.

102 IDL GJ2X/302 IDL GJ2Y

Please Print

_____

FIRST NAME

_____

LAST NAME

_____

ADDRESS

_____

APT.#   CITY

_____

STATE/PROV.   ZIP/POSTAL CODE

Visit us online at
www.ReaderService.com

▲ © 2015 HARLEQUIN ENTERPRISES LIMITED. ® and ™ are trademarks owned and used by the trademark owner and/or its licensee. Printed in the U.S.A.

▲ Detach card and mail today! No stamp needed

The boy nodded and continued talking softly to the horse.

"Thanks for taking care of Sam," Seth said to Jacob, then took a deep breath and dashed into the freezing rain. Surely the temperature had dropped—the rain hadn't felt this cold earlier. His boots slid in the mud and water. He'd be glad when the early spring rains stopped and summer started.

Rebecca met him on the porch. "You didn't have to run in the rain," she scolded, offering him a towel to dry off with.

He ran the cloth over his arms and neck, not appreciating her annoying tone. "What did you need to see me about?"

"I wondered if you could take one of the boys out hunting tomorrow or the next day," she answered, not bothering to hide her irritation at his gruff attitude.

Fay stepped out onto the porch. "You two stop snapping at each other and get in here where it's warmer."

Like two obedient children, they did as she said. Seth followed Rebecca inside, wishing he hadn't been impatient with her. Fay closed the door behind them. "Why don't you go into the sitting room and stand by the fire," she said to Seth.

"Thanks, I believe I will." He pulled his hat from his head and walked across the hardwood floor. His boots made squishing noises as Seth marched past Rebecca toward the sound of crackling wood and the promise of warmth. Knowing he would have to apologize for his rude behavior had him pricklier than a wide-awake black bear in the wintertime.

What was it about Rebecca Young that sent a tickle of irritation up his neck? Not all the time, just when she spoke abruptly or accusingly. Could it simply be that the rain had put him in a bad mood? Or the fact that she'd summoned him to the house like a hired hand? Seth wasn't sure, but he knew he didn't like this feeling, not one little bit.

He wished at times like this that he could just be on his way. Let the Young family live their lives and he'd carry on with his. The thought sobered him.

Did he really want to leave them? Didn't the boys need him now more than ever? His gaze moved to Rebecca. Her hair hung down her back and her cheeks were rosy. Pretty blue eyes studied him and he wished he could take back the harshness of his words.

Just don't allow yourself to get too close to any of them, he thought. Seth prayed that he hadn't already.

Chapter Twelve

Rebecca sat down on her favorite chair and picked up her sewing. The weather had turned nasty and so had her temper. She silently asked the Lord to forgive her. What was it about Seth Armstrong that had her emotions all in a knot?

He stood with his back to her. Wide shoulders stretched the wet material of his shirt. The edges of his hair curled around his collar. Seth braced his hands against the fireplace mantel.

Very aware of the creaking sound of Fay's rocker, Rebecca tried to focus on her mending. She didn't know what to say to him. He'd snapped at her like an old turtle. All she'd wanted to do was ask him to go hunting. They needed fresh meat.

Tears stung her eyes, making Rebecca angry. She had no intention of crying. Rebecca told herself she had nothing to cry about.

His warm voice washed over her like a healing balm. "I'm sorry, Rebecca. I'll be happy to take the boys out hunting tomorrow. It will also give me the opportunity to see how well they can shoot a gun."

Her voice cracked as she said, "Thank you."

The rocking stopped. Seth spun around to look at her. Rebecca focused on her mending. She didn't want to face either Fay or Seth with tears in her eyes. What was she going to do? She couldn't wipe the moisture away; they'd know for sure she was on the verge of crying like a baby.

"Ma, can I have a cookie?" Joy asked as she entered the room.

Rebecca practically jumped to her feet. "Yes, I'll help you get one." She hurried out of the room, very aware that both Seth and Fay still watched her.

Once in the kitchen, she wiped her eyes, then pulled down the cookie jar and handed Joy a cookie. "Here you go, sweetie."

"Ma, are you crying?" Joy asked, taking the cookie but not eating it. Her eyes studied her mother's face for an explanation.

Rebecca kneeled down to her daughter's level. "No, but I could use a hug."

Joy immediately went into her mother's arms. Rebecca held her tightly and enjoyed the sweet smell of her little girl. Joy liked the smell of vanilla and often put some behind her little ears. Rebecca grinned and then released her. "You smell nice," she said.

"I smell like nilla."

"Vanilla," Rebecca said, correcting her.

Joy nodded. "That's what I said. Nilla."

Rebecca leaned away from her daughter. "I know you can say it correctly. Why don't you?"

The little girl smiled. "That's the way Pa used to say it. Remember? I don't want to forget him so I use his words."

"I remember." The bittersweet memories flooded her mind. Rebecca gave Joy another quick hug and then stood. John was also the one who used to dab vanilla behind Joy's ears and then pretend to "eat her up." Funny that she hadn't thought about that in a long time.

She took Joy's hand and walked back to the sitting room, where Seth and Fay waited. Her gaze moved to where he stood by the fireplace.

He looked up as she entered the room. She ignored the question in his eyes. Instead Rebecca asked one. "What are you planning to do with the boys tomorrow?"

Seth turned his back to the fire. "Well, Noah, Philip, Andrew and I will go hunting. I'm assuming you want to replenish your meat supply, so I'll have Jacob, Clayton, Thomas and Benjamin go fishing. Then when we get back I want them to work with their horses. Sometime tomorrow evening I plan to have them practice passing the postage bag to each other."

Rebecca watched Joy nibble on her cookie, aware that she looked from one adult to the other. Did she feel the tension between Seth and Rebecca? Rebecca wondered if she shouldn't speak to Seth in private from now on.

Joy scrunched up her cute little nose. "What's a postage bag?" she asked Seth.

"It's the bag that will have the mail inside."

"Oh. Can I practice, too?" she asked.

Rebecca shook her head. "No, you are not a Pony Express rider like the boys."

Joy placed her small hand on her hip and announced, "When I grow up, I'm going to be a Pony Express rider, too."

Seth chuckled. "I don't doubt that you will."

Rebecca enjoyed the warm sound that seemed to bubble up from his chest. He really was a good man. His patience with the kids, especially Joy, gave her renewed confidence in the man. Yes, his methods scared her, but she'd have to learn to trust him to keep his word.

Joy looked up at her mother. "Ma, can I go fishing with Beni tomorrow?" She stuck a thumb into her parted lips.

Picking up her sewing, Rebecca sat down before answering. "I don't know. Babies don't go fishing." She hated that Joy still sucked on her thumb. She'd tried everything to break the habit, but nothing worked.

A light pink filled the little girl's cheeks as she jerked her thumb out of her mouth. "I'm not a baby," Joy protested.

Rebecca smiled at her daughter. "No, you are not. We'll have to see how the weather is tomorrow. If it's raining out there like it is now, we don't want you catching your death from cold."

As if on cue, Seth sneezed.

Fay, who had been silent so far, looked up and said, "Speaking of catching your death, Seth, you should probably get into some warm, dry clothes."

He nodded. "I believe you are right." Seth turned to face Rebecca once more. "Is there anything else we need to discuss before I go?" Seth quirked an eyebrow at her.

"No, I think that will be all. Thank you for coming in and easing my mind a mite." She offered him her most sincere smile. The last thing she needed was to offend the station keeper. He didn't have to share his plans with her and she really did appreciate his willingness to do so.

Seth put on his soggy hat and walked to the front door. "Have a good evening, ladies."

"Aren't you coming back in for supper?" Joy asked as she followed him.

He kneeled down in front of Joy. "Not tonight. I'm wet and cold. I think I'll stay in my room and get warmed up."

Rebecca's breath caught in her throat as his green eyes collided with hers over Joy's head. Tenderness filled the beautiful orbs as he continued talking to her daughter.

"Maybe your ma will send a plate out to the bunkhouse. I wouldn't mind eating in my room tonight." He turned his attention back to the little girl.

Joy smiled at him. "She will. Won't you, Ma?"

"Of course."

Seth stood. "Thank you." He brushed the top of Joy's head with his hand. "I'll see you in the morning," he said and then he was gone.

"He really is a nice man, Rebecca," Fay said as she closed her Bible.

Rebecca nodded. "He seems to be." She turned her head and watched out the window as he jogged across the rain-soaked front yard.

His boots slipped and for a moment, Rebecca held her breath, afraid he'd fall. When he'd managed to right himself, she released a huge sigh.

"He's a handsome young man, too," Fay said. She now stood beside Rebecca's chair and also watched Seth dash into the bunkhouse.

Rebecca ignored Fay's last comment.

"How old do you think he is?" Fay asked.

"Don't start matchmaking, Fay." Rebecca laid her sewing to the side.

"What's matchmaking?" Joy asked, reminding the two women that they weren't alone.

Rebecca turned her daughter away from the window. "You never mind what matchmaking is. Go straighten your room." She gave Joy a gentle push in the direction of her bedroom.

"All right, Ma." Joy skipped off.

Rebecca headed to the kitchen, where her beef stew and corn bread were cooking. Her thoughts returned to Seth. Fay was right, he was a handsome man. Mentally she answered Fay's last question—she figured Seth was probably a little older than her. She stirred the stew and then pulled the hot corn bread out of the oven.

Raindrops hit the pipe on the stove, spitting and spewing and sending a shiver down her spine. Poor Seth, he'd been soaked to the skin. She wondered if Thomas was as wet.

In the coming months, Rebecca expected the boys to be both wet and cold. She hated that they would be exposed to the weather and wondered if there was anything she could do to give them comfort. Would Seth ride the Pony Express, too?

Why was he in her thoughts so much today? Was it because he'd made her angry? Or was it because Fay had hinted at matchmaking between the two of them?

Seth was handsome but Rebecca couldn't allow him into her heart. She had a farm to run, children to take care of, and she had to preserve the memory of John for her daughter's sake. And she also needed to keep her family together. If she became interested in Seth as a future husband, then he might uproot her from the farm.

No, it was better not to think along those lines. Even if he did have lovely green eyes and a smile that melted her anger.

The horse flew past Seth. He tossed the flour sack up at Philip on the horse's back. It hit the young man squarely in the chest, knocking him from his horse and into the mud.

The others hooted and hollered from the sidelines. Seth shook his head. So far, none of the boys had been able to catch the pretend saddlebag.

Noah climbed aboard his small mustang. Seth doubted that Noah would fare any better than the other boys had, but he had to give him a chance to try.

Benjamin sloshed through the mud and scooped up the flour sack. He handed it up to Seth with a grin. "They ain't doin' so good, are they, Seth?"

"No, they aren't," Seth agreed, turning his horse back to the starting line.

Noah went to the opposite side of the pasture and rounded his mount. The boy laid low over his horse's neck and then at the yelp from Jacob kicked his horse into action. The little mustang ate the ground between them with super speed.

Seth met him halfway and tossed the flour bag. He was shocked to see Noah grab it in midair and loop it over his saddle horn.

More hoots and yells came from the sidelines. This time no laughter filled the air, only praise and questions. Seth wheeled his horse around and observed the boys.

How was it that Noah, the youngest at the age of

twelve, was so much better at practically everything than the other boys? He rode his horse with more confidence than the others, shot a gun better and had a wicked way with his knife.

While hunting earlier in the morning, Seth noted that Noah seemed to be tracking the deer, unlike the others, who were simply hunting. When they'd finally come upon their prey, Noah had been the one to kill the first deer. Andrew had shot the second deer. Noah had also killed three rabbits with a flick of his wrist and a knife. He'd quickly shown Philip how he'd thrown the knife and together they killed two more rabbits. Noah had skills, but how had he acquired them? Seth doubted that they were taught such things in an orphanage.

Rebecca had been pleased with the two deer and five rabbits. Thankfully, the other boys had brought in a load of fish that would have made anyone proud. She praised them all on their hunting and fishing skills.

The boys were covered in mud, all except Jacob. He hadn't participated with the activity as he was the stock tender and more than likely wouldn't need to ride the trail. Then again...

Seth called out, "Jacob, saddle up. You might need to learn this, too."

Noah handed the bag to Jacob and then continued his conversation with his other brothers. Carrying the sack, Jacob walked back to the barn to get his horse. If the slump of his shoulders was any indication, Jacob wasn't happy with this new turn of events.

Seth rode over to where the other boys were still standing. "Come on, fellas. Team up into twos and practice running your horses toward each other. I want you to get as close as you can without touching your horses together. When you are coming in from a hard ride, you are going to need to be fast and accurate in your tossing of the mailbag." He watched as they hurried off to do his bidding.

A smile touched his lips as he thought of what Rebecca's reaction might have been if she'd seen the boys catapult from the backs of their horses. Would she have laughed, like he had? Or would she protest that her babies were treated too roughly?

A giggle behind him answered his question. Seth turned to see Rebecca cup a hand over her mouth. Her gaze was trained on Thomas and a smile lit up her eyes. "They are all covered in mud," she said between her fingers.

"Not yet, but they soon will be," Seth answered, pointing to a scowling Jacob. The young man had just swung into his saddle and slowly walked his horse toward them.

"Jacob is going to ride, too?"

Seth shrugged. "In an emergency, he might. I want him to be able to catch the mailbag if he has to." He winked down at Joy, who clung to her mama's skirts.

When Jacob came within distance, Seth asked, "Ready?"

"As I'll ever be," Jacob responded. He continued to walk his horse to the far end of the pasture.

Rebecca giggled. "He doesn't look very happy about this, does he?"

Seth shook his head. "Nope. Should be fun." He instinctively winked at Rebecca before turning Sam away.

Why had he done that? He shouldn't be trifling with the mother of eight. Seth glanced over his shoulder and saw that she wasn't watching him at all, but had her eyes locked on the boys as they practiced. Maybe she hadn't noticed his slip.

His gaze moved to Joy. The little girl's mouth was slit into the biggest grin he'd ever seen. Her little eyes sparkled with hope and Seth felt dread ease into his heart.

He didn't want to build Joy's hopes that he might be interested in her mother. No, Seth needed to get a grip on himself. The last thing he needed was for the Young women to set their sights on him as a potential husband and father.

Chapter Thirteen

Seth hit the ground with a swoosh. Jacob had nailed him with the flour bag. Cold mud seeped into his pants and made a sucking noise as he attempted to push out of it. His boots slipped and there was another whooshing sound.

With his thoughts on Rebecca and Joy, Seth had forgotten that Jacob had the sack. He frowned up at Jacob.

The twenty-year-old had the gall to grin down at him. "Looks like I'm not the only one who needs practice." He reached down a hand to pull up Seth.

Seth had the satisfaction of slapping cold mud into the other man's hand. He grinned when Jacob didn't flinch. With the strength of youth, Jacob pulled him to his feet.

"Don't forget our mud-covered saddlebag," Jacob said, whirling his mount around and waving cheekily to his mother and sister as he passed them.

Shaking the mud off his hands, Seth bent over and collected the sack. He looked to Sam, who stood to the right of him, seemingly ashamed of his master. He hung the bag on the horse's saddle horn and murmured into his ear, "You would have fallen off, too, if we had been in different positions."

The horse snorted and shook his massive head.

For the next hour, they practiced passing the saddlebag. Soon all of them were spending more time in the saddle and less in the mire. In a way, Seth was glad that the rain had created them a nice soft spot to land, but now they were all covered in mud. He didn't relish the idea of washing in the cold stream, but the idea of hauling water to the house and heating it appealed even less.

"Dinner will be in an hour," Rebecca called from the sidelines. She lifted Joy off the fence rail, where the little girl had been perched, laughing at her brothers.

"You heard her, men. Let's get some clean clothes and head to the stream." Seth didn't have to tell them twice. The boys dashed away on their horses straight toward the bunkhouse.

Jacob called after them, "Whatever mess you carry into the bunkhouse, you have to clean up." He continued on to the barn and his tack room.

Sometimes Seth envied Jacob. The boy had a building all to himself. Peace reigned in the barn. Not so in the bunkhouse. Brotherly rivalry and boyish jostling seemed to be the norm.

Noah trailed behind his brothers. Seth rode up beside him. "Why aren't you in a hurry to get to the bunkhouse?"

"You heard Jacob."

Seth looked to the retreating back of Jacob. "Yes."

A sly grin crossed Noah's lips. "If I'm the last one there, I can't be accused of making the mess."

Seth felt a laugh grow in his gut and then burst

forth. Once he'd gotten his mirth under control, he said, "Noah, you are wiser than your years."

"Not really—they are just foolish for their advanced ages." He gently touched his boots to his mount's sides, leaving Seth to ponder the boy's words.

Long after everyone else was supposed to be in bed, Rebecca felt as if a pot full of water rested between her shoulder blades. She finished wiping down the counter and looked to Fay. The older woman leaned a mop against the wall and pushed the hair away from her face.

"Is it just me or was this the longest day of the year?" Fay slipped into one of the kitchen chairs.

Rebecca joined her at the table. "I don't know about it being the longest, but it was one of the hardest."

"Next time you send the men out for fresh meat, make sure they bring it in a little at a time." Fay yawned, proving she was exhausted beyond her normal tiredness.

"Why don't you head on to bed, Fay? I can take care of this." Rebecca indicated the piles of meat that filled trays on the kitchen table.

Fay shook her head. "No, four hands are better than two. I'll help you. I know you're tired, too."

Seth came into the kitchen through the back door. When he saw them staring at him, he grinned. "I thought I might help you put this meat away." Andrew, Clayton, Thomas and Philip followed him inside. "And I brought help."

Fay chuckled. "You are a blessing. We dreaded hauling all this out to the icehouse."

"Then dread no more," Philip said, grabbing a large tray and heading back out the door.

"Ladies, we'll take care of this. You can call it a day, if you want to." Seth picked another tray of meat and headed back outside.

Fay took off her apron and hung it on the nail beside the door. "Thank you, boys. I'm going to retire." She smiled at Rebecca. "You might as well let them take care of it and get some rest yourself." Then she walked out of the kitchen, barely hiding her yawn.

Rebecca couldn't let them do all of it. She knew they were tired, too. She'd seen the boys as they'd done their day of work and it hadn't been easy on them, either. Besides, she wanted it put away where she'd know what was what. She grabbed one of the smaller trays and hurried after Andrew and Clayton.

The icehouse wasn't far from the back door. Rebecca loved the small building and enjoyed going out. John's mother had taught her how to place the meat so that she'd never have to search for the part she wanted. Roasts, steaks, ground meats and delicacy meats all had their places in the small structure. She wasn't about to let the men simply toss it inside.

"I told you she'd follow us," Philip said, still holding his tray of meat. "Ma likes things put away orderly." He smiled broadly at Rebecca, assumably to take the sting out of his words.

Rebecca continued into the building. She set down her load on the small table to the right of the door. "Just set it here and I'll put it where it belongs," she instructed needlessly as Philip and Seth had already joined her by the table.

The boys continued going back and forth between

the icehouse and the kitchen, until they'd delivered all the meat. "That's the last of it, Ma," Jacob said as he set down the last tray.

"Thank you, son." She looked up to see the retreating back of Andrew. Jacob stood smiling at her. His eyes looked tired. "Go on to bed and tell the other boys thank you, too. It would have taken Fay and us forever to get all that meat out here."

He nodded and left. Rebecca wondered if Seth had, like the boys, already returned to the bunkhouse. They hadn't had time to discuss tomorrow, but she was beginning to trust Seth, so didn't feel the need to fuss about it. Although she did miss him. She pushed the thought away and went back to her work.

Rebecca took her time placing everything where she wanted it. A sense of satisfaction filled her as she pushed straw about the last few packages of meat, even though her shoulders ached and her fingers felt frozen to the bone.

Thinking herself alone, Rebecca jumped when she straightened up and saw Seth leaning against the frame studying her.

She gasped and placed a hand over her heart. "You scared the life out of me," she protested. "I thought you'd gone to the bunkhouse with the boys."

Seth pushed away from the frame and held the door open for her to exit. "I thought about it but realized you'd be half-frozen by the time you finished up in here." He followed her out. "So I took the liberty of making a fresh pot of tea in the kitchen to warm you up. I hope you don't mind."

He'd made tea for her? She knew he favored strong coffee. Rebecca turned to look at him. "That was very thoughtful of you. Thanks." It had been a long time since someone other than Fay had done something so nice for her.

"It was no trouble."

Rebecca realized that he'd not followed her. She stopped and turned to look at him. He stood by the icehouse with his hands tucked into his coat pockets. "You must be cold, too. Would you like to join me for a cup of that tea?"

He looked as if he might refuse. The notion hit Rebecca hard and she realized that she truly would enjoy his company if he accepted her invitation. To sweeten the idea for him she added, "I have apple pie warming on the back of the stove."

"Who am I to refuse apple pie?" He walked toward her with a teasing grin. A tingling she tried her best to ignore started in the pit of Rebecca's stomach.

She opened the kitchen door and slipped inside, the warmth enveloping her like a blanket. She'd reserved two slices of the pie for herself and Fay as a special treat after all the hard work they'd done that day. But since Fay was unaware of the gesture and Seth had been thoughtful in both getting the boys to help her and making the tea, she felt it only fair to share it with him.

"Please, have a seat at the table and I'll get the pie," she said, indicating that he should sit down at the small table.

He ignored her and walked to the coffeepot. "That's very kind, but I think I'll pour the tea. The sooner we have both on the table, the sooner I'll get to savor the pie." Seth carried the pot to the cabinet that housed the dishes and set it down, then reached for the cups.

How long had it been since a man had considered her feelings and overrode them for her benefit? Rebecca's emotions took a nosedive. Or maybe they soared out the top of her head. She couldn't be quite sure, but tears burned the backs of her eyelids and she fought a strong impulse to give in to them. She felt uncertain if her melancholy stemmed from his kindness or her overly tired body.

Taking a deep breath, she carried the pie plate to the table and grabbed two forks from the ceramic crock.

Seth set down the two steaming cups and together they slipped into chairs and sighed. He laughed. "Long day for the both of us, I'd wager."

"I hadn't considered the amount of work it takes to cure meat for storage." She offered him a tired smile.

He nodded. "Next time, we'll space out how much we bring back and the boys and I will do more of the work." Seth forked a bite of apple pie from his slice and slipped it into his mouth.

Rebecca followed the fork's action and realized that his top lip was thin, but the bottom one was full. His tongue snaked out and cleaned up the syrup left behind by the pie. She looked away, realizing that she'd been staring at his mouth.

Heat filled her face. She looked down at the pie plate, realizing she should probably say something. "Thank you. That would be nice."

"Your apple pie tastes like my grandmother's," Seth said, closing his eyes and savoring the sweetness.

She took a tiny bite and let the cinnamon flavor coat her tongue. Apple pie was something else John's mother had taught her to make. Her own mother had left her and her brother at the orphanage when Rebecca was eight years old and her brother ten. Meals in the orphanage weren't fancy and the children were kept out of the kitchen. It wasn't until she came to help John's mother that she learned how to cook.

He chuckled. "That was a compliment. No need to look so sad."

Rebecca smiled. "I'm sorry. I was just remembering John's mother. She taught me how to cook. I miss her." It was all true, just not the complete reason for her look of sorrow.

"I imagine you do miss her," Seth said, taking a sip of the fresh tea.

She nodded. "Yes, like you miss your grandmother."

He set down his fork and cupped the mug in his hands. "I do miss her."

They sat in silence for several moments, each lost in their thoughts.

Rebecca glanced at him. Had he suffered a lot of loss in his life? She wondered what had happened to his parents and other family members. Had Seth had a brother or sister at some point in his life?

Her brother, Daniel, had been made to leave the orphanage at age twelve. Without a parent who truly loved him and prepared him for the world, he'd been totally clueless as to how to fend for himself. He should never have been on the streets trying to survive during winter. He'd failed, and she blamed the orphanage for his loss of life.

It was the next summer before Rebecca found out her brother had died. Grief such as she'd never known had cracked the fragile shell she'd built around herself when Daniel left the orphanage. Unaware even that she'd formed a wall of protection, when it came crashing down, despair became her daily companion.

She'd had nightmares, and the staff had her treated for depression. Later, she'd suffered from a sense of hopelessness. If she couldn't help Daniel, the outcome of her own life appeared bleak.

But God had a plan. She learned early on to trust in Him and He had become her mainstay. Her life had taken a series of turns quite different from the ones Daniel had suffered.

Rebecca had vowed she would never pass up a chance to help those less fortunate. Thankfully, John had understood her need to keep as many boys off the streets as she could and had allowed her to adopt her boys. Those boys were her life now and she loved them all deeply.

"You have a very pretty smile," Seth said, pulling her back to the present.

Unaware she'd been smiling, Rebecca ducked her head in embarrassment. "Thank you." He must think her insane—in the past few minutes he'd seen her go from exhausted to tired and then to smiling.

"Does it bother you when I compliment you?" She glanced up to find him regarding her inquisitively.

Rebecca thought about it for a moment before answering. "No, it doesn't bother me. It just feels surprising to know that someone even considers my smile." She shrugged. "It's been a long time."

"You're a great lady, Rebecca. Someone should compliment you every day of your life." He pushed back his chair. "I'll see what I can do about that."

A tumble of confused thoughts and feelings assailed her. She let out a long, audible breath, but her voice deserted her. She could only stare at him. Crimson color slipped up the sides of his face and ears.

Seth walked to the door. "Umm, thanks for the tea and pie. I really should turn in now."

She picked up the pie plate and cups as she followed him. "Me, too."

"Right after breakfast, I'm taking the boys on a long ride. We'll cover the trail they'll be riding in a few weeks." He ran his hand over the back of his neck. "Just thought you'd like to know."

She nodded. "Would you like for me to pack some sandwiches?"

"If you don't mind. I'm only taking three of the boys tomorrow and then three the following day." Seth stood with his hand on the door.

"You're taking Jacob, too?"

Seth nodded. "Yep, he may have to be a relief rider. But more than likely he won't actually go out very often. Plus, as the stock tender I want him to learn the trail so that he'll know which horse to send out." The red color seeped from his face. Now that they were talking normally, he seemed to no longer feel embarrassed.

Rebecca spoke her thoughts aloud. "Which in turn will decide which boy will travel which trail."

"Sounds right."

She tilted her head to look at him better. "Wouldn't it be best to take all the boys at the same time, just in case they need to ride in both directions?"

He nodded approvingly. "Yes. And I will take them out again and go in the opposite direction than what they'll be traveling over the next couple of days."

Why didn't he just take them all tomorrow and again the next day? Rebecca didn't understand his job, but to her that made more sense.

As if he could read her thoughts, Seth yawned and said, "I'm taking them a few at a time to keep the focus on the job at hand. I want to make sure that they understand the trail and the dangers on it. All together they turn into a bunch of cutups."

His yawn had her mimicking the action. Rebecca covered her mouth. A warm chuckle drew her gaze to him once more.

"Good night, Rebecca."

"Seth?" Rebecca's courage almost failed when he turned to look at her. "Thanks for tonight."

"No thanks needed. Next time we won't bring back as much meat."

She took a deep breath and smiled. "No, I meant the other. It does a woman's heart good to have nice things said to her occasionally. And the tea, well, that was a sweet gesture, too."

They stared at each other, a spark of some indefinable emotion in his eyes. Did he feel the attraction, too? Or was she simply overtired and seeing too much in him and his actions?

"Good night, Rebecca." He pushed open the door and disappeared into the night.

It seemed silly but Rebecca missed him already. She whispered, "Sweet dreams, Seth." Then she picked up the lantern and walked to her bedroom.

As she prepared for bed, Rebecca continued to focus on Seth and the work he was doing. He'd been working hard with her boys and she could already see that their self-confidence had grown. Even little Benjamin walked with straighter shoulders.

As she'd tucked him into bed, he'd told her that Seth and Jacob had taught him how to check the horse's legs to make sure they were straight and strong. His eyes shone and his cheeks puffed in pride at his newfound knowledge. How could she not love the new excitement her boys showed each time she talked to them? And it was due to Seth's way of treating them and the confidence he instilled.

The stage was due in the morning. Would Seth's mail-order bride be on it? Or would someone on the stage know who Charlotte was or where to locate her? She pulled back the covers on her bed and climbed inside.

Blowing out the lamp, Rebecca relaxed and sank into the cushioning softness. A thought niggled at her tired mind. Did she want Seth to find his fiancée?

Over the past couple of weeks she'd grown to like Seth Armstrong. He cared about her boys. She smiled into the darkness. They weren't boys anymore; they were men. Still, another man might break their spirits, not understand them like Seth did. His gentleness was one of the things she liked most about him.

In the stillness of the dark night, Rebecca faced her real fear. Did she have feelings for Seth? Feelings that went beyond friendship? No? Then why had her heart flip-flopped when he'd told her she had a pretty smile? Why did the pulse at the base of her throat jump every time their eyes met? And last but not least, why had it felt so good to have him compliment her?

She tossed over to her side.

These feelings were caused by tiredness, that was all. But that little voice just wouldn't keep quiet in her mind. She'd felt all that before today, so it stood to reason that tiredness played no part in her feelings.

Rebecca thumped her pillow in frustration. Why,

why, why did she have to complicate matters with feelings? He'd complimented her, making her feel special. So what? He probably did that to anyone that cooked and cleaned for him. Yes, that had to be it.

She turned over to the other side and tucked her hand under her pillow. She wasn't acquiring feelings for Seth. She wouldn't allow it. Falling in love wasn't a part of her future, not with Seth, not with any man. Her children were her whole focus.

Her hand snaked across the bed and touched John's pillow. Besides, she wouldn't betray John's memory. The children had already faced many changes. Adding another man in their lives, well, to her way of thinking that just wouldn't be wise.

Chapter Fourteen

Seth didn't want to admit it, but his stomach felt as twisted as that apron. April had arrived with clear skies and anticipation in the air. He'd had two months to work with the boys and he felt they were as ready as they'd ever be. Since Noah was still his best horseman Seth decided to give him the first run. The uncertainty had plagued him all through the night.

Rebecca stood on the porch watching as they waited for the Pony Express rider from the east to arrive. Noah sat on his horse looking relaxed and ready to go. Rebecca twisted her apron in her hands, the only indicator that she was nervous.

Finally, unable to stand the tension, Seth sprinted up to the porch. Before he changed his mind he blurted out, "I'm going with him." Rebecca clasped her hands against her heart and pure relief washed over her features. She nodded.

It felt good. It was the right thing to do. Seth then turned and ran to the barn for his horse, Sam.

He couldn't let her fuss over the youngest rider and Seth felt certain it would drive him insane not knowing if the boy had made his run without mishap. No matter how hard he tried, Seth couldn't help but care for the Young family.

Jacob met him halfway with Sam. "I thought you might need him," he said, handing the reins to Seth, an expression of satisfaction showing in his eyes.

"Thanks." Seth clapped a hand on his shoulder in appreciation. The boy had the makings of a great leader, discernment being one of the most important gifts to have been blessed with. It was for sure he'd gotten this situation sized correctly. "I'll be back as quick as I can. You're in charge. Be sure and write down the time that the rider coming in arrives." Seth jumped into the saddle.

He moved into position a few feet behind Noah. The boy turned in his saddle. Noah lifted an eyebrow in question then asked, "What's going on?"

"Change of plans. I'm going with you," Seth called to him, just as a bugle rang out, announcing the arrival of the other Pony Express rider.

With pride, Seth watched them exchange the saddlebag. Noah caught it in midair, whooped loudly and then put his heels to his pony's sides. The young boy shot off and Seth followed.

He paced Sam and allowed Noah his lead. As far as he knew none of the other Pony Express station keepers had two riders going at the same time, meaning a fresh mount would be waiting for Noah, but not for him.

Noah turned in his saddle, seeing that Seth rode farther and farther behind, and spun his horse and returned. "You're gonna have to ride faster than that if we are to make our time," he called.

When Noah was within hearing distance, Seth

called to him, "Go on and ride like thunder. I'll follow more slowly and will catch up with you. Don't wait for me."

Noah didn't have to be told twice. The mail had to go through and it had to go through fast. They were on a timeline. They had ten days to get the mail from St. Joseph, Missouri, to Sacramento, California. Noah and the other boys had vowed to do a good job for the founders of the Pony Express and they all intended to see to it that they kept their word.

Four relay stations later, Seth caught up with Noah at the home station in Willow Springs. Noah sat on the front porch waiting for him. His feet were propped up on the porch rail. He had a satisfied grin on his face.

Seth climbed down off Sam. He patted his horse and then turned toward the home-station house.

"I made my time, Seth," he stated as Seth walked up the steps.

Seth nodded. "I'm proud of you."

Noah stood. "Now that you are here, I'm going to hit a bunk. Didn't get much sleep last night."

"Me, either," Seth confessed, following Noah off the porch and taking Sam by the reins and heading to the barn. "Soon as I get Sam tucked in, I may join you for some shut-eye."

Noah walked the short distance to a small bunk-house. It wasn't nearly as big as the one at Dove Creek. Of course, Seth doubted there were as many boys here who called Willow Springs their home station, either.

The stock tender greeted him as he entered the barn. "I'm almost done with this one, Mr. Armstrong. If you want me to take care of your horse I'll be a couple of minutes."

When Seth couldn't remember the man's name, he realized he was tired. More so than he'd first thought. After crossing streams and being in the saddle for about seventy-five miles, he realized why they wanted to hire younger men. "I'll take care of him."

As he groomed Sam, his thoughts went to Rebecca. Over the past few weeks, she'd put distance between them. He missed her coming out to see what her boys were doing. She hadn't been rude during their nightly meetings, but kept to the point as to what she needed done.

The stagecoach hadn't produced the results he'd hoped for in finding Charlotte. Maybe it was time to try something else, but what? He yawned.

"I think you've brushed his coat enough, Mr. Armstrong," the stock tender said, bringing a bag of oats for Sam.

The sweet smell caused Seth's stomach to rumble. "Thank you." He nodded toward the oats.

"Cook has beans and corn bread on the stove, if you'd like," the man offered, patting Sam on the neck.

Seth had the feeling the stock tender would like nothing better than for him to leave and let him get on with his work. He realized that he'd have to make some form of reimbursement for the care of the extra horse if he teamed up his boys to travel the trail. They couldn't expect the other home stations to feed their animals and extra mouths.

He thanked the man once more and then headed back to the house. The station keeper, Joe Cantrell, sat on the porch. Good, Seth needed to talk to the man and now was the perfect time.

"Come on up and have a seat, Seth," Joe insisted.

Grey hair topped the man's head and curled on his neck. Seth would guess his age to be about sixty. He held a piece of straw between his teeth and had the look of a man who wanted to talk.

"I believe I will." Seth climbed the stairs for a second time. He sank into the rocker that Noah had sat in earlier.

They rocked in silence for a couple of minutes. Then Joe spoke. "Your boy did good. Came in like a pro." He took the straw out of his mouth and studied the end of it. "I was a bit surprised when he told me you weren't far behind. What brings you my way?"

Seth liked Joe. He was a straight talker and didn't mince his words. "Well," he said, leaning his arms on his knees, "his ma was worried about him and I felt compelled to come along and make sure this first ride went smoothly."

"Yep, that's what I figured." Joe leaned back in the rocker and closed his eyes.

Seth didn't dare close his eyes. He'd be asleep in no time. Even though Joe's eyes were closed, Seth knew the station keeper wasn't sleeping. There was more to be said, so he waited to hear what it was.

Joe cleared his throat. "Wondered if having the boys' ma around would cause trouble."

"Naw, she isn't any trouble. Just worried about her boys." Seth wasn't about to tell Joe or anyone else how Rebecca had clucked about the boys like a mother hen when he'd first arrived.

Joe stopped the rocking of the chair. "That's good."

"I do need to compensate you for the care of my horse and if it isn't too much trouble for a meal." Seth's stomach rumbled again, reminding him it had been a long time since he'd eaten.

"Is this going to become a habit? You riding along with the boys?" Joe asked, opening his eyes and searching Seth's face.

Seth stood. "No, I won't be coming, but one of the other men might. It really depends on you," he admitted.

"How so?"

He didn't want to tell Joe that Rebecca would be a nervous Nellie as long as her boys were out alone, but if they had someone to go with them on their rides, could team up, so to speak, Seth felt sure she'd feel much better. "I'm thinking of having my boys travel in teams of two. But if I do that I'll have horses eating here and an extra boy eating and sleeping here. You'll need some kind of payment for the extra mouths you'll be feeding."

Joe nodded and rubbed his chin, as if thinking about it. "Well, do you have any good hunters in your group?"

Seth grinned. "The best in the bunch is sleeping in your bunkhouse right now."

Disbelief filled the station keeper's eyes. "That slip of a boy is a good hunter?"

"The best I've seen in a long time."

Joe stood and stretched out his back. "Well, fresh meat is what we need. If your boy is as good as you think he is, I believe that will take care of the boy's meals. As for the horses, do you reckon you can spare the supplies to feed them?"

Seth nodded. "Yep, when they deliver Pony Express hay to Dove Creek, I'll just have them send part of the supplies here to you."

The older man slapped Seth on the back. "Go grab some grub and some sleep and tomorrow we'll take that boy of yours out to see if he can hunt."

Seth did as he was told, all the while wishing there was some way he could let Rebecca know that Noah had made it safe and sound. He already missed her and the other boys.

Rebecca hurried to the Young family cemetery just as the sun set. She wanted to clean off the graves and admire the new fence the boys and Seth had placed around it.

It had been two weeks since the Pony Express started running. A few days earlier the country had celebrated the fact that the boys who rode the trail were able to do so in ten days. She felt so proud and still a bit amazed that her boys were part of the event that made mail travel so much faster. Nowadays Rebecca hardly saw the boys since they came and went as they did.

Happily surprised when she found Andrew standing within the fence of the cemetery, Rebecca waved to him. She finished climbing the small hill just as Andrew hurried to open the little gate for her. "Hi, Ma. What are you doing up here so late?" he asked as she walked past him.

Her gaze moved to John's grave. There was no need to worry about it being cluttered with leaves; someone had already cleaned it up. She looked to John's parents' graves and saw them clean, as well. "I came to take care of the family plots but I see someone has already done so." For a moment she allowed sadness to fill her. Without the excuse of cleaning, she really had no reason to linger up here with her son.

Sensing her sorrow, Andrew said, "I'm sorry. I took care of it this afternoon. If I had known you wanted to do it, I wouldn't have done so." He slapped his hat against his leg.

"Oh, Andrew, I'm not upset that you took care of them." She gave him a quick hug. "Thank you for taking care of Papa John's grave." She extended her hand. "And the others, too."

"I still miss him." Andrew kept his arm around her shoulders.

Rebecca nodded. "Me, too."

"But you know, Ma, Papa John wouldn't want you pining after him. He'd want you to start fresh."

She took a step back and looked up into her son's handsome face. "No, I'm sure he wouldn't, but what are you getting at, Andrew?"

A pink flush filled his ears. "Oh, nothing." He held up his hands as he studied her face. "Really."

"Then why did you say that?" she asked as she bent down to pick up a small stick and toss it over the fence.

Andrew put his hat on his head and dug his hands into his front pockets. "Well, I've been thinking about my own future as well as yours."

Fear clutched her throat. *Please, Lord, don't let him say he is leaving.* The silent prayer flew from her mind and she prayed it would reach heaven's gates before Andrew spoke again. "I see. And what have you been thinking?"

"Well, even though we are all orphans, Seth says we can still have a bright future, even you." He rocked on his boot heels.

"Seth said this, about me?" What else had Seth said about her? It dawned on her that Andrew said, *we can still have a bright future, even you.* "How does Seth know I was an orphan?"

Seemingly unaware of her building anger, Andrew answered, "We were talking one day and I mentioned it."

Trying hard not to let her frustration at being talked about come through in her voice, she asked, "Do you often speak of me?"

"Sure we do." A big grin crossed his face. "We're all very proud of you. You're a great ma."

His sweet words filled her heart but she still wanted to know if they were just talking and mentioned her, or if Seth had been putting his nose where it didn't belong, which was in her business. "Thanks, son. I'm proud of you, too."

"Every evening, after your visit with Seth, he comes to the bunkhouse and those of us that are there, except Jacob, read a little of the Bible and discuss what we've read." He opened the gate to leave.

Rebecca followed him out. She had no idea they were having a nightly Bible study. And the fact that Andrew was willing to participate surprised her, too. He and Jacob had quit reading with her and the younger ones after John's death.

"Did you know that there is a Scripture that talks about orphans and widows?"

Absentmindedly, Rebecca nodded.

"Seth says that since you are both, we need to take especially good care of you." He latched the gate behind them.

Rebecca stood in his path. "Andrew, has he been asking questions about me?"

Andrew shrugged. "Sometimes, but he asks questions about all of us. He even wanted to know about Papa John and his parents."

"I see." She glanced up at the sky. Stars were beginning to shine even though the sun wasn't completely down.

"Ma, I need to go. It's my turn to take the mail and the other rider will be here soon. Will you be all right walking back to the house?" Andrew looked in the direction of the woods.

Rebecca noticed that his horse stood there, munching on the new spring grass as if he and Andrew came here often. "Go on, son. I'll be fine. I'll take the road back to the house." She smiled at him.

"Walk off to the side. I'd hate for the pony rider to accidentally hit you." He sprinted to his horse and grabbed his reins.

"I'll be careful," she called to him. Rebecca watched him walk his horse to the road then spring into the saddle. Man and horse disappeared as they raced to the house.

Rebecca followed slowly. How dare Seth Armstrong discuss her with her boys! What had he thought? That he'd learn something new about her? And if so, what did he plan to do with this new knowledge? The speed of her footsteps increased. She'd have a few choice words for him this evening. She'd set him straight and since he didn't know her boundaries, Rebecca had every intention of sharing them.

Chapter Fifteen

Seth both looked forward to his discussion with Rebecca tonight and dreaded it. He wanted to tell her how wonderfully the boys were doing and that he'd noticed that the south fence needed repairing. But over dinner he'd felt a deep tension coming from her direction. She'd refused to look him straight in the eye while eating, and that didn't bode well for his peace of mind. When his grandmother behaved this way, she usually had a burr under her saddle.

He walked up the steps and found Rebecca sitting on the porch. "Oh, I didn't realize we were meeting out here tonight." In two strides he was beside the swing she sat in. "It's nice enough. I'm enjoying this warmer weather."

Still she silently rocked. Yep, there was a burr somewhere. He leaned against the porch rail and waited for her to speak. When it was obvious she didn't have anything to add to his comments, he asked, "Is there something wrong?"

In a crisp, cold tone, she answered, "Depends."

Yep, definitely something ate at her. "Care to share?"

Her head snapped up and her blue eyes reminded him of blue ice. "I don't appreciate you talking to my boys about me, Seth Armstrong. You have no business asking them questions about me. If you want to know something, ask me yourself. Do not worry my boys with questions. And that goes for questions about John, too." She blew the hair off her forehead.

He studied her red cheeks. What had he asked that would have offended her? Come to think of it, Seth couldn't recall asking personal questions about her or John. He and the boys often discussed family, especially during Bible study, but as far as he could remember, Seth had never pried into her personal life.

"Well, what do you have to say for yourself?" she demanded in a soft yet dangerous voice.

Seth rubbed his jaw. "Well, for starters, I apologize. I wasn't aware I had pried. But evidently I have. For that I am sorry." And he truly meant the words.

Rebecca nodded, still looking as if she wanted to argue with him. "And another thing, I appreciate you starting up nightly Bible study with the boys. You've reminded me that this family goes to church on Sundays. Now, I know—" she held up her hand to stop his protest "—I've been negligent in that since you've been here, but starting this Sunday we are *all* going to church." She put great emphasis on the word *all*.

"Rebecca, I appreciate the sentiment behind your statement. It's a good thing to be faithful to church. But even you can see that at least one of the boys will need to ride." He stood a little taller. What would she say to that?

She inhaled and stood. "Then I suggest you start looking for a relief rider on Sundays because me and my boys are going to church and that's final. Since their father is gone, the responsibility for their spiritual raising is now mine and it's time I started taking it seriously." Rebecca pulled her shawl closer to her body and lifted her head. When he didn't immediately respond, she left him standing on the porch.

A chuckle sounded off to his right. Seth squinted his eyes and looked into the shadows. "Think that's funny, do you, Jacob?"

Jacob moved into the light that streamed from the window. "Sure do. You really ruffled Ma's feathers."

"Any idea how that happened?" Seth wondered if Jacob had been the one to tell Rebecca of the nightly Bible studies.

"Nope. I knew she was in a mood so I was going to come talk to her when I saw you walk up. Glad you got to her first. Now I know to stay away for a while." Jacob turned and walked in the direction of the barn.

Seth followed him. He wanted to ask if Rebecca held on to her anger long, but decided that asking probably wasn't the best thing. To his reckoning, that might be what she considered prying. As he entered the barn Seth settled it in his mind that those types of questions had been what had gotten him into trouble tonight. "Any idea who we can get to ride on Sunday?" He walked over to Sam's stall.

"You can always ask Bill tomorrow if he'll stay a couple of extra days and take Clayton's place. Or you can make the ride yourself." With that Jacob walked into the tack room and shut the door.

Seth rubbed Sam's nose. It would be nice to attend

the Sunday service. He'd ask Bill if he'd take the ride, but if Bill refused Seth knew he'd ride in place of Clayton.

Rebecca Young was one stubborn woman. He knew she wouldn't back down and now he had to find a rider to take his boys' place every Sunday. His job just got a little harder.

He stepped out into the night and looked to the house, where Rebecca could be seen through the sitting room window. His grandmother had been stubborn and now Rebecca acted the same way. Both women intended to get what they wanted. Seth shook his head and muttered, "Lord, deliver me from stubborn women."

A star twinkled off in the distance. Would the Lord answer his prayer? And would Charlotte be just as stubborn as Rebecca and his grandmother? Seth frowned. He hadn't thought of his mail-order bride in a long time.

His gaze returned to the window. Rebecca sat in her chair rocking. It looked as if she was working on something in her lap. There was a stubborn tilt to her chin. Stubbornness was part of the reason Seth liked Rebecca. That and the fact that she stood up for what she believed in.

He shook his head. "Get a grip, ol' boy. One moment you like her, the next you want to wring her neck. Can't have it both ways. You can't like her too much anyway 'cause you're promised to another and don't you forget it." The thought came to him that Rebecca was the type of woman who would insist that love would be the only reason to get involved with a man. And love was not something he wanted or needed.

* * *

Sunday morning, Rebecca gathered her things and led her children out the church doors. She heard Seth's voice behind her as he shook the preacher's hand and thanked him for the sermon. He'd surprised her by attending. Not that she didn't believe him a God-fearing man, but she'd expected him to stay behind and take Clayton's place on the Pony Express trail.

Fay stayed behind. Said her rheumatism was acting up. She also promised to make sure that Bill had a big lunch before he took off for his ride.

It really was too bad that the Pony Express didn't take off Sundays. From what Rebecca had seen of Bill, he could have used a morning in church. The young man seemed rough around the edges, but most of the young men that came through Dove Creek's home station looked as if they could use a mother's care.

"What did you pack for lunch?" Philip asked, reaching toward the two baskets that Rebecca had shoved under the wagon seat.

She slapped at his hands. "Get out of there. You'll find out as soon as we get to the meadow." She scooted over and let Jacob take the reins.

Philip laughed and hopped onto his horse. "Then let's go. I'm starving."

"Ma, can I ride with Seth?" Joy asked, pulling at her skirt.

Rebecca turned to look at her daughter. Joy looked pretty with a light blue bow in her long blond hair. Seth sat on top of Sam not more than a foot away from them.

"It's up to Seth, sweetheart."

Joy squealed. She jumped up and Rebecca grabbed

the back of her dress to keep her from falling out of the wagon.

"If you keep jumping around like that, I'm going to change my mind," Rebecca warned. She wished she hadn't agreed, when Seth bent over and scooped up the little girl.

He winked at Joy. "Too late."

Rebecca couldn't get over how nice he looked with his hair combed into place, wearing a light green shirt covered by a tan jacket with what looked like leather patches on the elbows. His jeans looked new and his black boots shined. The black hat he wore on his head was pushed back and he gave her a playful grin.

"It's never too late for me to change my mind, Seth Armstrong, and don't you forget it," she teased back.

The wagon lurched as it took off. Her other boys all mounted their horses and surrounded the wagon as it pulled out of the churchyard.

A smile touched her lips as she heard Benjamin tell Seth, "Yep, she changes her mind if you make her mad. You and Joy better be nice."

She cut her eyes and looked at Seth and Joy. Joy looked happier than a girl with two playful kittens. Her blue-green eyes stared up at Seth adoringly.

The boys laughed and talked as they drove to the meadow. Only Jacob rode in silence. Rebecca looped her arm in his and laid her head on his shoulder. In a quiet voice she asked, "What did you think of the service this morning, Jacob?"

He shrugged. "It was fine."

Rebecca knew of all the young men in her care that Jacob was the only one who either didn't believe in God or had simply given up on Him. She didn't know how to reach the boy. Since John's death he'd been quiet and reserved, especially when it came to talking about his Maker.

"Ma, can I put the blanket out?" Benjamin asked.

She lifted her head. "Sure you can, but I get to pick the spot."

"Is this meadow much farther?" Seth asked.

Thomas answered. "Just over that rise. I'll race you."

"You're on!" Seth replied.

Rebecca watched them shoot off in front of the wagon. Seth's arms wrapped around the little girl's waist protectively.

Joy's blond hair flew out behind them. Her giggles filled the air as she hung on to the saddle horn.

Was her daughter getting too close to the station keeper? Rebecca watched them top the rise and go over the other side. As soon as Seth could find his mail-order bride, he'd be gone; she knew this to be true. Maybe she should limit Joy's time with the handsome man. Rebecca stopped herself. Had she just thought of Seth as a handsome man?

He was, but Rebecca didn't think it wise to think of him that way. She made a mental note to stop thinking about him altogether. The wagon topped the hill and she looked down into the meadow to find Seth tossing Joy into the air as if she was a sack of flour. Her joyful laughter couldn't be ignored. Joy was falling in love with Seth. Not in the way a woman fell in love with a man, but as a friend she was going to miss terribly when he left.

Jacob spoke. "Everyone likes him."

Had she said her thoughts aloud? No, Rebecca was pretty sure she hadn't. "True. He's a nice man."

"Yes, he is." He stopped the wagon, set the brake and hopped down to help Rebecca unload the food.

The boys were all tying their horses up to keep them from wandering too far. Rebecca lowered her voice and asked Jacob, "Do you think Joy is getting too attached to him?"

He looked to where Seth swung Joy around and around in a circle. "Possibly. All the boys are. I don't think it can be helped."

Jacob was probably right. Rebecca handed him the last box and then climbed down from the wagon. She looked at the meadow and smiled. "I love it here."

Benjamin hurried to her side. "Ma, can I put the blanket down now?" His eager eyes met hers. He clutched the old quilt close to his heart.

Rebecca laughed. The boy only wanted to spread the cover so that they could start lunch. He'd grown a full two inches in the past few weeks and eating had become a favorite pastime for him. "Yes, over by that small grove of trees." She pointed to where a group of cottonwood trees stood proudly.

Her gaze moved to Seth once more. Was she becoming too attached to him, too? If so, how could she put more distance between them?

Seth clutched his stomach and groaned. "Rebecca, I think that was the best lunch I've had in a very long time."

Benjamin nodded his agreement. "Ma makes the best fried chicken around."

"I agree." Seth closed his eyes and leaned his back against the tree. "But I believe I ate too much."

"Seth, come play with me." Joy grabbed his hand and pulled.

He cracked an eye and said, "Oh, Joy, girl. My tummy is too full to play right now."

Thomas stood and stretched. "I'll play with you, Joy."

"Can we play duck, duck, goose?" Joy jumped up and down.

Seth listened as first Philip, then Noah and Benjamin, agreed to play duck, duck, goose. They walked a short ways from the picnic area and began to form a circle for the game.

He watched as the boys slowed their running speed so that their sister could outrun them and take their place in the grass. All except young Benjamin. He always beat his little sister and crowed to the others that he was the fastest one there. Seth chuckled.

The three older boys stood beside the wagon. He couldn't make out their conversation but knew it was friendly by the way one or the other would laugh from time to time. This was the most relaxed he'd seen the family and to tell the truth, Seth enjoyed it.

Rebecca began to gather up the food and place it in the boxes. He was amazed at how well she'd packed their meal and had even packed tin cups for them to drink cold cider out of.

Seth sat up to help her. He handed her a jar that had once held pickles. His hand brushed hers and warmth traveled up his arm where their skin connected.

"Thank you, Seth, but I can do this." She looked down at her hand where it had touched his.

Had she felt the warmth also? He wasn't ready to leave just yet and from the looks of the happy kids, Seth didn't think they would be ready to go, either. "Can't you sit a while and enjoy the sun on your face? You work hard all the time. Surely you can spare an hour or so to relax and have some thinking time."

She put the lid and ring on the pickle jar and placed it in the basket. Gathering her skirt in one hand, she sat beside Seth with her back pressed against the same tree.

"What's this thinking time you're talking about, Seth?" Her voice sounded a little shaky to his ears. So perhaps she had felt the warmth they'd just shared.

"My grandmother used to make me take a nap every Sunday afternoon. But after I turned ten and no longer wanted to take naps, she said for me to get out away from the house so I wouldn't wake up her. She told me to go think on things."

"And did you?"

He nodded. "That became my favorite time of the week."

She drew an invisible pattern between them on the quilt. "What did you think on?"

"Oh, the things that had happened in the past. Things I wanted to do in the future." He chewed on a piece of grass. "I'd map out a plan in my head how to accomplish more."

"Is that all?"

He turned his head to face her, allowing a teasing expression to enter his eyes. "What? You don't think that was enough?"

"No," she said, bumping his shoulder lightly with her own. "I'm sure you thought on lots of things and I think that's one of the best suggestions I've heard.

But you misunderstood. I wanted to know all that you accomplished."

He stretched his legs out in front of him, crossed his arms on his chest and put his head back against the tree. "I guess the main thing I thought about was how to make myself into the type of person I wanted to be. I already had a strong opinion as to what I didn't want, but at ten had a hard time figuring out what I did want."

"Deep thoughts for a ten-year-old."

"Maybe. But I see myself in Beni. He tries so hard to be good all the time, but occasionally the mischievousness sneaks out. I try to convince him that's normal, but each time you punish him, he thinks it's a direct hit against his character."

She chuckled and he turned to study her profile. Wisps of hair framed her oval face. Her face showed a strength that did not lessen her femininity. The beginnings of a smile tipped the corners of her mouth. One dimple winked in his direction. "I'm thinking he already has you wrapped around his little finger."

"No," he growled, turning her smile into an infectious grin. "Why would you think that?"

"Because that little rascal kept playing John and me against each other. John would make him stand in the corner and he would look at me with those big eyes and say, 'I'm a bad boy, Ma. You need to pray for me.' Then I would tell John that we were wounding his spirit. I became upset and John would dismiss the punishment."

"Oh, no, that's not good. How did it turn out?"

"Well, one day we heard Beni bragging to Philip. 'I just pucker my lips like I'm gonna cry and tell Ma I'm a bad boy. She doesn't ever want me to think I'm a bad boy. She makes Pa let me go.'"

Seth couldn't help it. He guffawed. "That little faker. Then what happened?"

"Next time John put him in the corner, I agreed that he was a bad boy and that he would stand even longer in the corner because that's what happened to bad boys. He knew we were onto him. He never tried it again, but he did go overboard trying to be good to prove he wasn't bad."

"That explains a lot. I bet you have stories like this on all the boys, don't you?"

She looked at him, her expression suddenly somber. The silence lengthened between them, making him uncomfortable. What had he said wrong? He studied her face. "Why are you looking at me like that?"

"Are you asking because you care about the boys or so you can use the stories against them?"

Seth breathed in shallow gasps. The tension between them increased with frightening speed. He glowered at her then turned away, jumping up to gather their things. He'd been so stupid.

For a second it had felt as if they were courting, but the look on her face said that wasn't the case and probably never would be. "Thank you for letting me tag along with your family today, Rebecca. I thoroughly enjoyed myself."

Regret filled her voice. "Seth, wait."

"Let it alone, Rebecca. I understand." Seth felt an acute sense of loss. She would never trust him, that was evident, so how could they continue working together? How would he make it without the boys he'd come to love?

He looked to where the kids were now playing freeze tag. Joy squealed as Benjamin tagged her. She froze into place and yelled for Philip to unfreeze her. They really were a great bunch of kids. He was glad he got to see them so relaxed and acting like kids.

"Come on, kids! Time to pack up and head home," Rebecca called to them. She looked at Seth. "I'm sorry I spoiled our fun."

Seth swallowed with difficulty but found his voice. "It was time to leave anyway. The boys need to feed the livestock." Seth watched the older boys walk over and take the boxes back to the wagon. Jacob shook the blanket out and then folded it.

"Aw, Ma, do we have to go?" Benjamin protested. He dragged his boots across the grass and looked dejected.

"Yes."

The boys all headed for their horses, but Joy came running to Seth. "Can I ride home with you, Seth?"

Rebecca answered before he could. "Not this time, Joy. I want you to ride with me."

"But, Ma. I don't get to ride all the time like the boys do," she protested.

Seth wondered why Rebecca didn't want the little girl to ride with him. He waited to see what Rebecca would say.

"No buts, Joy. Go to Jacob. He'll help you into the wagon." Rebecca didn't meet Seth's inquisitive look. She simply followed her daughter.

How did women do that? He was the one offended, but she acted as if he'd hurt her. He shook his head in disbelief and mounted his horse.

On the ride back to the farm, Seth took the time to

think. He'd thought they were getting on well together. But a relationship without trust could never survive, even one that wasn't romantic.

Chapter Sixteen

Rebecca kept watch over the road that led past her house. The stagecoach should be rolling in any minute and she was also expecting Thomas and Philip's return. She hung the last of the boys' shirts on the line to dry, placed the empty basket on her hip and headed back to the house.

Fay met her at the door. "I put the sweetbread and sandwiches out on the sideboard."

"Thank you, Fay. I'll make a fresh pot of coffee…"

"That's already been done, too." Fay wiped her hands on her apron. A light coating of flour dusted the smock that covered her house dress. "I hope you don't mind, but I thought I'd get a start on the dough for tonight's biscuits."

Rebecca smiled. "Mind? I don't know what I would have done without you over the last few weeks. I'm so glad you decided to stay out here with us."

"Me, too," Joy said from her place on the rug.

Her daughter was surrounded by doll clothes that Fay had made for Joy's baby. It was amazing how much one woman could do to change the dynamics of the family. Rebecca couldn't imagine life without her.

"Me three." Fay grinned down at Joy then she looked back up at Rebecca. "You and your family have given me new life and a new purpose."

The sound of the stage pulling into the yard alerted the women it was time to get to work. Rebecca pulled her wet apron from her waist and tied on a clean one. She patted her hair into place and then pushed through the door that separated the kitchen from the main living space. Fay followed.

A quick glance around confirmed that the room was in order and ready to receive their guests. Earlier in the week she and Fay had set up the small table that had been in the kitchen for their guests to eat. Fay had already set out the food and fluffed the pillows that rested on the settee. All that was left was to answer the door.

Two ladies entered the room. Neither looked very happy. The youngest one said to the other, "I thought they were going to overtake us. Didn't you?"

"I already told you, yes, Grace. I'd really rather not think about it for a few minutes."

"Winifred, how can we not think about it? We have to get back into that contraption and pray they don't give chase again," Grace answered in a huffy voice.

Rebecca cleared her throat. "Ladies, if you would like refreshments, the sideboard is this way." She motioned toward where the food sat waiting.

"Thank you," Winifred answered. She walked to the sideboard and began loading a plate with sandwiches and sweetbread.

Had she seen the sign? Rebecca started to point

it out, but then Winifred dug into her handbag and dropped the money into the crock.

Fay waited until they sat down and then asked, "Who was chasing you, dear?"

Grace looked as if she were about to explode with the news. "Road bandits. They chased us for a long time. I felt sure they would catch up with us." She shoved a bite of sweetbread into her mouth. Around the treat, Grace continued, "They would have taken all our money."

Winifred shook her head, seemingly annoyed at her companion.

"Well, they would have," Grace said.

A huge sigh whooshed from Winifred. "They could have killed us or worse," the older woman said.

"How many were there?" Rebecca asked. She poured herself a cup of coffee and sat down on the couch. Would they chase her boys? Thomas and Philip still hadn't returned. *Lord, please keep my boys safe.*

"Just two," Grace answered. "But they looked big and mean."

The stagecoach driver opened the door. "Ladies, we'll be leaving in five minutes."

Rebecca got the ladies a piece of cheesecloth to wrap up their leftovers.

Winifred took it. "Thank you. This was very nice and has settled my nerves somewhat." She stood to leave.

"You're welcome." Rebecca walked them to the door. "Oh, before you go, do either of you know a Charlotte Fisher?"

Both women shook their heads. Grace answered,

"No, but if we meet her we'll tell her you inquired about her."

Rebecca felt both disappointed and a little glad. She wasn't ready for Seth to take off. Her boys respected him and she didn't know who Mr. Bromley might send as his replacement. At least that was what she told herself. "Thank you. Safe traveling, ladies."

When they left, Rebecca closed the door. "What do you think of that?" she asked Fay.

The older woman shook her head. "The bandits are getting braver. The men on the last stage said they'd not chased them once they realized they had guns at the ready. Most likely they thought the women were no threat to them."

Rebecca looked at her. "I didn't realize that you'd talked to the men about road bandits."

"You stepped out of the room to help Joy with something," Fay explained as she picked up the plate of sandwiches and sweetbread. "I think I'll run these outside to the boys, if that's all right with you."

"Sure, I know they will enjoy them." Rebecca carried the coffeepot back to the kitchen.

Road bandits were a concern for everyone. They seemed to be getting braver or maybe she'd just not heard about them much since the station hadn't been on the stagecoach route. Either way, she wasn't happy with knowing they were out there.

As Rebecca cooked and cleaned the rest of the evening, she prayed for her boys and the people on the stagecoach. Her nerves were stretched taut when Seth and the boys came to the house for dinner.

"It smells good, Ma," Andrew said enthusiastically as he took his seat at the table.

Rebecca grinned at him. "It should—it's your favorite." She set a platter of steaks on the table.

Fay added baked potatoes and hot rolls. She turned and took a bowl of hot green beans from Joy's small hands.

Andrew laughed. "This is everyone's favorite meal." He poured milk into his glass.

Rebecca patted him on the shoulder. "True."

A few minutes later, Seth said the blessing and they passed around the plates of food. Rebecca looked to Jacob's, Thomas's and Philip's empty chairs.

"They should be back any minute now," Seth said, taking a potato and putting it on his plate.

She swallowed as the urge to cry almost overtook her. "I know." Rebecca wished her voice didn't sound so weak.

Fay reached over and patted her hand. "The boys are fine, Rebecca. Don't borrow trouble."

To prove Fay's words, the door banged open and both Thomas and Philip entered the house. Excitement flowed from them in invisible waves.

Jacob followed behind them and shut the door. "Sorry we're late, Ma." He slid into his chair.

The other two boys were already in their chairs and reaching for the plates of food. "Us, too," Thomas said around a mouthful of bread.

"We ran into a little trouble," Philip said, sharing a grin with Thomas.

Benjamin looked up from his plate. His brandy-colored eyes sparkled with excitement. "What kind of trouble?"

Thomas leaned forward for dramatic effect. "Indians."

"Really? You saw Indians?" Benjamin all but bounced in his chair.

Philip answered, "Sure did. We had to outrun them."

Thomas waved his fork in the air. "They were easy to outrun."

Rebecca's gaze met Seth's across the table. Was he thinking the same thing she was? Did the boys seem to be enjoying this adventure just a little too much? Hadn't Seth taught them that Indians were a real threat? She wanted to scream at him to say something. Scold them. Anything but just sit there.

When he didn't obey her silent orders, Rebecca decided she'd need to talk to him about emphasizing the real dangers of riding the Pony Express. Because from the way Thomas and Philip were going on now, he obviously had not done his job with them.

Seth could almost hear her thoughts. She was angry and scared. Her eyes screamed at him, but he refused to reprimand the boys at the dinner table.

He cleared his throat to get their attention. Everyone looked to him except Rebecca—suddenly she was very interested in the pattern on the edge of her plate. "Boys, let your vittles fill your mouth." Seth looked pointedly to Rebecca.

Understanding crossed their features. Both boys took great interest in their supper. The rest of the family found other things to talk about.

Everyone but Benjamin. "But I want to hear about the Indians," he protested.

Seth caught his eye. Keeping his voice calm but firm he said, "The dinner table is no place for such talk."

Benjamin dropped his gaze. "All right, Seth." Under

his voice he mumbled, "But I'm going to the bunkhouse with the men tonight and learn about them Indians."

Grins split Thomas's and Philip's faces as they chewed. When Benjamin looked up at them with awe in his eyes, Philip winked at him.

Yes, they needed a talking-to. Indians weren't to be taken lightly and yes, Benjamin needed to hear what Seth had to say, too. Between the Indians and the road bandits, the Pony Express trail was becoming more and more dangerous.

Rebecca pushed her food around on her plate. It didn't take an educated man to know that she was upset and rightly so. Seth dreaded tonight's meeting. The way she shot sharp looks in his direction told him that she had a lot on her mind and that he was going to get the brunt of it.

Fay kept Joy entertained with talk about needle-work. The two discussed an alphabet sampler that Joy was working on. "We'll have to see about getting some new colors of thread," Fay said.

Joy grinned. "Blue? Can we get blue?"

"No, I think you should get your favorite color," Clayton said around a mouth full of potatoes.

"But blue is my favorite color," Joy protested.

Clayton hid a smile. "Oh, well then maybe you should get my favorite color. Can you guess what it is?"

"Red?" Joy asked.

He shook his head. "Try again."

She tapped her bottom lip with her fork. Her gaze moved across the table to Andrew, who mouthed *yellow*. "Yellow." She beamed at Clayton.

"Very good."

Joy giggled. "I will look for yellow, too."

Dinner continued with small talk of the day and then everyone was leaving the table. The boys all thanked their mother for the meal, took their plates to the kitchen and then made their way back to the bunkhouse.

Seth stopped Thomas and Philip as they hurried to the door. In a soft voice he said, "Hold all Indian talk until I get out there. I want to hear all the details. So wait for me."

"Sure, Seth," Thomas said and then the boys walked a little slower out of the house.

Seth turned to the table. Fay and Rebecca were already clearing the remaining dirty dishes. "Let me give you ladies a hand," he offered, picking up the food bowls and carrying them to the kitchen.

Fay grinned at him. "There's no need for that."

"I think there is. You two work hard all day. A little help from me will give you a little more time to relax." He returned to the dining room to pick up dirty glasses.

His gaze moved to Joy, who now sat in the parlor with her needlework. She looked up and he grinned at her. "My favorite color is blue-green," he said winking at her.

"Hey, Ma says my eyes are blue-green."

He laughed. "So they are." Seth carried the glasses into the kitchen.

Rebecca was pouring hot water into the washtub. She scraped soap off into the water and swished it around. It didn't create many bubbles but would clean the dishes well enough.

He picked up a dish towel and stood beside her. "I'll rinse and dry if you'll wash."

Rebecca looked at him. "All right. Thanks."

"I'll scrub down the table and chairs," Fay said, grabbing a cloth and wetting it in Rebecca's dishwater. She then returned to the dining room.

As soon as she was out of the room, Rebecca demanded, "Didn't you teach those boys that Indians could be dangerous?"

He rinsed and dried the glass she handed him. "Yes, but obviously, I didn't do a very good job. Tonight I'll have a good talking-to with them about both the Indians and the road bandits. Then tomorrow I plan on having all the boys practice using their guns and rifles." He put the glass to the side and reached for another.

"Thank you. I hate that they have to learn to point a gun at another human being."

"So do I. But both the Indians and the bandits have guns and know how to use them. God never intended for us to shoot each other with them, but sometimes for our own safety, we have to."

When he finished talking, Rebecca answered, "I know. John taught me how to use a Colt but I never really wanted to."

Seth dried another plate. "I promise, I will emphasize to them that taking another person's life is not the purpose of carrying the gun. It's to be used only if necessary."

They continued working in silence. Fay entered the room and got the broom, then returned to the dining room. Seth wanted to talk to Rebecca, assure her he had the boys' best intentions at heart, but didn't know how to do so. Talking to women was often hard, especially when their emotions were involved.

Would he be able to talk to Charlotte should he find her? Did he want to? Part of him wanted to give up the search for his fiancée, but Seth knew he had to keep his promise to his grandmother.

When the last dish was dried, Seth hung his wet towel on a hook by the basin area. "Well, I need to get out there where the boys are." He walked to the back door.

"Seth?"

He turned at her questioning voice. "Yes."

"Today when the stage came, two women were on it. They talked about road bandits. Would you caution the boys about them, as well?"

"I will." She looked so lost and scared that he wanted to walk across the room and hug her fears away.

But Fay chose that moment to come back into the kitchen. "Seth, we asked about Miss Charlotte but the two women on the stage had never heard of her." She set the broom back against the wall by the kitchen door.

"Thank you for asking. I'm not sure I'll find her this way." He leaned his hip against the doorjamb.

Fay shook her head. "It's a long shot for sure."

"We'll keep asking," Rebecca assured him.

Seth nodded and then pushed away from the door frame. "Good night, ladies."

Both echoed back. "Good night."

He stepped out into the cool night air. Maybe he should start thinking about moving on so that he could find Charlotte. If Fay hadn't come back in when she had, Seth was pretty sure he would have acted on his feelings and hugged Rebecca.

His thoughts went to the excitement and joy that the boys had gotten from running into the Indians, and he knew he still had work to do here at Dove Creek. He couldn't leave knowing the Young men weren't well trained. It was his job to keep them safe.

His inner voice taunted him, *Are you sure it's because you want to keep them safe, or have you allowed yourself to become attached to the Young family? Especially Rebecca Young?*

Chapter Seventeen

Seth watched as the boys took turns racing past a fence post and trying to shoot a can off it. They all were able to knock it off on their first run-through.

Jacob stood beside him. "The target needs to be moving."

"Any suggestions on how to make that happen? We can't have them shooting at each other." His frustration was showing but Seth didn't care.

"I think so."

Seth turned to face him. "Let's hear it."

"Well, you could tie a rope around a can, toss it over a limb of a tree. Get behind the tree, so they don't shoot you, and then pull on the rope to make the can go up and down. They ride their horses past and try to shoot the can." He grinned.

It wasn't a bad idea, as long as he stayed behind the tree. "I noticed you said *I* could hold the rope and hide behind the tree."

Jacob tried to look serious, but his eyes danced with merriment. "Well, you wouldn't want them to have to live with killing their oldest brother if they were to miss, would you?"

Seth laughed. "I might be willing to risk it." He slapped Jacob on the back. "Go get the rope."

By the end of the day, Seth's nerves were shot. The young men were great at shooting nonmoving objects, but terrible at shooting moving ones. Earlier in the day he'd made the mistake of stepping out from behind the tree and a bullet had whizzed past his right ear. The poor tree had more holes in it than one of Rebecca's colanders.

It hadn't helped that Jacob had stood by the barn door and laughed. Seth didn't really see what was so funny and was beginning to lose his sense of humor. He'd noticed Rebecca had come out and stood on the porch for a few minutes watching. Her pretty face had confusion written all over it. What she had to be confused about, he had no idea.

Still standing behind the tree, Seth called the boys to a stop. He waited a couple of minutes before stepping out. Jacob walked across the yard to join him.

"Want me to wave the can for a bit?" Jacob asked. When Seth didn't answer immediately, he suggested, "You might be able to tell the boys what they are doing wrong."

Why not let Jacob stand behind the tree and have bullets whiz around him for a few minutes? Who knew, Jacob might realize how serious this was. Jacob might even feel bad for laughing at him. "All right."

Jacob looked to his brothers and raised his chin as if to say "take your best shot, boys." He went behind the tree and began pulling on the rope.

Seth watched as the Young men lined up to practice

again. He rubbed his hands together gleefully at the lesson Jacob was about to learn. They'd already decided they'd go in order of oldest to youngest.

Andrew raced toward the can and swerved just as he came within a few feet of it. He fired off his shot and the sound of metal hitting metal pinged in the afternoon air.

He'd hit it! Seth couldn't believe it. Andrew tipped his hat at him as he rode past and went to the end of the line.

Clayton took off at a dead run. His horse was surefooted and, using both hands, Clayton sighted his rifle at the moving can. He fired his rifle and within seconds the sound of the bullet hitting the can echoed in the yard.

He'd hit it, too! Seth stared at the moving can that now had two bullet holes in it. Clayton also tipped his hat at Seth as he rode past.

Thomas and Philip decided to go together. Their argument earlier in the day was that since they always rode the trail together, they should train together, too. Their horses raced toward the tree and at the last minute both boys fired on the moving can. Thomas hit it high, Philip hit it low. They passed him, eyes dancing and lips twitching.

He'd been had. Seth didn't know whether to be angry or amused. All afternoon he'd heard their bullets whiz over his head and around the tree. Not once had any of them hit the can.

As Noah raced past, Seth knew he would hit the can. Noah was the best shot of all. Using his Colt, he emptied it into the can. Why hadn't he realized sooner that the boys had been playing with him? He should have known that Noah could hit a moving target. Just weeks before the boy had brought down a running elk.

Benjamin grinned as he passed Seth. Seth spread his legs and waited for the boy to miss. Beni was only eight years old. Seth fully expected the youngster to miss. Metal hitting metal brought the realization that he was wrong again. The boy whooped as he raced back to his brothers.

Jacob came out from behind the tree. He rubbed his chin. "I don't know how they got so good so fast."

The other boys rode over to them.

Seth looked from one to the other. He tried to keep his face stern as he met each of their laughing eyes. "I guess they've had a lot of practice."

Jacob and all the boys howled their merriment.

Seth tucked his hands in his back pockets and waited them out. He was proud of them. Each would be able to hold their own on the trail, even Beni. But he didn't enjoy the fact that they'd let him believe they were horrible shots all afternoon.

When he quit laughing, Jacob said, "Aw, Seth. You taught them all well."

Seth shook his head. "Not me. I believe your Papa John taught you all well."

It was Andrew who spoke for all of them this time. "With guns and rifles, yes. But not about safety. We all listened last night and realized we haven't been taking the dangers of the trail serious enough."

He didn't understand what that had to do with them tricking him all day. They'd been able to shoot the can, so why hadn't they?

As if to answer his question, Andrew continued, "Don't be angry, Seth. If we had all hit the can earlier, would you feel as confident about our shooting abilities then as you do now? We wanted to show you that given the choice, we can hit the target or we can hit close enough to the target to scare it. Like you said, never take a life if you don't have to."

The dinner bell began clanging. Each boy—no, each man—looked at him, waiting to be dismissed. They were good men and they could do their job. He was proud of them.

"Go on. Enjoy your dinner."

They didn't have to be told twice. Six of the boys took off for the porch. They each tied off their horses and hurried to the washbasin outside the back door.

Jacob stood beside him. "Are you angry with us?" Weariness filled his eyes.

Seth grinned. "No, I'm proud of you."

The young man continued to study his face. "Don't think we don't need you anymore. We do." He turned to join his brothers at the house.

Seth called after him, "Jacob, would you mind asking your ma if she'll fix me a plate and bring it to me after you all are done with supper?"

Jacob nodded. "Be happy to."

Seth walked to his room in the bunkhouse. He wanted to believe that the Young men needed him, but was beginning to think he'd been fooling himself. His legs felt like lead as he walked. He had some powerful praying to do. Maybe it was time for him to go. Time to fulfill his promise to his grandmother. Time to leave the Young farm. He'd ask the Lord. If he felt God release him to go search for Charlotte, he'd leave.

Over the next few days, Rebecca noticed that Seth was quieter than usual. Their nightly visits were all business, and half the time he took his meals in his room. She missed him.

Today he and the four of the boys were mending fences. Noah was hunting and Benjamin was in his room with a cold. Andrew was on the trail.

Fay stepped out on the porch with her. "The stage is late."

"Yes. Do you think we should send for Seth?" Rebecca asked. Her gaze scanned the direction in which she'd seen the boys leave.

Joy came out on the porch carrying her dolly. "I'll go get him," she offered.

"Oh, no, you won't." Rebecca ran her hand over the little girl's silky blond hair.

"Want me to wake Beni up? He can go get Seth," Joy said, not the least bit upset that her mother had told her no.

"No, he's too sick to be going out to the pasture." Rebecca looked at Fay. "Will you watch the kids for me? I'll go see what Seth and Jacob think about the stage being almost an hour late."

"Be happy to," Fay answered. She looked down at Joy. "Let's go sample those sugar cookies. We can take a couple up to Beni, too."

Joy ran to the door and yanked it open. "All right."

Fay laughed. "I wish I still had that kind of energy or knew a good store where they sold it."

Rebecca grinned. She knew just how the older woman felt. "I'll be right back."

It had been a while since Rebecca had ridden a horse and she wasn't sure she wanted to take the time to saddle one now. She looked down the road again. An uneasy feeling crept up her spine and into her hair, causing goose bumps to run up and down her arms. The need to hurry had her jogging across the yard and heading toward the north pasture. Saddling a horse would be time wasted.

Her thoughts went to Andrew as she ran. The long grass pulled at her shoes and skirt. Rebecca slowed to a fast walk. It wouldn't do for her to step into a gopher hole and twist her ankle.

She didn't know how long she'd been searching, but Rebecca was glad when she heard a horse whinny a greeting. Turning in the direction of the sound, Rebecca began to jog.

Seth saw her first and stopped hammering. He said something to Jacob, who had been holding the log in place. Both men dropped what they were doing and got on their horses to meet her.

Jacob got to her first. "Ma, is everything all right? Is it Beni?"

Seth joined them.

"Everything is fine at the house but the stage is over an hour late." She looked up at Seth. "I thought I'd better tell you. I have an uneasy feeling about it."

"I'm glad you did." Seth looked to Jacob. "Go tell the others to finish up here and then head to the house. You and I are going to go ahead and check on the stage."

Jacob nodded and then returned to his brothers.

Seth kicked his foot out of the stirrup and leaned over with his hand extended to Rebecca. "You can ride with me back to the house."

She eyed the big horse. "I don't know, Seth. It's not really proper."

"Jacob's horse is a Pony Express horse." He wiggled his fingers at her as an invitation to take his hand.

Rebecca didn't know what the significance was of Jacob's horse being a Pony Express horse. But her feet were aching from walking across the uneven pasture and she decided no one was going to see her on Seth's horse anyway. She put her hand in his, put one foot in the stirrup and then swung up behind him.

Jacob joined them as Rebecca was tucking her skirt modestly under her legs. "Done." His gaze moved to Rebecca and he grinned.

Seth nodded. "Good." He touched his heels to the big horse's sides and took off back to the house at a gallop.

Rebecca wrapped her arms around Seth's waist and hung on. She hadn't expected him to run the horse back. Did he sense, like her, that the stage was in trouble? Could road bandits or Indians have attacked them? She rested her cheek against his warm back and silently prayed for the people aboard the stage.

Chapter Eighteen

Seth enjoyed the feel of Rebecca's arms wound tightly around his waist. He almost hated to see the house come into view, but also felt an urgency to find the stagecoach. Since it wasn't sitting in front of the house, he assumed it hadn't arrived.

He kicked his boot out of the stirrup once more and helped Rebecca swing down from Sam's back. He missed her closeness immediately.

Fay stepped out onto the porch.

"Any sign of them?" Seth asked.

She shook her head and answered with a worried frown. "No, and now they are really late."

"Jacob and I will see if we can find them." Seth spun Sam around without waiting to see if Jacob was in agreement with him or not. He headed in the direction that the stage should have arrived from.

"What do you think happened to them?" Jacob asked, pulling along beside him.

Seth looked in his direction. "I'm not sure. Perhaps they broke a wheel."

They rounded a bend about a mile and a half from

the farm and there stood the stagecoach. The driver sat on the seat of the coach in just his pants. No hat, shirt or boots. No horses, either.

Seth recognized him as Ty Walker. He reached the stage first. "What happened, Ty?"

"Bandits." The poor driver sounded downtrodden. "Three of them, came in hard and fast. Hit us before we knew what had happened."

"Is anyone hurt?" Seth asked.

"Just our pride," Ty answered. He kept his gaze focused on the horizon.

"Why didn't you walk the rest of the way to the farm?" Jacob asked. His gaze was on the alert in case the bandits were still about.

"Can't get the womenfolk to budge." He continued to look straight ahead as if looking back at the carriage might scald his eyeballs.

Seth got down and started to walk to the coach. He had a feeling he understood the coachman's strange behavior when he heard a woman's voice call out from inside the wagon. "Stay there. Don't come any closer."

Jacob frowned. "What is going on here?"

"I gather the bandits took everything?" Seth asked as he walked back to Sam and began to remove his saddle.

"Just about."

"Jacob, I believe we are going to need your saddle blanket." He laid his own saddle on the ground and pulled the blanket that it rested on from the horse.

Giving the blanket a good shake, he waited for Jacob to finish unsaddling his horse. Jacob looked confused but did as Seth asked him to. Within a matter of minutes Seth had both blankets and was walking back to the wagon.

"I've got a couple of blankets you ladies can wrap up in. Do you want me to hand them to you through the door?" Seth asked.

"Yes, please." A hand snaked out the door and a woman's fingers wiggled as if to say "give it here."

Seth placed the blankets in her hand and then walked back to the other two men. Jacob's ears had turned a soft pink and the stagecoach driver tried not to smile. The man now wore Jacob's jacket for a shirt.

Jacob dropped his saddle back on his horse's back and tied the cinch. "What now?" he asked Seth. "We can't ride them back without saddle blankets."

"It's not that far—we'll walk," Seth answered.

They could hear the women in the carriage fussing.

"I don't think this is much better," one complained.

The other answered, "Would you like to try this one instead?"

"No, yours is smaller and I need the bigger one. Make sure it covers me completely." After a couple of seconds she demanded, "Well?"

"You are decently covered."

Seth picked up his saddle and put it on Sam's back. He called over his shoulder, "Ladies, we need to get going. Those bandits might decide to return."

They shot out of the coach like two cats in a room full of rocking chairs. Like the coachman, they wore no shoes or hats. Wrapped in the blankets they were decent enough, but their dispositions were not to be trifled with.

"If you ladies are ready, Jacob and I will lead the way." Seth led Sam back down the road they had just traveled. He didn't look back and he tried not to chuckle as the ladies followed the two horses and three men back to the farm.

Sam's blanket barely covered the robust woman behind him. She was short and fat with a double chin and black ringlets that hung about her shoulders. The other woman was tall and slender and looked to be about Jacob's age. She was pretty with light brown hair and blue eyes the color of a clear riverbed.

Seth glanced to Jacob. If the young man had noticed the young woman, he showed no sign of it. He walked beside his horse and looked forward.

"We sure are blessed you came along, Seth," Ty said, hobbling along beside him. "Not sure what I would have done, if the sun had set on us."

Seth nodded. "It still gets chilly here at night. You would have been cold, that's for sure."

Jacob glanced over his shoulder. Then turned back around.

"How they doing?" the driver asked in a low voice.

"Seem to be doin' just fine," Jacob answered. "I don't think they're very happy about the way things have turned out."

"None of us are," the driver answered. "If only I could have gotten to my gun faster."

Seth shook his head. "If you had, you might be dead right now. Didn't you say there were three of them?"

"Yep, and nasty, too. Could have killed us. They had no trouble stripping us down to our unmentionables and taking everything." He glanced over his shoulder, then turned around. In a low voice he continued, "But that big one, she gave them what for. Said she'd have her husband hunt them down like a couple of foxes and skin them alive." He chuckled. "You should have seen their faces."

Jacob looked to Seth, who shrugged. Like Jacob, he couldn't see the humor in it, but then again, he hadn't faced death and lived to tell about it, either.

Rebecca, Fay and Joy stood on the front porch waiting for them. Seth focused on Rebecca's sweet smile. Her twin dimples winked in her cheeks. She said something to Joy and the little girl ran into the house.

Both women hurried off the porch and came out to meet them. Rebecca spoke first. "Is everyone all right?" she asked, rushing to the older woman's side and wrapping a supportive arm around her thick waist.

"We're much better now," the older woman said.

"I'm Rebecca Young and this is Fay Miller. I sent my little girl to get you both clean blankets to wrap up in. I'm so sorry to see you've had trouble."

"Thank you, Mrs. Young. I'm Martha Ranger and this is Emma Jordan. A clean blanket will be nice. Not that I'm complaining, mind you. It was nice of the men to loan us their saddle blankets in our time of need." Martha sneezed.

"Please, call me Rebecca." The women walked past the men as if unaware that they'd stopped walking and let them pass.

"Then you must call us Martha and Emma. I hope we aren't too much trouble. Those scoundrels took all our dresses and shoes. It might be a while before we can replace them." She pulled the blanket up to her chin.

Rebecca helped her up the porch just as Joy burst through the door.

"Here are the clean blankets, Ma." She stopped and stared up at the newcomers.

"Thank you, Joy." Rebecca took the blankets and draped them over her arm. She looked to Seth. "Would you take Mr. Walker to the bunkhouse and see if he can wear any of the boys' extra boots?"

Seth felt like one of her children. "I'll be happy to," he answered.

"Jacob, I'll send Joy out to the barn in a couple of minutes with your horse blankets." Rebecca held the door open for the women, who hurried inside. She turned to look over her shoulder at Seth.

He didn't know what to make of her glance. Her gaze connected with his and she offered a soft smile. Was she simply grateful they had found the passengers? Or had she been concerned for him? Seth didn't know and he didn't want to read too much into that expression.

As the women told her and Fay what happened when the bandits attacked them, Rebecca worried more and more about Andrew. He was out there alone. Her gaze moved to the window, praying that her son would arrive soon.

The sound of a bugle filled the air. Rebecca ran to the window and watched as Andrew raced into the yard. His horse stopped in front of the barn, where another rider was prepared to take the mailbag.

Andrew jumped from the horse and tossed the bag to the other rider. He turned to the house and waved to his mother. Relief washed over her even as she prayed for the other young man, who now was alone on the

Pony Express trail. She bowed her head. "Thank You, Lord, for bringing my boy home."

She felt a hand on her shoulder. Rebecca turned to look at the young woman beside her. "Praying was the only thing that kept me calm during the robbery. I'm glad God brought your son home."

"Thank you, Emma." Rebecca patted her hand and then turned to face her. "That dress looks pretty on you."

Emma twirled about. "It fits me nicely. Thank you for sharing it."

Pretty pink material swirled about Emma's slim ankles. It brought the color out in her cheeks, giving her a fresh, happy appearance. Rebecca smiled. "I'm not sharing it, Emma. I'm giving it to you."

The girl stopped turning. Her face sobered. "You are? Why?"

"Because it gives you pleasure and I want you to have it." Rebecca watched as the girl studied her face. It was as if Emma was looking for an alternative reason to be given the gift.

Emma ran her hands down the soft fabric. "Thank you. This is the nicest gift I've ever received."

Martha stepped out of Rebecca's bedroom. Rebecca had given the older woman one of her mother-in-law's dresses. It had to be taken out a little on the sides, but with Fay's swift needle, they had altered the dress to fit the older woman.

"You look lovely," Rebecca said.

The older woman huffed. "Well, it isn't as nice as what I'm accustomed to, but it will do." She looked at Emma. "It's nice to see you wearing something appropriate for your station."

Did the woman realize how rude she sounded? Or was it just her social position that caused her to speak in such an impolite manner?

Emma looked away. Her joy from a moment earlier now seemed clouded. "Thank you." She walked to the window and looked out across the yard.

"What are you looking at?" Martha demanded, coming to stand beside her.

Rebecca's gaze moved past the women. The boys were returning from mending the fence. It was obvious that they'd raced back to the house.

Joy stood between Jacob and Andrew. Her little face lit up at the sight of her brothers.

Martha huffed. "Rebecca, I don't believe I'd let my little girl socialize with the help. It's not the proper way to raise a young lady." She turned from the window.

It took all Rebecca could do to smile. "The hired help, as you call them, are her brothers. I guess we need to get something straight."

Martha raised her chin. "Yes?"

"As long as you are staying here, under my roof, I expect you to treat everyone as equals, including Emma. This is first and foremost my home and I will have peace and politeness at all times." Rebecca crossed her arms over her chest and held the woman's gaze.

Fay stepped through the bedroom door behind Martha and nodded her approval.

"I can treat her any way I please." Martha mimicked Rebecca's stance.

Rebecca nodded. "But this is my home and Emma is my guest, just as you are. Now, if you want one of the boys to take you to town, I'll be happy to make the arrangements." Martha started to interrupt but Rebecca held up her hand. "But there is only one place to stay in town and they don't accept credit."

Anger filled Martha's eyes. "So what you are telling me is that I really have no choice. Abide by your rules or find myself out in the cold." Martha dropped onto the couch. Her lips were pinched into a pucker.

Behind Martha's back, a small grin twitched at Emma's lips. She covered her mouth with her hand to hide her pleasure at seeing Martha made to show respect for others.

"I think you'll find it easier to do than what you think. And it may only be for one night," Rebecca added. She turned to walk into the kitchen. "Emma, would you mind helping me peel potatoes for dinner?"

Emma followed her. "No, I don't mind."

Rebecca told the young woman where the root cellar was and asked her to gather twenty-six potatoes. She figured two potatoes per person would be enough. While the girl was gone, Rebecca wondered if she'd been too hard on Martha.

A few months ago she'd been living quietly with her boys and Joy. Then Seth had arrived and they'd all adjusted, to the point where it felt as if he belonged with them. Fay had joined them shortly after Seth and she, too, now felt like a member of the family.

Instinctively, Rebecca knew that once more everything was about to change. How long would Martha, Emma and Mr. Walker be her guests? Would Martha make things harder than they needed to be? Once the boys saw how pretty Emma was, Rebecca knew she could be facing a whole other set of problems. Even Seth might find the girl attractive.

Something in her heart ached at the thought. Would he be interested in Emma? If so, would he give up his search for Charlotte? Rebecca took a deep breath. She'd allowed herself to care for Seth and now she wasn't so sure she wanted to see him become involved with another woman.

Perhaps Emma was too young for Seth. Still, he had his heart set on marrying Charlotte. Plus, John's memory was too important to the kids for her to even think that she might have feelings for the station keeper.

But a part of her ached at the thought that he would be moving on as soon as he found out where Charlotte might be. If only she hadn't promised to help him search for her. Rebecca knew she wouldn't go back on her word, even if her word broke her heart.

Chapter Nineteen

Over dinner Seth and Ty made plans to ride into town the following morning to tell the sheriff about the holdup. It was also decided that after dinner, the boys would go get the stagecoach and bring it to the farm. Seth asked them to all go, because he felt there was safety in numbers.

The stage would be moving on after they returned from town the following day with fresh horses to pull it. Mr. Walker seemed happy at the idea of getting a good night's sleep and a couple of hot meals before he continued on with his job.

Martha and Emma also seemed content to enjoy the food and beds that Rebecca supplied. It had been established that Martha would be staying in Fay's room with her and Emma would be sleeping in Rebecca's room. Martha didn't say much to anyone, just simply ate her food and avoided eye contact with the rest of the women.

Benjamin sat at the table looking tired, but the fever had left his cheeks and the sparkle was back in his eyes.

His voice sounded as if a small bullfrog had crawled into his throat. Joy laughed every time Beni spoke.

Seth noticed that Rebecca seemed quiet and wondered if she was feeling the strain of having added guests. Her attention seemed focused on Beni and Joy. None of the older boys seemed to notice their mother's silence. They were too interested in Emma.

The young woman smiled shyly at them as they passed her plates of food. Thomas and Philip seemed to compete for her attention. Although, Seth couldn't help but notice that Emma appeared to be more interested in Andrew.

He turned his attention back to Rebecca. Her gaze told him she'd caught him staring at Emma and the boys. What must she think? Seth realized his attention had been on the younger woman for too long. Rebecca's cheeks were a soft pink. She broke away from his gaze.

Had he seen jealousy in her expression? Surely not. Rebecca hadn't conveyed any interest in him. Why would she start now? And how would he feel if she was attracted to him?

He wasn't looking for love. And he had a mail-order bride to find. Seth panicked and pushed away from the table. He had to get out of the house. There was too much going on around him and he felt trapped in the thoughts that were threatening him.

Everyone turned to look at him. "I just realized I need to go check on something in the barn."

Jacob moved to go with him.

Seth stopped him. "No, Jacob. Stay and finish your dinner." He left his half-eaten dinner and hurried out of the house and into the fresh night air.

He walked to the barn and opened the heavy door.

Warmth and the scents of hay and horse welcomed him. What was wrong with him? Was he so afraid of Rebecca's feelings that he'd run from the house like a scared mouse?

He was and he had. The realization hit him in the gut. Seth knew without a shadow of a doubt that he cared for Rebecca.

Rebecca yawned and crawled into bed. Emma was already there. "Thank you for letting me stay with you tonight. It's been a long time since I've slept in a soft bed like this one," the young woman said, also yawning.

"You're welcome." The sheets felt cool and welcoming.

Rebecca blew out the lamp and listened to Emma's breathing. She liked the girl and was glad to see that she hadn't egged on the boys tonight. But Rebecca hadn't liked the fact that Seth had studied the girl so intently at dinner. He hadn't come to the house for their nightly chat, but she supposed that was because he'd already told everyone that he and Mr. Walker would be running to town the following morning.

"Rebecca?"

She tried to make her voice sound sleepy. "Uh-huh?"

"Thank you for making Mrs. Ranger be nice to me." Her voice sounded sad in the darkness. "She doesn't like it, but it's nice for a change."

Curiosity ate at her. "Why do you work for Martha, Emma?"

Emma sighed. "My pa sold me to her. So I don't exactly work for her. She owns me."

Rebecca knew that people had slaves, but since

Emma was white, she hadn't expected her to be a slave. Her heart went out to the young girl. "I'm sorry. I guess my making her be nice to you isn't going to help you later, is it?"

"No, but for now I don't care," Emma admitted. "She bought me when I was thirteen years old and most of the time she's kind, but sometimes, well..." Her words trailed off into the thick darkness.

To Rebecca's way of thinking it wasn't right for anyone to own another person, no matter what color their skin. It wasn't right. She tried to keep the conviction out of her voice as she asked, "How long have you been with her?"

"Five years."

Rebecca couldn't imagine being a slave for five years. When she'd come to work for the Young family at the age of sixteen, they had treated her like family. Taught her how to cook and clean, but not as a slave. At the orphanage she'd been treated harshly, but that was the way everyone was treated. It was just the way things were.

Emma's soft breathing told Rebecca the girl had gone to sleep. It broke her heart to think that Emma had no freedom to call her own.

Rebecca woke very early with the same thoughts running through her mind. The sun was nowhere on the horizon, but she couldn't go back to sleep. Emma needed to be free. But how? She got up and let the girl sleep.

Fay sat at the kitchen table nursing a cup of coffee. A frown marred her features and she stared out the dark window.

"You're up early," Rebecca said, helping herself to the fresh-brewed coffee.

"I've a lot on my mind this morning," Fay answered, rocking the cup back and forth between her hands. "Why are you up so early?"

Rebecca slid into the chair across from Fay. "Same reason. Couldn't sleep."

Fay leaned forward and whispered, "Is it our house-guests that are keeping you awake?"

She took a sip from her coffee. "Yes. I learned something last night that has me concerned."

"I bet it's the same thing I learned." Fay sighed and took a sip from her cup. "It always amazes me how we humans can be so cruel to one another."

Rebecca sat her cup down. "Did Martha tell you that she owns Emma?"

Fay nodded. "Oh, yes. She plans on selling her in Missouri."

The news shocked Rebecca. "I wonder if Emma knows."

Fay shook her head. "No, I don't believe she does. Martha is pretty angry with her right now and I think she made the decision last night. At least that's the impression I got."

A plan began to form in Rebecca's mind. She couldn't stand the idea of Martha selling off Emma like a piece of livestock. "How much does a slave cost?"

"I heard that they were running about eight hundred dollars." Fay set down her cup. "Are you thinking about buying one?"

Rebecca nodded. "Yes, but that's a bit high. Did Martha say how much she wanted for Emma?"

"Can't say that she did." Fay ran her finger over the

rim of the coffee mug. "You know, I think I'll talk to her and see what she might be asking for the girl. It would be easy for me to play the old-lady card and say I needed the girl's help. Do you think you could come up with the money?"

Rebecca licked her bottom lip. "I'm not sure. The boys might be willing to help. The Pony Express pays them fifty dollars each, every two weeks, to be riders." She knew they'd gotten paid a few days earlier and hated to ask them for their money, but to save Emma, she'd do it.

Fay's gaze moved out the window again. "The light just came on in the bunkhouse."

Rebecca stood. "I'll ask them and come right back." She grabbed her shawl off the hook by the door and quietly left the house.

The mornings were still cool, but the air felt nice on her hot cheeks. Would the boys be willing to help her? She wouldn't demand their help but hoped they'd offer it. Raising her fist, she knocked quietly on the door.

Andrew opened it a crack and looked out. "Ma? Is everything all right?"

She pushed past him. The scent of unwashed clothes assaulted her senses. Rebecca had more pressing matters to discuss, so she tried to ignore the odor. "Yes and no. Are all the boys awake?"

He shook his head. "No, but I can wake them." He pulled on his shirt as he went to each bunk and woke his brothers.

Rebecca sat down by the woodstove and waited for them. Hair tousled, clothes half-on and rubbing sleep from their eyes, they slowly came to sit around her. "Noah, would you go get Jacob, please? And be as quiet as you can in doing so. Don't wake Mr. Walker, if you can help it."

With a nod, Noah slipped out the door.

Andrew looked at Rebecca. "What's this about?"

"When Noah and Jacob get back, I'll tell everyone at once. I'm sorry to get you all up so early and I wouldn't have done so if it wasn't necessary." Rebecca folded her hands in her lap and waited. She thought about mentioning the smell in the room and then decided against it. It wouldn't do to put them on the offensive before asking for a favor.

Her gaze moved to the closed door that led to Seth's quarters. Was he awake? If so, would he join them? She couldn't ask him to help so she prayed he'd stay in his room, at least until her business with the boys was finished.

Jacob and Noah slipped into the bunkhouse. The concern on her oldest son's face caused her to feel guilty.

"Come on in, boys." She motioned for them to sit down.

Noah sat down on the floor at her feet. Jacob pulled a chair from the table that sat against the wall.

As soon as they were seated, Rebecca began. "Last night, I learned something that really bothered me." She looked at each boy in turn to make sure she had their total attention. "Emma is a slave."

"What?" Thomas and Philip looked at each other, as they both had the same reaction.

"Martha and her husband own her," Rebecca answered.

Thomas jumped to his feet. "What can we do to free her?"

"We could kidnap her and take her away from here," Philip answered.

Jacob growled from his chair, "Shut up and let Ma talk."

Rebecca shook her head. "No, they'd just have the sheriff find you and both of you would be in trouble with the law."

Philip clamped his mouth shut. Rebecca knew the boy hadn't given up on his idea.

"Fay and I have another idea. Fay is going to offer to buy Emma from Martha." Rebecca watched their faces go from furious indignation to surprise. She smiled. "Once Martha leaves, we will give Emma her freedom."

The boys all began to talk and ask questions at once. The room buzzed with their excited voices. Andrew's topped the others.

He asked, "What can we do to help?"

Silence filled the room as they all looked to her expectantly. "We need the money to buy her."

Jacob stood up and walked to the stove. "How much?"

Rebecca knew this was the moment of truth. Her boys would either give her the money or tell her she asked too much. She met each boy's eyes before answering. "Whatever you want to give us. I'm not telling you how much—you all have worked hard for your money. If you don't want to give it to me, I understand." Rebecca knew she was asking a lot from the boys.

The boys looked at each other and then slowly each rose from their sitting places. Thomas dug into his front pocket and handed Rebecca his pay. Philip moved to his bunk and pulled out a small box, then returned to hand her his money. Jacob slipped out the door.

Rebecca hadn't thought that Jacob would refuse to

help, but she couldn't bring herself to be upset with him. She knew he was saving his money—he'd never said so but she was sure Jacob planned on someday going in search of his real mother.

Andrew and Clayton each gave her their wages. Noah handed her his money, as well.

"Thank you, boys. I know how much this means to you." She held the money out in front of her. "It may not be enough. Fay said that slaves are sold for about eight hundred dollars each. I'm going to add money to this and we'll all need to pray that it's enough. If Martha refuses, I'll make sure you get your money back."

Jacob slipped back into the bunkhouse. He walked up to his mother and gave her his money. She knew he got paid more than his brothers as a stock tender. She didn't look at the amount of money he handed her, simply tucked it with the rest. His eyes met hers and he said, "No one should be held a slave."

"Thank you, son." She met each boy's eyes. Her boys were no longer children, but grown men. "Thank you, all."

They looked away, embarrassed by the look of pride Rebecca was sure shone on her face. "Before I go I have to tell you what Fay and I have in mind."

The young men all sat back down. They leaned forward to hear her better. Each face told her that whatever she said, they would accept.

"Fay is going to offer to buy Emma. She's going to pretend that she's getting too old to take care of herself and needs a slave to help her." Rebecca looked at them.

Clayton asked, "Why don't you just buy her?"

Rebecca shook her head. "Martha doesn't like me.

I've made her treat Emma with respect while they are here. I think she would refuse out of spite."

Thomas grinned. "What if one of us offered to marry her?"

Philip punched him in the arm. "She's not going to let me marry Emma. She wants the money."

"I wasn't talking about you, chicken head." Thomas punched him back.

"Knock it off, you two," Jacob growled at them. "No one is going to marry her."

"You just want her for yourself," Philip mumbled.

Rebecca spoke sharply. "Boys. We're going to stick to the plan of Fay offering to buy her. But I don't want you boys acting like you know anything about it. Not that Emma is a slave. Not that Martha is planning on selling her. And most important, not that Fay is interested in buying her. Don't even mention this to Mr. Walker or Seth. Let's keep it in the family. If we want things to go smoothly, we are going to have to trust Fay to make it happen. Do you understand?"

They nodded in turn. Rebecca stood and tucked the money into her dress pocket. "Good. I need to get back in the house before I'm missed." She walked to the door. But before she slipped out, Rebecca turned to look at them. In a stern voice she said, "You need to air this place out and bring your filthy clothes to the house. It reeks in here."

The young men looked surprised and even a little embarrassed. Noah sniffed the air. "Told you so," he said to the room at large.

Rebecca hurried back to the house. She decided to go through the kitchen. Since the boys were up, they'd be wanting breakfast soon.

As Rebecca walked her mind worked. Had Martha woken yet? Would she be willing to sell Emma to Fay? Even thinking about buying another human being felt odd. She knew she'd have to heed her own words and not show her true emotions and knowledge that Fay was offering to buy Emma. Rebecca silently prayed that they had enough money to purchase the girl's freedom.

Chapter Twenty

Seth stood on his side of the door, listening as Rebecca told her boys what she wanted and needed from them. His admiration for the woman went up as she explained that Emma was a slave and Fay was going to use their money to buy her. Since he couldn't see them, Seth could only assume that each of the young men had handed over their hard-earned wages.

The sound of the bunkhouse door closing again told him Rebecca had left. Her parting shot about the smell had him chuckling. Women noticed such things, where men didn't. Thanks to her, he now had more jobs to keep the young men busy while he and the coach driver were in town.

As he dressed, Seth decided to give to the fund to buy Emma's freedom. Slavery was an ugly thing. He pulled on his boots and went to his Bible, where he'd tucked his earnings.

As he took out a hundred dollars, Seth wondered how he was going to get the money to Rebecca. He couldn't just hand it to her—she'd think one of the boys had told him and he'd heard her telling them not to let on to him about what was going on. He had to admit that it had stung when she'd said it. It was true that he wasn't a part of their family and he'd do well to remember that. Even if at times he felt as if he was.

Rebecca Young was a private person—hadn't she been upset when she'd thought he'd been snooping into her life? If she figured out that he'd been eavesdropping on her conversation with her sons, that might cause more trust issues between them. He sighed and sat down on the edge of his cot.

The money rested in his hands, money he'd intended to use to help him find Charlotte. So far there had been no leads on his mail-order bride through the stage-coach line…maybe there never would be. Seth knew that soon he'd need to move on, keep looking for her. He'd promised his grandmother he'd find Charlotte, but he also felt drawn to help free Emma.

Seth bowed his head and silently prayed. Only the Lord could give his mind peace as to what to do with the money. After several long minutes, he felt the urge to help Emma outweigh the need to go in search for Charlotte. He took that as an answer to his unspoken prayer.

He tucked the money into his pants pocket and laid the Bible back down on the table. He put on his jacket and prepared to leave the room.

Seth opened the adjourning door in the bunkhouse and stepped into the boys' living quarters. They looked up at him as he entered. "Good morning." He walked over to the coffeepot and poured himself a cup. "You fellas are up awful early."

No one responded to his comment.

Seth tipped the cup to his lips and grimaced as

the thick brew coated his tongue. He swallowed and frowned. "Who had coffee duty? This stuff tastes like blackened mud."

Thomas chuckled. "We found something Noah isn't good at."

Noah ducked his head. The back of his neck turned red.

Seth chuckled. "Good to know he's human." He put down his cup.

They all chuckled. When they'd quieted down again, Seth continued, "Ty and I will be heading to town after breakfast. Be on the lookout for Indians and road bandits. I want you to team up if you decide to leave the farmhouse. Also, don't leave the women without at least one of you here."

Phillip asked, "Do you think they'll cause trouble here at the station?"

"Only time will tell but it's better to be safe than sorry," Seth answered. He waited to see if there were more questions. When it didn't seem that there were, he said, "Jacob will be in charge today. We're not expecting a rider but if one comes in, I believe it's Clayton's turn to head out."

Clayton nodded his agreement. "I'll be ready."

"Good." Seth walked toward the door. While he'd been talking he'd decided to give the money to Fay, not Rebecca. It would probably be easier to slip the money to the older woman than to explain to Rebecca how he knew they needed it.

Jacob stood. "Last night I noticed that one of the carriage wheels is cracking. You might want to take a look before you leave." He pulled his jacket off a hook by the door and slipped his arms inside.

"Why don't you show me now and I'll give you the list of chores for the day." Seth pulled the door open. He stopped and looked at each young man. "Why don't you boys air this place out today. It's beginning to smell like something died in here." He stepped outside with Jacob right behind him.

He half expected Jacob to say his ma had said the same thing, but the young man kept quiet. Seth followed Jacob to where the boys had unhitched the coach beside the barn. Ty stood beside it, looking at the wheel.

"I was just about to show Seth that wheel," Jacob said.

Ty rubbed the back of his neck. "It's cracked. Can't take the chance of it busting on the trail."

"Looks like we'll need to haul it to town in our wagon," Seth said, looking to Jacob.

Jacob nodded. "I'll see that we get the wheel off and the wagon hitched up."

"Don't go bothering yourself with taking it off, son. It's my coach. I'll take it off." Ty rolled up his sleeves and kneeled beside the wagon.

Jacob nodded. "I'll hitch up the wagon. I assume you'll want to leave right after breakfast," he said, looking to Seth for the answer to the unasked question.

Seth realized the trip to town was going to take longer than he'd first anticipated. He nodded.

Rebecca stepped out on the porch and began clanging the dinner bell. The boys tumbled out of the bunkhouse, reminding Seth of a gangly bunch of puppies. He watched as they hurried to the farmhouse.

She looked pretty this morning with her light brown hair pulled back in a ponytail. The brown dress with a white apron covering her middle hugged her shape. The smile on her face as she watched her sons warmed his heart. Seth didn't want to admit it, but her kindness and generosity for Emma had melted another section of his heart toward her.

He shook off the thought. "Men, let's go grab some breakfast before that pack eats it all," Seth said to Jacob and Ty. He walked to the house.

Jacob fell into step beside him. Seth knew Jacob knew what to do to keep the boys busy, but began telling him what he expected, just in case Jacob decided to take it easy on his brothers. "Have the boys feed and exercise the horses today. Especially the Pony Express horses. Also, have them clean the barn, muck the stalls, make sure the hay is stacked and dry. We should be getting another supply of feed this week— have them clear out a spot to put it in. Have them haul up fresh water and make sure they air out the bunkhouse. If that's not enough, have them rub oil into the saddles and bridles."

Ty chuckled behind them. "And I thought my job was hard."

Seth glanced over his shoulder. "Just wait until you try to convince the men in town to give you credit for fixing your wheel and two new horses. You'll think we have it easy out here."

The older man groaned. "Don't remind me."

They all washed their hands in the basin and proceeded into the house. Seth looked for Fay but didn't see her at the table. Martha and Emma were there and like the night before Thomas and Philip sat on each side of the young woman, hoping to get her attention.

Beni looked much better. The little boy smiled at

him and said, "Seth, tell Ma I'm well enough to go back to work."

Rebecca gave the little boy a stern look. She handed him a bowl filled with what looked like oatmeal.

Seth laughed. "Sorry, partner. You have to get permission from your doctor before you can come back to work. If she says you are up to it, then I'm sure Jacob can find you something to do."

Rebecca looked over the little boy's head and smiled her thanks. Her twin dimples brightened his day.

He didn't see Fay at the table. Seth hoped he'd find her in the kitchen. Everyone was filling their plates and chatting among themselves. He slipped out of the dining room and was relieved to see Fay dishing up biscuits at the stove.

Seth pulled the money from his pocket. He hurried to her side and tucked it into her apron pocket. "That's for Emma," he whispered.

She looked at him with wise eyes. "Thank you, Seth, that's very kind of you."

He shook his head. "Kindness has nothing to do with it. I want her free—everyone deserves to be free."

Fay nodded. "That they do." She thrust a plate full of buttered biscuits in his hands.

"Um, Fay. Would you keep this between us? I don't want Rebecca to know I know what you two are up to." He stared down at the bread, praying she wouldn't ask him how he knew in the first place, if Rebecca hadn't told him.

She patted his arm. "Your thoughtfulness is safe with me."

Seth glanced up to find her looking at him with

warmth in her eyes. He nodded, happy to know she wouldn't say anything about the money. "Thanks."

"Now take that bread out before it gets cold," she ordered, returning to the pan of biscuits and butter.

He did as he was told, feeling much like a little boy again. His grandmother often had him toting plates of food to the table. Sorrow cut into his chest. He missed his grandmother, but Fay was swiftly filling that empty spot in his heart. Oh, she could never replace his grandmother, but she did make missing her a little easier.

When he reentered the dining room, Rebecca looked up. She was slowly filling an empty space in his heart, too. Seth handed the plate to Jacob. He silently prayed, *Lord, please don't let me get any more attached to this family.*

Rebecca dried the last breakfast dish and then began to wash a pot of beans. Chili beans sounded good for dinner, with corn bread. She smiled as she looked to the table, where Beni and Joy were looking at a picture book.

"We're done, Ma. Can I go help Jacob now?" Beni asked.

She set her beans to the side and went to the little boy. Rebecca gave him a hug. "Yes, but only until lunchtime. I know you think you are all well, but I think you will need a rest time this afternoon."

He pulled out of her embrace. "All right." Beni ran for the door and yanked it open.

"Wait!" Rebecca called after him.

He stopped and came back. "You said I could go."

"Yes, I did, but not without your coat."

"But, Ma, it's not cold outside."

"Benjamin Theo Young, you will wear your coat or you can go back to bed." She pointed at the coat hanging by the door.

He pulled it off the hook and slipped his arms into it. "It's on," Benjamin said, his voice a croak.

"I want to go, too." Joy reached for her cloak.

Rebecca shook her head. "Not today, Joy. You have a bedroom to clean."

The little girl frowned. "I don't want to clean my room."

Fay came into the room laughing. "I don't want to clean mine, either, but it needs to be done. Why don't I help you clean yours and then you can help me clean mine?"

Joy smiled broadly. "All right."

As soon as they were gone, Rebecca noticed Martha sitting on the couch. She walked over to her and asked, "Would you like to come into the kitchen with me?"

"Why? So you can put me to work, too?"

Rebecca forced a smile. The woman was almost impossible to get along with but she'd try. "No, I thought you might like some company and I know I would."

"Well, if you insist." Martha stood. "Where is Emma?"

Rebecca grimaced. "I sent her out to collect the eggs." She walked toward the kitchen, waiting for a mean comment.

Martha followed. "Good, that girl needs to be working."

"Do you know her very well?" Rebecca asked, swishing the beans about in the water.

Martha sat down at the kitchen table. She picked up

the kids' picture book and leafed through the pages. "Well enough."

Rebecca worked in silence, thinking about what she could say that wouldn't get her head taken off. "That's good." She wondered how Seth and Mr. Walker were getting along. Had they made it to town yet? Bought the wheel? Horses?

"She makes a good traveling companion," Martha said out of the blue.

"Where are you headed?" Rebecca asked, pouring the dirty water off the beans.

"Missouri. My husband went there a few months ago on a business trip. We're joining him there."

Rebecca looked over her shoulder at the older woman. Could she be selling Emma because the girl was getting older and more attractive? Could she be afraid the younger woman might attract her husband's attentions?

"This is a cute book," Martha said.

"Yes, I enjoy reading it to the kids and they love the colorful pictures." Rebecca poured fresh water over the pot of beans and set it on the back of the stove to start boiling.

She poured herself a cup of coffee and one for Martha. Then she put several cookies on a plate and carried them to the table. "Care to join me in a snack?"

The older woman looked up and grinned. "Thank you." She took one of the coffee cups and a cookie.

Rebecca pulled out a chair and sat down. "Emma mentioned earlier that you came from California."

Martha nodded. "Yes, my husband sells mining equipment. With the gold rush, we ended up in Sacramento." She broke her cookie in half.

"Sounds interesting."

She shook her head. "Not really. There aren't a lot of women there and those that are work from sunup to sundown, unless they have husbands who can work for them." Martha laughed.

Rebecca wasn't sure why the older woman laughed, but decided that since she was in such a good mood she'd ask about Charlotte. "By any chance do you know a woman named Charlotte Fisher?"

Martha studied her for a few minutes. "Charlotte isn't in my social circle but I have seen her working at one of the eating establishments there."

"You've met her?" Rebecca asked, unable to keep the excitement out of her voice.

The older woman set down her cup. "Yes, a couple of times. Emma probably knows her better. How do you know Charlotte?"

"She's…"

Emma came through the back door humming a soft tune. She looked to the two women, who had stopped talking and were staring at her. "Is something wrong?"

Rebecca jumped to her feet. "No, everything is great!" She took the egg basket out of Emma's hands. "Do you know Charlotte Fisher?" She set the basket on the counter and pulled Emma to a kitchen chair.

The young girl's eyes widened and she looked to Martha.

"Answer her," Martha barked.

"Y-yes."

Rebecca tried to calm herself. She reached over and patted Emma's hands. "You aren't in any trouble, Emma. I've been helping Seth look for Charlotte. You are the first people who know her. I'm just excited. Not angry."

Emma grinned and her shoulders relaxed. "Oh, Charlotte is a very nice person. She can't remember anything about her life before she arrived in Sacramento. I'm not sure why she can't remember. We never really discussed that. I only know her from short trips to get Martha lunch. How do you know her?"

Rebecca explained that she really didn't know the young woman but that she'd been asking passengers of the stagecoach about Charlotte for Seth. She didn't say that Charlotte was his mail-order bride or that he'd been searching for her for months. Instead she patted Emma's hand again and then got up to get the girl a cup of coffee.

Dread and excitement filled Rebecca at the thought of telling Seth that they'd found his Charlotte. His Charlotte. The words echoed in her mind like the hammering of nails in a coffin.

What was life going to be like after he was gone? Deep sorrow melted the excitement of a few minutes ago. Seth would probably be leaving them soon. Rebecca couldn't explain it, but her heart ached.

Chapter Twenty-One

Seth felt as if someone had punched him. The trip to town had been a total waste of time. As he'd predicted the businessmen in town refused to give Ty credit for a new wheel and horses. He and the ladies would have to stay put until the stagecoach line sent fresh horses and money to fix the wheel.

If that wasn't bad enough, the sheriff didn't seem too interested in catching the road bandits. He'd promised to keep a lookout for them, but had no intentions of calling together a posse, his excuse being that it was planting season and too many farmers were preparing their fields for future crops and didn't have time to enforce the law.

Ty sighed as he climbed down from the wagon. "Thanks for loaning me the wagon, Seth. It's a shame the men in town are so untrusting."

Seth nodded. He looked to the house longingly. Had Rebecca saved him and Ty dinner trays? Or would it be a miss-a-meal night, as his grandmother used to call it when he'd returned after supper and dishes had been washed and put away?

Jacob walked out of the barn. "How'd it go in town?" he asked as he helped unhitch the horses from the wagon.

"Can't say it went well," Ty answered.

The young man shook his head. "That's too bad. Ma saved you both a plate. She said for you to go on up to the house when you got back." He pulled one of the horses into the barn. Ty followed him with the second.

Seth knew Sam had to be taken care of before he filled his belly with fine cooking. He wondered how Rebecca was going to feel with the extra women in the house for a few days. At least with them having more time, maybe Fay could talk Martha into selling Emma to her at a reasonable price.

His thoughts moved to the young men in his care as he unsaddled his horse. It didn't take much for him to realize he'd come to care for them and that to ensure their safety they needed a plan. There was no doubt in his mind that the road bandits would strike again.

Jacob came to stand beside him. "Why don't you go on up to the house and eat, and I'll take care of Sam. Ma seemed excited to see you as soon as you got back."

Rebecca missed him? Seth handed him the horse comb. "Thanks." He turned to Ty. "Come on with me. You can finish that later."

Ty yawned. "Would you mind asking the missus if you can bring my plate out here? I'm mighty tired and not fit for female companionship." He made a point of covering his mouth as if to stifle another big yawn.

Was it all an act? Ty hadn't seemed that tired a few minutes earlier. Was the older man trying to give him some privacy with Rebecca? Or avoid his passengers and their many questions? "Be happy to."

He walked to the house and entered it through the kitchen. The warm smell of buttery corn bread greeted his hungry belly. He moved to the stove, where a plate sat on the back and there was a big pot beside it. Seth lifted the lid of the pot and inhaled the scent of chili beans. His stomach growled its appreciation.

Rebecca entered the kitchen from the dining area. Her hair was down and hung about her shoulders in soft waves. Big blue eyes searched his. "Did you get everything done in town?" she asked, pulling two bowls and plates out from under the cabinet.

"No, I'm afraid the stagecoach passengers will need to stay on with us for a few more days." Seth leaned a hip against the counter and simply looked at her. Her hair looked silky soft. How upset would she be if he reached out and touched it? He stuck his hands in his pockets to keep them from acting on their own.

"Oh." Her blue eyes met his. "Sit down and I'll get your supper ready," she ordered, gently nudging him to the side so that she could get to the beans and corn bread.

Seth did as she asked and sat down at the table. "Ty would like to eat out in the barn. Says he's too tired to eat in the house. I'll run it out to him real quick if you'll pack it up."

"Benjamin can take it out to him. I have something important I want to tell you." She dished up two bowls of chili beans and put corn bread on two plates. Rebecca sat one in front of him and then said, "I'll get Benjamin to take this out and then I need to talk to you." Rebecca left to get her son.

She'd already said that she needed to talk to him.

Her serious face and low voice alerted him to the fact that whatever Rebecca had to say was important.

Jacob had said she was excited but she didn't seem excited to him. She almost seemed depressed. Had something happened with Emma? Had Martha refused to sell her slave to Fay?

He said a quick prayer over his supper and then nibbled at the bread. Rebecca and Benjamin entered the kitchen.

"Hi, Seth. Ma let me work with Jacob this morning." His little throat still sounded scratchy but it was obvious that Benjamin was on the mend.

"I'm glad to hear that." His thoughts went to the story Rebecca had told him about the little boy on the day of their picnic and he smiled.

Rebecca handed the boy a tray with a covered plate and bowl on it. "Take this to Mr. Walker in the barn."

"Can you give him some cookies, too?" the boy asked, looking longingly at the cookie jar.

She walked over and took out one cookie. Rebecca wrapped it in cheesecloth and laid it beside the plate. "There, I'll have to ask him in the morning if he enjoyed his cookie as much as you enjoyed yours."

Benjamin twisted his face up in thought. "You know, I could have him eat it first and then I can tell you how he liked it." He licked his lips in anticipation.

Seth hid his grin behind a spoonful of chili.

"That won't be necessary." Rebecca planted both hands on her hips. "I expect you back in this house and in bed before he has time to eat his cookie. Now scoot."

Benjamin frowned. "Yes, Ma." The back door closed with a bang behind him.

Seth chuckled. "He really is a little scamp, isn't he?"

Rebecca finally released her pent-up grin. "That he is."

She came to the table and sat down.

He picked up his spoon and sampled the chili. It really was very good. Seth continued to eat while Rebecca drew imaginary circles on the table. After several long minutes of this, he couldn't remain quiet a moment longer. "I believe you said you have something to tell me." He tore his bread apart and took a big bite.

She straightened in her chair. "I do. Today I asked Martha if she'd ever met Charlotte."

His hand stopped halfway to his mouth. "And?"

"And both she and Emma know Charlotte. She's living in Sacramento and is a server at one of the restaurants there." Rebecca studied his face. What was she looking for?

Seth put down his spoon.

Benjamin banged back into the house. "I'm back," he announced breathlessly.

"Good. Thank you. Now go get back into bed. I'll tuck you in again in a few minutes." Rebecca motioned for Benjamin to leave the room.

He stopped by the table. "You all right, Seth?"

Seth looked at the little boy. Was his shock that plain on his face? "I'm fine, Benjamin. See you in the morning." He really hadn't expected Rebecca to find Charlotte. At first it had seemed like a good idea, but after so many people had said they hadn't heard of her, he'd begun to think of it as a long shot.

"'Night." Benjamin left the kitchen slowly.

As soon as the little boy was gone, Seth turned his attention back on Rebecca. "So what did they say?" Did he sound excited or worried? Seth didn't know.

"Just that she's living in Sacramento and that she only knows her name. Charlotte told Emma she can't remember anything before she arrived." Rebecca wiped at imaginary crumbs on the table.

"If she couldn't remember where she was going, that would explain why she didn't show up in St. Joseph," Seth said absently. He pushed his plate away, no longer hungry. His emotions were torn. "What I need is more answers. Are the ladies already retired for the night?"

"Yes, but I'm sure they will be happy to answer any questions you have for them in the morning." She picked up his dishes.

Seth stood. "I think I'll turn in myself." This was crazy. He'd been looking for Charlotte. Wanted to find her to fulfill his promise to his grandmother. Now he wasn't sure what he wanted to do.

The Young family had become very dear to him. He couldn't leave now. Not with bandits robbing people and Indians chasing the boys on the trail.

"Seth?"

He looked to Rebecca. She stood before him, holding out a cookie. "Don't forget your dessert." Her soft smile only made his decision harder.

Without thinking, Seth pulled her to him and kissed her lips. His hands moved to hold her head close to his. Her hair felt silky soft and smelled like lavender soap. He gently messaged her scalp and savored the taste of sugar cookie on her lips.

He didn't rush the action. It might be the only time in his life that he would get to kiss her. Moving his lips softly against hers, he felt her arms travel around his waist and her hands press against his back. Seth didn't care if Fay or anyone else walked in. He wanted to enjoy knowing that for a few moments he could express his feelings for her.

It happened so fast that Rebecca was caught off guard. The last thing she'd expected was for Seth to kiss her. And the second-to-last thing she'd expected was that she'd relish his kiss.

She'd always enjoyed kissing John, but kissing Seth took her breath away. Rebecca stepped deeper into his embrace. His hands in her hair felt wonderful.

When he released her she felt dazed. Her fingers moved up to the tingling in her lips. Rebecca looked into his face and saw a tenderness there that she'd never seen on anyone's face before. Then he spun on his booted heels and headed for the door.

Seth stopped and turned to face her again. With one hand on the door he said, "I'm sorry. I shouldn't have done that." And then he was gone.

Rebecca couldn't sleep after being thoroughly kissed. She tossed and turned all night. How could he kiss her like that and then go find Charlotte? Did the kiss mean anything? Was he really sorry that he'd kissed her?

Those questions and more troubled her all night. She continued to replay the kiss in her mind. It had felt so right, but was it? What if one of the boys had walked in? Or Fay?

When morning finally arrived, Rebecca still hadn't found sleep. She pulled on her housecoat and went to the kitchen to start the coffee and breakfast.

The smells of scrambled eggs, coffee and bacon soon filled the kitchen. She could hear her houseguests coming into the dining room and stepped out on the porch to ring the dinner bell.

Fay and Emma entered the kitchen. "Can we help you get this on the table?" Fay asked, picking up a platter of eggs.

"Yes, thank you. If you can set the table, I'll go get dressed." At their nods of agreement, Rebecca hurried to her room to change into a day dress and pull her hair into a braid.

By the time she returned to the dining room everyone was seated. Jacob said the blessing and then the plates were being passed around. She tried to avoid Seth's gaze by focusing on helping Joy with her plate.

She noticed that the little girl's hair was braided and had a pretty pink ribbon in it. "You look very pretty this morning."

"Emma helped me fix my hair." Joy beamed across at her new friend.

Rebecca smiled. "Thank you, Emma. That was very nice of you."

Emma winked at Joy. "It was fun. Wasn't it, Joy?"

"Yep. I like the way she braided my hair," Joy answered. "She made it look like yours."

Rebecca hugged Joy to her. "Yes, she did."

The rest of breakfast was a noisy time. Everyone talked and ate. The boys were getting ready to go do their chores when Seth's strong voice stopped them.

"Before everyone leaves the table I have an announcement to make."

Rebecca held her breath. Was he leaving? Her heart broke and Rebecca knew she'd fallen in love with Seth. She'd known it for some time now, but hadn't faced the fact. How could she? She still loved John. Was she betraying his love and memory? What if Seth loved her back? Would he break his promise to his grandmother and not marry Charlotte? No, Seth was a man of his word.

"This concerns you all. Until the road bandits are captured, I want you all to stick close to the farm. If you need to go to town, I think instead of taking the main road you should take one that's less traveled. According to the sheriff the bandits seem to be sticking close to the main road. Also, go in twos or more. No one should travel alone. It's not safe. Is this agreeable to everyone?" Seth met each person's gaze and waited for their nod of consent before moving on to the next person.

Rebecca felt as if the oxygen had been sucked out of the room when he looked to her. His gaze bored into hers and he waited for her to nod. She did so and tore her eyes from his.

"Does anyone have any questions or want to add anything more?" Seth asked, looking about the table.

When no one answered he smiled. "Good, then I guess we can start our day."

The boys all shoved back their chairs, picked up their dirty dishes, carried them to the kitchen and then filed out of the house.

Seth waited until they were all gone and then turned back to the table. "Mrs. Ranger and Miss Jordan, yesterday we learned that you will need to stay here until the stage company sends more horses and money to fix the wheel on your coach. I hope you don't mind."

"We don't mind," Martha answered for both of them.

Joy clapped her hands with happiness. "Emma, you get to stay longer." She jumped from her chair and hurried to stand by the young woman. "Want to go look at my picture books?"

Emma ran her hand over the little girl's head. "Sure."

"Miss Jordan, would you wait just a few more minutes? I need to ask you and Mrs. Ranger a couple of questions about Charlotte Fisher." Seth rested his hands on the back of the chair.

Rebecca stood. "If you will excuse me, I'll clean the dishes." She quickly began to gather up the remaining dirty dishes.

"I'll help you." Fay stood also and picked up hers and Joy's plates.

Once in the kitchen Rebecca realized her hands were shaking. She prepared the dishwater and scraped the food from the plates the boys had left.

Fay added her plates to them and then stepped back to look at her. "What's wrong with you this morning? Are you feeling bad?"

"No, I'm just a little tired. I had trouble sleeping last night." It was the truth.

Fay nodded. "That explains the dark circles under your eyes." She began washing the cups.

Rebecca touched the skin under her eyes. Did she really have dark circles? She grabbed a pot and tried to see her reflection in it.

In a low voice Fay said, "I spoke to Martha last night about buying Emma."

She lowered the pot and walked closer to Fay. "What did she say?"

"Said she wants five hundred for her," Fay answered.

Rebecca sighed. "We only have four. What are we going to do?"

"I already paid her the five hundred." Fay smiled

over her shoulder at Rebecca. "I had a hundred you didn't know about."

"Did you get papers?" Rebecca asked, trying to hide the excitement in her voice.

"Yep, and to keep them safe I hid them in your room. But she made me promise not to tell Emma."

"Why not?" Rebecca didn't like the sound of that. What games was the other woman playing?

Fay passed her a clean plate to dry. "Said she wants to tell her just before she leaves so the girl won't carry on."

"Do you believe her?" Rebecca put the plate in the cupboard.

Fay shrugged. "I have papers that say Emma Kate Jordan is legally mine. And I have a bill of sale to prove it."

Rebecca nodded. Something didn't feel right. She thought Martha would have either fought to keep Emma from Fay, or she would have gloated to the girl that she sold her. The desire to talk to Seth about it pulled at her. But she knew he had other things on his mind. Like finding his lost mail-order bride. His conversation with Martha and Emma now proved he'd decided to go look for his future bride. Would she be able to forget him after he left? Or would she forever have a hole in her heart?

Chapter Twenty-Two

Seth was disappointed that Emma and Martha didn't know any more about Charlotte than what they'd shared with Rebecca. All day he'd tossed their words around in his head. It seemed Charlotte couldn't remember her life before arriving in Sacramento. Emma said she was a sweet woman and very pretty with auburn-colored hair and green eyes.

He knew he couldn't leave the Pony Express station until the road bandits had been captured and his friends were no long in danger. Also, before he left he'd need to contact Mr. Bromley and let him know that he was quitting and why. Then he'd need to wait for his replacement.

The thought of leaving the farm, Rebecca and the boys made him sad. He'd learned to care deeply for the family and wasn't looking forward to saying goodbye, especially to Rebecca. Seth knew he'd fallen in love with the pretty lady.

But he had no intention of telling her. He'd made a promise to his grandmother and he intended to keep it. If he left now, he'd not have to worry about Rebecca breaking his heart or leaving him, like his mother had his father.

Not that she'd given him any indication that she cared or loved him. As a matter of fact, she'd acted as if he didn't exist today. How could she do that? He was aware of her presence even when they weren't in the same room. *Because she doesn't love you.* The thought hurt more than he cared to admit.

He stepped up on the front porch. Deep in thought, he was surprised when the porch swing squeaked. Seth looked to where Rebecca sat waiting for him. "I thought you'd be inside," he said, walking over to her.

"I needed fresh air. It's a little crowded in there," she answered, gently swinging.

Through the window he could see Martha sat on the sofa reading a book. Emma, Benjamin and Joy were working on what looked like a puzzle at the table and Fay sat in her rocker by the window sewing what looked like a quilt block. "It does look a mite crowded in there," he said, leaning against the porch rail.

"Did you learn anything new from Martha and Emma about Charlotte?" Rebecca asked.

He shook his head. "No, other than what they told you, they don't seem to know her."

Her voice sounded husky when she asked, "Are you going to be leaving soon to find her now that you know she's in Sacramento?"

Did she care about him after all? Or was she coming down with Benjamin's cold? "No, I'm not going until after the sheriff catches those road bandits."

"What if he doesn't catch them? Are you never going to find her?" Rebecca asked. She sniffled.

"Are you coming down with Benjamin's cold?" Seth

asked, moving closer to her so that he could see her face better.

Rebecca touched her cheeks as if checking for a fever. "I don't think so."

He wanted to reach out and feel her face. Not only to check for a fever, but just to feel her warmth. Seth stared into her beautiful blue eyes. He was going to miss her when he left.

"Seth?"

Mentally he shook himself. "Yes?"

"What if the sheriff doesn't catch the bandits? Then what?"

She dropped her hands back into her lap and searched his face.

He straightened. "They will make a mistake and he'll catch them. Bad guys always make a mistake." Seth offered her a grin to lighten the mood.

Rebecca stood and pulled her shawl closer to her body. She looked him in the eyes and said, "I hope so." She reached out and touched his arm, then pulled her hand away quickly. "I think I'll go in now. I'm not feeling very well."

Seth watched her hurry back into the house. She stopped by Fay's chair, said something in a low voice and then disappeared from sight. Did she really feel bad? Or was she just tired of being with him? Why had she cared so much whether or not he was going to go look for Charlotte? Did she want him to leave? Or stay?

His emotions felt as ragged as frayed rope. Seth turned to go to his room. What he needed was time with the Lord.

The next morning, Seth was still no closer to knowing what to do. Just when he thought that the Lord had assured him that all would be well, he'd worry again about what to do about Charlotte and Rebecca.

He was rubbing oil into his saddle when Jacob sat down on the hay bale beside him. Dust puffed up and Seth sneezed.

In his normal straight-to-the-point way, Jacob said, "You know, Seth, you could always send Miss Charlotte a letter using the Pony Express boys."

Seth cut his eyes at Jacob. Why hadn't he thought of that? He couldn't send it in the mailbag, but maybe the boys could pass it off to one another until it reached Sacramento. The last rider could hand deliver it to Charlotte. "That's a good idea."

"Next rider's expected in an hour." Jacob got up and went to saddle up Clayton's horse. "I'm sure Clayton would be happy to start the letter on its way."

He set the oil and saddle to the side. "I'll be in my room, if anyone needs me." Seth walked out of the barn even though he felt like running. The sooner he got the letter on its way, the sooner he'd know what to do about Charlotte, the Pony Express job and, most important, Rebecca. If Charlotte set him free from his commitment, he'd be able to tell Rebecca how he felt about her.

Even as he found paper and a pencil, Seth couldn't shake the fear that if he told Rebecca he loved her she would break his heart. Would she stay with him or, like his mother, would she desert him?

Rebecca spent the next three days avoiding Seth and fighting Benjamin's cold. She felt worn to a frazzle. Since she'd sold Emma to Fay, Martha hadn't changed much. She still spent her days in the sitting room, reading or complaining. Emma seemed happier than ever.

Now that Fay had given her her papers and told Emma she was free, the young woman had blossomed even more. Rebecca had offered Emma a home for as long as she wanted. Even though it wasn't expected, Emma tried to help out as much as possible. She and Fay made sure that Rebecca didn't overexert herself.

Her chest ached but she couldn't decide if it was from the cold or if it was simply her heart breaking knowing that Seth would be leaving soon. Rebecca found herself reliving their one and only kiss and wishing for more time with him.

She stretched and yawned. Thanks to Fay's thoughtfulness, Rebecca had enjoyed a long afternoon nap. She pulled on her shoes and walked into the sitting room. It was empty. The house was quieter than usual. She'd gotten used to lots of talking and laughter.

Rebecca headed to the kitchen, where she found a note propped up next to the cookie jar.

Rebecca,
The stage horses finally arrived and Martha and Mr. Walker left shortly afterward. Clayton agreed to take myself, Emma and Joy into town. Emma is happy to be free and we are going to buy fabric to make her a new dress to celebrate. We'll be home in time for dinner.
Love, Fay

A relieved sigh eased through her dry lips. Martha Ranger had been a thorn in her side ever since she'd arrived. Rebecca was glad to see that she was gone. The house felt warmer than usual so Rebecca opened the back door to let in a cool breeze.

She'd not eaten much for lunch and decided to make herself a fried egg and potato. It wasn't often that Rebecca fixed a meal for herself alone, but today she wanted to celebrate Martha's departure with her favorite meal, breakfast.

Her face and neck felt as if they were on fire and she wondered if perhaps she had a fever. Then she decided that it was probably just the afternoon heat that was making her feel feverish.

Pulling a potato from the bin, Rebecca found her sharpest knife and began to peel it. It wasn't a large potato, but would be the perfect size for one person. She'd just about finished when a hacking cough squeezed through her lungs. The knife slipped and cut a long, deep line through the center of her palm.

Blood poured from the wound. It burned like wildfire and brought tears to Rebecca's eyes. She grabbed a tea towel and pressed it to the wound. Within a few moments the cloth was saturated. She pulled the cloth away but couldn't see how deep the wound was because blood continued to pour from it.

She needed a doctor to look at it. Rebecca grabbed a clean towel and wrapped it tightly around her palm. Without being told, she knew that her hand would need stitches. She walked out to the barn to see if one of the boys could ride with her to town.

Jacob looked up and grinned when she came into the barn. "Hey, Ma, how are you feeling?"

"Better but I cut my hand and need to go let the doctor have a look at it." Rebecca kept her palm closed so that Jacob couldn't see how bad the cut was. "Is Andrew or Clayton around so they can go with me?"

He shook his head. "No, Clayton took the women

into town and Andrew and the rest of the men, except for me and Noah, are out in the back pasture trying to round up calves." Jacob looked down at her hand. "How bad is it?"

Rebecca put more pressure on her palm. She knew Clayton was with Fay; she'd simply forgotten. "Oh, not too bad. Noah, saddle Brownie for me." She turned her attention back to Jacob. "I'll just take Brownie and the back road to town."

Worry etched his young features. "Ma, if you would wait I could go with you. The other rider should be here in a few minutes and then I'll be free to go."

Noah pulled Brownie toward her. His dark eyes studied her face and Rebecca had the feeling that he understood her urgency to get to town. He held Brownie still while she pulled herself up into the saddle with her good hand. "When you get finished here, you can catch up with me, Jacob. If it's just a few minutes, I won't be in any danger."

She didn't give him time to argue. Rebecca could feel blood seeping through the thick towel. Her head felt fuzzy. She hated being sick and hoped that the doctor could give her some medicine for her cold, too. "I'll see you soon, son," she called over her shoulder as Brownie headed to town.

Half a mile down the back road, Rebecca looked down at the cloth. Blood darkened the fabric until she could no longer see the pattern. She felt light-headed and sleepy. A yawn forced its way past her dry lips. With her free hand she felt her forehead. It was hot. Feverish and bleeding, Rebecca welcomed the sound of horse's hooves coming up behind her.

She turned, expecting to see Jacob.

Instead two men with cloth across their faces were whipping their horses to catch up with her. Rebecca put her heels into the little mare's side, prompting her to run. But Brownie was no match for the two younger horses.

One of the men leaned over and grabbed the reins from Rebecca's good hand. "Whoa!" he yelled and pulled on Brownie's bit until she came to a stop.

"Give us your money," the other barked as he pointed a gun at Rebecca.

She swayed in the saddle. "I don't have any money."

"That's what they all say, lady," the second man growled.

His voice sounded familiar. Rebecca squinted at him. "Do I know you?"

The other bandit laughed. "Nope, but we know you. Now give us your money and get down from that horse." He waved the gun at her.

Rebecca felt foolish. Why hadn't she followed Seth's orders and waited for Jacob to come with her? She swayed in the saddle, but hung on to the horn.

Would she see Seth or the boys again? What would these men do to her? She wished she'd told Seth she loved him. Rebecca had been so concerned about John and the boys' feelings that she hadn't expressed her own. Now it might be too late.

Seth arrived back at the farm just as Noah and his horse shot off down the road carrying the Pony Express mailbag. The thrill of the ride flashed across the boy's face as he passed him. He raised a hand and prayed for Noah's safety before heading to the barn.

Jacob came running to him and slid to a stop to the side of Sam. His eyes held worry and frustration.

Seth could sense that something was wrong, dreadfully wrong. His gaze moved to the house. Was Rebecca feeling worse?

Fear filled Jacob's voice as he said, "Seth, Ma took off for town alone. She hurt her hand and wouldn't wait for me to go with her to the doctor."

"How long has she been gone?" Seth asked, trying to control the pounding of his heart.

Jacob's answer sounded clipped and frantic. "About a half hour. The rider was late and I couldn't leave Noah here alone. Someone had to document the time of the rider's arrival. I've already saddled a horse to go after her."

"No, you stay here. I'll find her, Jacob." He put his heels in Sam's side. The horse took off like a bullet from a smoking gun. Seth leaned low over Sam's neck and prayed. What had the woman been thinking? He'd warned them all to stay in groups when leaving the ranch.

Seth pushed Sam harder than ever before. He felt that still small voice telling him to hurry. Deep down, Seth knew Rebecca was in trouble. If anything happened to her, he'd be heartbroken. The thought seemed ironic. He'd kept his distance from her to keep his heart safe and now the threat of separation from her caused it to ache anyway.

When he topped the small rise and saw Rebecca trapped between two masked men, Seth pulled his Colt from its holster and aimed for the sky. If he didn't have to kill the men, but could scare them off, he would. He pulled the trigger and pushed Sam to race faster toward the woman he knew that he loved.

The men turned. One ran at the sight of Seth barreling down toward them. The other pointed his gun at Seth and fired.

Seth pressed his body close to Sam's and continued racing forward. He watched in horror as Rebecca went limp and slipped off Brownie's back.

The big man fired again at Seth. Anger seeped from the man's eyes. His stance said that as soon as Seth was in range, he'd kill him.

Seth aimed for the man's shooting arm and returned fire. He hated shooting but had to get to Rebecca. Had the man shot her? Or had she fainted?

His bullet hit true—the bandit grabbed his shoulder and turned his horse to follow his fellow outlaw. They disappeared over the next hill just as Seth jumped from Sam's back to Rebecca's side.

Rebecca groaned as he kneeled beside her and lifted her up into his arms. He cradled her hot body against his chest and arms. She was burning up with a fever. Smears of blood covered the front of her dress.

She opened her eyes, and her dimples winked at him. "Seth? You came for me?" Her glazed eyes told him that she was no longer aware of pain or heat from the fever.

"Yes, I came for you. Where are you hurt?" he asked, feeling her arms and torso for gunshot wounds.

She waved a bloody hand in front of his face. "I cut myself."

Satisfied she hadn't been shot, Seth picked up the bloody rag she'd used to cover the cut. He wrapped her hand and said, "I can see that."

She closed her eyes and he gently laid her back down on the ground. Gathering Brownie's reins and keeping a close watch out for the road bandits, he tied the little mare to the back of Sam's saddle, then hurried back to Rebecca.

Rebecca opened her eyes and looked at him. Her eyes had turned from their clear exquisiteness to that of a beautiful storm, dark but filled with a haze that only a summer storm could produce, or in this case pain and fever. "Are you taking me home, Seth?" she asked in a drowsy voice.

"No, I'm taking you to the doctor, but first we need to get you up on Sam. Can you stand up?" He leaned over and helped her stand. She closed her eyes and swayed against him. "Stay with me, Rebecca."

She opened her eyes and reached up and touched his jaw. "Always." Once more she slumped against him.

With more strength than he knew he possessed, Seth scooped her up against him and walked over to Sam. How was he going to get her on? *Lord, I need Your help here.* He looked up into the clear blue sky and quietly pleaded with God to help him get her on the horse.

Sam snorted and then buckled his front legs, then his back. He turned his big head and stared at Seth as if to say, *Well, what are you waiting for?*

Seth put Rebecca into the saddle and while holding her upright climbed on behind her. Sam stood. "Thank You, Lord!" Seth shouted and then grabbed the reins while holding on to Rebecca.

The trip into town felt as if it was taking forever. Seth continued to pray over Rebecca. She'd lost a lot of blood and the fever wasn't helping her. He rode in as fast as Sam could go and still tow her horse behind them.

The doctor stood on the sidewalk in front of his home and office. He hurried to help Seth get Rebecca off the horse. "What happened?"

"Jacob says she cut her hand."

"With what, a rusty knife? She's burning up with fever." The doctor allowed Seth to sweep Rebecca into his arms. He held the door to let them inside.

"She's been sick for a couple of days. I had no idea she was running a fever until I found her on the trail and brought her here." Seth laid her down on the cot that the doctor pointed to.

"You'll have to wait outside, young man." The doctor was already peeling the cloth from Rebecca's hand.

Seth walked to the door, but before exiting, he turned to look at Rebecca's pale face. Dark brown eyelashes fanned out under her eyes. He wished those eyes were open now, but she seemed to be sleeping. Her cheeks sported two red spots, making the rest of her face look powdery white.

Her hair had fallen down in his hurry to get her to town and now rested around her head on the pillow. His mind went to the silky softness of the strands. He'd only touched them once and that had been while kissing her.

The doctor cleared his throat and pointedly looked at the door. "I can't help her until you leave."

Seth left. He stepped out onto the porch. A rocker invited him to sit down but he couldn't. Sam and Brownie needed to be taken care of. He called through the door, "I'll be at the livery. If not there, the sheriff's office."

He heard the doctor grunt and took that as an indication that the man had heard him. Seth walked Sam to the livery, and Brownie followed, still tied to Sam's saddle.

Thank You, Lord for helping me get her here. And, Lord, please make her well. Her sons need her. He paused, lowered his head and confessed in a quiet voice, "I need her."

Even as he said the words, Seth knew that he didn't have a future with Rebecca. He really didn't want to confess, even to himself, that he loved her, but deep down he knew he did. Was it wrong to resent the promise he'd made to his grandmother? To Charlotte? Would he be able to live with the fact that he was marrying one woman but in love with another?

Chapter Twenty-Three

The next day, Rebecca woke up at the doctor's office. She knew she'd suffered from fever throughout the night and that her hand burned as if someone had branded her palm. A white bandage covered the cut.

During her fever-induced sleep, she recalled Seth coming over a hill with his gun blazing in the air.

The doctor came into the room. "Oh, good, you're awake." He smiled kindly at her and touched the back of his hand to her forehead. "And the fever is gone. That's a good sign."

She pushed up on her elbows. "Where's Seth? Did he make it through the gunfight all right?"

"There was a gunfight?" The doctor grinned at her. "Honey, I think you dreamed that."

"No, he shot at the road bandits who were trying to rob me." She fell back against the pillow. Had she dreamed it?

The doctor unwrapped her hand and inspected his handiwork.

The soft sound of the door clicking into place told her someone else had entered the room. "She's right,

Doc. I did shoot at the men trying to hold her up." He came around and grinned at Rebecca. "I'm glad to see you awake. How do you feel?"

The tenderness in his eyes touched her heart. "Well, my hand feels as if someone stuck a branding iron to it, but other than that, I feel better."

The doctor shook his head. "Someday, when we both have a little time, you'll have to tell me all about that gunfight, Seth."

Seth laughed. "It really wasn't much of a gunfight, but I'll be happy to tell you all about it."

"As for you, young lady, if Seth here wants to take you home, you have to promise to keep those stitches clean and let them heal. I'll come out in a few days and see if we can take them out." He rewrapped her hand and gave her a gentle pat on the arm.

"It would be my pleasure to take her home," Seth answered. "I'll just leave you to get ready." He stepped back out the door.

The doctor handed Rebecca a small pouch. "This has some herbs in it. I want you to take a teaspoon a day out, soak them in water and then use the water to wash that hand. They'll speed along the healing." At her nod, he continued, "Your dress is hanging over there. The missus tried to get the blood out for you, but I'm afraid it might still be stained."

"Thank you for the herbs. I'd like to thank her before I leave," Rebecca said, looking at her dress. She didn't see any stains.

"Good. I'm sending her in to help you with those buttons, so you'll have your chance." The doctor left her alone. Rebecca pushed off the sheet and stood slowly. Her hand throbbed so she held it up.

The door opened again. The doctor's wife, a plump woman with a sweet face, entered the room. "Doc says you are ready to go home. How do you feel?"

Rebecca wondered how often she'd have to answer that question before the day was over. "Better, Mrs. Bridges. We're blessed to have a good doctor in town."

The other woman walked over and pulled down Rebecca's dress. "You're blessed to have such a handsome young man who worries about you." She helped her step into the dress. "He stayed all night, sat in that chair."

Seth had stayed all night with her? She smiled. "That was sweet of him." Why would he do such a thing? Why hadn't he just had Fay come sit with her? Rebecca didn't want to think too much of the situation. So she pushed those thoughts to the back of her mind and focused on getting dressed.

After the dress was buttoned, Mrs. Bridges helped Rebecca with her shoes. "Thank you for getting the stains out of my dress," Rebecca said. It felt odd to have someone else button her shoes for her.

"It was no trouble at all. I was glad to help." She stepped back and looked Rebecca over. "Would you like me to brush your hair for you? It's a little wild-looking."

Rebecca looked down at her hand and nodded. She'd not realized how much help she was going to need over the next few days, but she couldn't even comb her own hair.

Mrs. Bridges chattered about the church bake sale that was coming up while she combed Rebecca's hair out and then pulled it up into a bun on top of her head. "I'll be making my spice cake this year." She stepped back and looked at her handiwork. "All done." The doctor's wife smiled at her.

"Thank you."

Seth called through the door, "About ready?"

Mrs. Bridges opened the door. "She's ready." She beamed at Rebecca.

Rebecca walked slowly to Seth. Her head still felt a little light, but she didn't say anything because she wanted to go home. "Thank you for everything." Tears stung her eyes as she realized just how much this woman had done for her.

"It was my pleasure."

Rebecca followed Seth out onto the porch. She expected to see Brownie and Sam standing in the road, but instead she saw that both of them were hooked up to a wagon. "You didn't have to get a wagon, Seth. I could have ridden Brownie home."

"Um, no, you couldn't. I want to make sure I get you back to the farm in one piece. Those boys of yours would skin me alive if you fell off and broke your neck." He held his hand out to help her up.

As soon as she was seated, Seth pulled himself up onto the wagon and took the reins in his hands. Rebecca didn't know what to say. She clutched the herb pouch in her hands and enjoyed the cool breeze on her face.

"You look pretty," Seth said once they'd passed the town's border.

Rebecca rubbed her lips together. "Thank you. I'm sure I look like death warmed over." She studied her hands.

"No, that's how you looked yesterday when I brought you to town. Now with a little color in your cheeks you are as pretty as those pink evening primroses over there." He pointed off to his right and grinned at her.

She felt heat fill her face and ducked her chin. Was that sweet talk? Or was he just trying to be kind? Rebecca turned her head to look at the field of flowers. They were pretty.

Unsure what to say but knowing that she wanted to tell him how much he meant to her, Rebecca decided not to say anything at all. He had a mail-order bride that he'd soon be going to see and possibly wed. Sorrow filled her at the thought, but she decided to ignore it and enjoy the beautiful flowers that were blooming all around her. Her telling Seth that she was in love with him wouldn't change anything.

Seth pulled into the yard just as the sun was setting. Everyone had been watching for them and within minutes the wagon was surrounded.

Jacob reached up and helped his mother down. He hugged her close and growled, "If you ever do that again, I will…"

Whatever he was going to threaten was lost among the others pushing him away and taking their turn hugging her. Each boy greeted Rebecca with hugs and pats. Little Benjamin hugged her about the waist and Joy clung to one leg.

Fay called from the door, "Come on, everyone. Let's get her inside."

Andrew scooped up Joy, and Benjamin released her waist. Seth gently took Rebecca's elbow and walked with her to the house.

Fay and Emma met her at the door. The two women

hugged her and fussed over her injured hand. Seth guided her to the sofa.

Benjamin rushed to her side. "Tell us about the bad men, Ma."

She pulled him closer to her side with her good hand. "Well, Benjamin, I learned a lesson from those bad men." Rebecca looked down into his brandy-colored eyes.

Awe filled his voice and he said, "You did?"

"Uh-huh."

"What did you learn?" he asked, never breaking eye contact.

Rebecca looked to Seth. "Well, first off, I learned never disobey Seth. If I hadn't taken off by myself, I might never have had to face those two men."

"Yeah, Jacob said that was foolish of you." Benjamin looked to his older brother.

"Oh, he did, did he?" Rebecca also looked to her oldest son.

Happy to be the center of attention, Benjamin continued, "Yep, he said even mas can do foolish things sometimes."

Rebecca smiled at Jacob. "He's right, Benjamin. It was foolish of me to take off on my own. I put myself in danger, and Seth. He could have been shot."

Joy wasn't going to be left out. She pushed out of Andrew's arms and crawled into Rebecca's lap. Her thumb went into her mouth and she laid her head on her mother's chest.

"I'm sorry I worried everyone. I promise from now on I won't leave the farm without a companion. Those men were mean and could have done a lot of harm to me. I should have listened to Seth and Jacob." She looked around the room at each person.

They were her family, even Emma and Fay. And the care she saw in their eyes touched her heart. Rebecca recognized that the boys would eventually leave the farm, but knowing they loved her so much made the realization a little more bearable.

Clayton drew everyone's attention off his mother. "What did the sheriff say, Seth?"

Seth leaned against the fireplace. "He said they'd keep a lookout for the road bandits."

"That's it?" Thomas demanded. "After what they tried to do to Ma, that's all he's going to do about it?"

The rest of the boys began to grumble, too.

Fay broke in to their complaining. "Now, see here, boys. The sheriff will do what he can to find them. That's all we can ask."

Philip grunted. "No, he could round up some men and go find those low-down..."

"Philip!" Rebecca wasn't sure what her son was going to call them, but she felt sure it wasn't nice or appropriate in a room full of children and women.

Jacob spoke up. "Listen, we stick to the rules. Don't go anywhere without someone with you. Don't leave the farm unless you have to. And let the sheriff do his job the way he sees fit." He eyed each of his younger brothers. "We are not the law or above the law."

Seth nodded. "Jacob is right. We have a job to do for the Pony Express. What is that job?"

"The mail must go through!" seven young voices boomed all at once.

The room burst into laughter. Rebecca smiled at her

family. They began visiting and playing around. It felt good to be home. She yawned.

Fay leaned down over the back of the couch and asked, "Are you ready to retire?"

"Not yet." Rebecca patted the hand that rested on her shoulder. "I want to enjoy my family for a little longer."

Emma sat on the arm of the chair. "Are you hungry, Rebecca? I made corned beef and cabbage for dinner. I'll be happy to dish you up a plate." She stood, waiting for Rebecca's consent.

"That sounds wonderful, Emma. Thank you."

The young girl beamed and hurried off to the kitchen.

Fay called after her, "Grab her a hot biscuit, too."

As soon as Emma left the room, Fay complimented her. "That girl can cook. Just wait until you taste her biscuits."

Rebecca watched her boys. Thomas and Philip were obvious in their admiration for Emma, but it was Andrew who caught her attention. He watched the young woman prance from the room and a small smile teased his lips before Andrew pulled his facial features back into serious lines. Was he interested in Emma? Or did she simply amuse him?

The next day, Rebecca felt useless as Fay and Emma prepared for the incoming stagecoach. Her hand felt stiff, but other than that Rebecca didn't feel any different. She wanted to make cookies, wipe down the tables and do her job. But Fay was having no part of it.

"You work too hard. Just relax and let us take care of you for a change." The older woman fussed as she pulled out the tray of sweetbreads she'd made.

"All right, I'm going to the sitting room." Rebecca

used her good hand and pushed through the door that joined the two rooms.

Joy sat by the fireplace playing with her doll. She looked up when her mother came in and smiled. "Look, Ma, Emma fixed my doll's hair like mine."

Rebecca grinned. "She sure did. It is very pretty."

The little girl nodded and went back to changing the doll's dress. Rebecca moved to the window and watched as several of the boys applied whitewash to the corral fence. She couldn't hear what they were saying, but their laughter drifted on the breeze toward the house.

Noah was standing in front of the barn with his horse. He seemed to be examining one of the horse's front hooves. His pant legs looked a little short on his boots. Had the boy had a growth spurt? When he stood up and flexed his shoulders she saw that the material appeared tight across his back. Yes, it was time to take him shopping again.

The stagecoach pulled in and all the boys looked toward it. Seth came out of the barn. He saw her standing in the window and waved before going into the bunkhouse. Rebecca turned her attention to the stage.

A beautiful young woman came out first. Her auburn hair shone in the sunlight. She was dressed in a simple green traveling dress and black shoes showed under her skirt. Next came a man. He wore a black business suit and his hat was smaller than the hats her boys and Seth wore.

Rebecca tried to remember what it was called but the name escaped her mind.

Fay and Emma hurried into the room. Each had a plate and were carrying them to the sideboard. Coffee and tea were ready, along with cups and saucers for serving. Emma took Joy's hand and returned to the kitchen.

Rebecca moved to the door and opened it just as the pair stepped onto the front porch. "Welcome. I hope you've had a safe trip so far."

The woman smiled sweetly at her. Rebecca was taken aback by the pure beauty of her emerald-green eyes. "Thank you. We've been blessed with no mishaps," she said as she passed.

The gentleman smiled at her, too, as he walked past. "This is the Dove Creek Pony Express station. Is that correct?" he asked.

Rebecca shut the door. "Yes, it is. Would either of you like a refreshment before you continue on your journey?"

"That would be lovely," the woman said as she walked toward Fay and the table. The light scent of rose water traveled with her.

Seth walked up behind Rebecca. "I see our guests are helping themselves to your fine cooking," he whispered against her ear.

She shivered and looked to the ground. "Not mine. Fay wouldn't let me help in the kitchen," Rebecca whispered back. She found herself wanting to lean into him.

He chuckled. "Good for her."

Rebecca felt someone watching them. She looked up to find the woman staring at Seth with interested eyes.

"Do you think Fay would slap my hand if I snatched a sandwich and maybe a slice of that sweetbread?" he asked, glancing at the table.

"Are you kidding? She'd let you take both plates if you wanted to," Rebecca answered. It was true. Fay thought that Seth could do no wrong, especially after he told how he'd rescued Rebecca from the outlaws.

He grinned. "I'll settle for one sandwich and a slice of bread." Seth walked over to Fay.

Rebecca turned her attention to the passengers. They both sat at the table. The woman's gaze continued to follow Seth. Why was she so interested in him? He was a handsome man, but so was her companion. So what did she find so intriguing about Seth?

Rebecca felt uncomfortable and she knew why. This woman was beautiful and she was interested in Seth. And for the first time in her life, Rebecca experienced jealousy.

Chapter Twenty-Four

Seth felt the woman's gaze upon him, but decided to ignore her. The thought that she was trying to make her companion jealous bothered him and he decided that as soon as he finished his sandwich he'd head back out to the barn.

Fay handed him a glass with tea in it. "Here, this should help wash that bread down."

He smiled his thanks, took a sip and then asked, "How is she doing today?"

Fay glanced over at Rebecca. She'd moved to the rocker by the window and picked up Fay's Bible. "Good. She wants to help but I told her she has to let her hand rest a few days before she starts using it."

"I'm glad she has you watching over her," Seth said, taking a big bite out of the sandwich.

Fay frowned at him. "If you keep gulping your food, you're going to choke."

He chewed and swallowed. "I'm just in a hurry to get back to the barn," Seth explained. He took a swallow of the tea.

Fay teased him in a quiet voice. "Why? Because our guests are making you uncomfortable?"

"You feel it, too?" he whispered.

She laughed softly. "No, I don't feel anything but I can see that you have drawn some attention from the woman. I think she likes you," Fay whispered back.

Seth stuffed the last of the sandwich in his mouth. He already had two women to worry about; he didn't want or need to add another. As soon as he could swallow, he drank the last of his tea and handed Fay back the glass. "Thanks for the sandwich." He turned to leave but her voice stopped him.

"Aren't you going to take a slice of sweetbread with you?"

He turned back to her. She'd wrapped it in a soft piece of cloth and handed it to him. From the corner of his eye, Seth could see that the passengers were finishing up their meal and were standing to leave. "Thank you, Fay." He thought to go back out the kitchen.

A male voice stopped him. "Excuse me, but are you Seth Armstrong?" he asked.

Seth inhaled through his nose and released the air through his mouth. Then he turned to face the man with a smile. At least he hoped it was a smile and not a grimace. "Yes, I am."

The man walked toward him with an outstretched hand. "I'm Ben Wheeler. May we speak to you outside?"

Seth shook the man's hand. "Of course." His gaze moved to the woman and for the first time he really looked at her. Emma's words about Charlotte came back to him. *She's a sweet woman with auburn hair and green eyes.* Seth realized he was looking in the face of his mail-order bride.

She extended her hand also. "Seth, I'm Charlotte. Charlotte Fisher."

He took her delicate hand in his. His gaze moved to Rebecca, who stared back at him with big blue eyes. Seth felt the air leave his lungs.

Mr. Wheeler cleared his throat. "Is there someplace private we can talk?" he asked.

Seth released Charlotte's hand. "Yes, yes, there is." He opened the front door and inhaled the scent of roses as Charlotte passed him.

Once outside, Seth looked around for a place to take them. He knew that if they stayed on the porch, Rebecca would be able to hear every word they said.

Charlotte motioned toward the stage. "We could sit inside the coach and talk."

"That's an excellent idea," Mr. Wheeler agreed, leading the way.

Mr. Wheeler helped Charlotte into the stage and then motioned for Seth to follow her. "This is between the two of you." He made eye contact with Seth and said, "I hope you make the right decision." Mr. Wheeler nodded his head and closed the door on the coach.

Charlotte folded her hands in her lap and searched Seth's face. "I can't believe we are finally meeting."

He looked around the carriage. "Me, either. This wasn't exactly how I thought it would happen." Seth studied her face. "I'm sorry I didn't find you as fast as I'd planned."

Charlotte shook her head. "No, it was my fault. Let me explain."

Seth nodded, happy to finally find out what had happened to her.

"I left on the day I sent you that last letter but to get to the station I had to walk through a cold rainstorm. When the stage left I was soaked and already starting to feel bad. We got about halfway to St. Joseph and I was very sick. Fever and chills shook my body. The ladies on the coach were afraid I was going to make them sick, too. So they talked the driver into leaving me behind." Her green eyes took on a faraway look as if she was reliving those moments.

"Why didn't you take the next stage and continue on? I would have taken care of you." He leaned forward and took her hands in his.

Charlotte smiled. "I'm sure you would have, but I didn't have any more money and the next stage wouldn't arrive for another two days. The lady at the stagecoach stop said I could sleep in the barn. So I stumbled to the barn and tried to get better. When the stagecoach arrived I was weak from lack of food and the fever that had consumed me. But I was determined to get to you." Her green eyes searched his.

Seth couldn't believe how cruel the women had treated Charlotte. She was beautiful and jealousy was a cruel beast that some women fought. Of course, jealousy may have had nothing to do with their treatment of Charlotte; it could have been their fear of getting sick. "I'm sorry I didn't get to you first," he confessed. "You don't have to tell me this, if it is too painful. You are here now and that's what is important."

"No, I have to tell you the whole story." She pulled her hands from his. "I made it out of the barn but tripped when I took a step to get into the coach." Her hand went to her head. "The fall knocked me out and when I awoke, I had no idea who I was or where I'd been going." She dropped her hand back in her lap. "But thankfully, Mr. Wheeler was on that stage. He's a doctor. He found out from the woman at the station that my name was Charlotte Fisher." A gentle smile touched her lips. "Ben says he fell in love with me the moment he saw me. Can you believe that?"

Seth sat back in his seat. So the man outside the door was in love with Charlotte. He smiled at her. "Yes, I can. You are a very beautiful woman."

She giggled. "Well, that day I was anything but beautiful. Anyway, he nursed me back to health, took me back to Sacramento and helped me find a job at the restaurant."

Seth was confused. It was obvious that Charlotte was in love with Ben also, so why was she here? He knew she hadn't had time to get his letter. How did she know where he was? If she didn't know he was here and it was a complete accident, how had they known he was Seth Armstrong?

"I'm almost done, I promise." Charlotte sat up straighter. "I was working one day when I heard a conversation between two men who had just arrived on the afternoon stage. One of the men asked the other if he thought they might run into Charlotte Fisher, that gal that Seth Armstrong was looking for in Dove Creek. I don't know why it happened but hearing both our names in the same sentence had my memories flooding back to me. I remembered why I was on the stage. That night I told Ben and explained to him that I had to come find you." She inhaled deeply.

Seth searched her face. "But you love Ben, so why did you come here looking for me?"

"I came to ask you to release me from my promise. I know I said I'd marry you and I will, if you won't release me, but please, Seth. Ben wants to marry me, and my heart will shatter into a million pieces if I can't marry him. He's the first man who hasn't looked at me and only seen outside beauty. He saw me when I was sick, dirty and starving, and he loved me on sight." Her hands shook in her lap. Tears filled her eyes and spilled down her cheeks.

Seth leaned forward and placed his hands on hers once more. "It's all right. I release you, Charlotte."

She grabbed him and hugged him, then leaned back. "But what about your promise to your grandmother?"

He shifted on the hard seat. "She made me promise to get married. She didn't say it had to be to you."

A smile tipped her lips once more. "You're happy I'm releasing you, aren't you?"

Seth nodded. His heart was about to explode out of his chest with happiness. Now that he knew what had happened to Charlotte and she'd asked him to release her, he was free to tell Rebecca how he felt about her.

"It's the woman from the house, isn't it? The one with the bandaged hand." She wisely crossed her arms over her chest and gave him a stern look.

Seth laughed. "Yes, but she doesn't know how I feel, so I'm a little unsure what the future holds now. Thank you for coming and telling me what had happened to you. I wish you and Mr. Wheeler the best." Seth stood to exit the coach.

"I wish you the best, too, Seth. If you tell her that you love her, I'm sure your future will be bright."

How could Charlotte be so sure? Would Rebecca believe that he loved her? Would she say yes if he asked her to marry him?

Lord, let Your will be done. He silently prayed that his will and God's will were in alignment.

Rebecca watched from the window as Seth climbed out of the coach. Charlotte followed, looking happier now that they'd had their talk. What had she said to him? They'd been in the coach so long.

"What do you think they talked about?" Emma asked, standing beside her.

Fay answered from the sofa. "It's none of our business, ladies."

Rebecca ignored Fay. "I don't know but look how happy she is now."

Emma nodded. "But she's getting back in the coach and so is the man. Are they leaving?"

The coach pulled away from the house and continued on its route, carrying Charlotte and Mr. Wheeler with it. Rebecca watched as Seth hurried to the bunkhouse. "He never even looked back." She turned from the window. "I'm tired. I think I'll go lie down for a little while." Rebecca started to walk out of the room but stopped. "Thank you both for taking care of the passengers today."

Emma asked, "Rebecca, are you feeling all right?"

"I'm fine. I just need to rest." She didn't tell them that her heart was breaking. Seth seemed happy, Charlotte seemed happy and Rebecca couldn't help but feel miserable.

She went to her room and shut the door. The desire to throw herself across the bed and weep pulled strongly at her. Was Charlotte going on to St. Joseph to wait for Seth? Were they still planning on getting married?

Deep down Rebecca felt sure that they hadn't broken off their marriage since they both looked so happy. Even Charlotte's companion had looked pleased.

Rebecca avoided the bed and moved to the stuffed chair that sat beside the window. She picked up her Bible off the side table and opened it to Proverbs.

To her, Proverbs was the book of wisdom—at least that was what she liked to think. She read Proverbs, chapter sixteen, verse nine, out loud. "'A man's heart deviseth his way: but the Lord directeth his steps.'"

Peace washed over her. God was in control. Seth may have been in her life for a little while and if he left, she'd be fine because God would never leave her.

She closed the Bible and lay across her bed. "Lord, I trust You to direct my steps." Rebecca closed her eyes, sadly wishing that her steps and Seth's walked side by side.

Seth paced the bunkhouse. He knew that God had brought him to the Young farm to teach him about love. When he'd arrived he'd sworn never to fall in love, to never let anyone hurt him like his mother had hurt him and his father. But all that had changed.

He loved Rebecca. He wanted to marry her. He also respected her sons enough to ask their permission.

Philip entered the bunkhouse first. When he saw Seth, he frowned. "Is everything all right?" he asked.

"Better than all right. Go tell the other boys to come here. I'd like to have a meeting with them."

Philip nodded. "Let me change out of these wet socks and I'll go get them."

It seemed to take forever for Philip to do the simple task of changing socks. And it took even longer for all the boys to make their way into the bunkhouse.

"This is everyone," Philip announced unnecessarily.

Seth walked to the stove and stood in front of it, facing them. "Today my mail-order bride came to the farm."

"What?"

"Where is she?"

"I didn't see her."

"Are you going to marry her here?"

"Does Ma like her?"

Jacob stopped the questions. "Shut up, and let him talk."

"She released me from marrying her. It would seem Charlotte has met someone more to her liking and so have I." Seth took a breath and was immediately interrupted again with questions and outrage.

"Who did she meet?"

"What does more to her liking mean?"

"Who have you met?"

"Enough!" Jacob yelled.

All the boys looked to him.

"If you interrupt Seth one more time, I am going to thrash you."

They seemed to take their older brother at his word and quieted down again. All eyes turned to Seth.

Seth answered their questions. "She met a doctor and they are going to get married. That's what I meant by more to her liking. As for who I have met." He paused.

For the first time he worried the Young men might reject him and his idea to marry their mother.

Jacob grinned. "Go on, tell them who you have met."

Seth swallowed and then rushed on. "I met your mother and I want to marry her."

Andrew stood. In a tense voice he asked, "Why?"

The two men locked gazes. "Because I love her," Seth answered.

Jacob stood, too. He stepped between Andrew and Seth as if he thought Andrew would start a fight. Jacob said, "Then you should marry her."

Andrew nodded his approval.

Clayton, Thomas and Philip grinned up at him.

Noah shrugged. "If you love her, then you should marry her."

Benjamin stood and looked up at Seth. He didn't say anything and he didn't nod. Seth kneeled down in front of him. This little boy meant the world to him and he needed his approval as much, or more, than the others'. "Beni, I can't marry her unless all the Young men approve. It wouldn't be right."

"Would I have to call you Papa Seth?"

The seriousness in Benjamin's voice reminded Seth that in Beni's eyes he was trying to take John's place in their lives. He shook his head. "No, you don't. I'll always be Seth to you. I can't take Papa John's place in your heart, Beni. No one can."

He looked to his other brothers, who nodded their heads at him. Benjamin looked back to Seth. "Then I reckon it's all right with me, if you want to marry Ma."

Seth stood and faced them once more. He swallowed. "Thanks."

They laughed and clapped him on the back. Andrew stood off to the side with his arms crossed over his chest. Seth turned to him. "Andrew, are you sure you're all right with me asking her to marry me?"

"Yep, I was just thinking. Now you have to actually ask her. These guys are acting like she's already said yes. She might say no." He turned and walked out of the bunkhouse.

Seth's heart sank. Andrew was right. What if she did say no? What if she did reject him? Would she feel like Beni, that no man could take her late husband's place?

Chapter Twenty-Five

The next morning, Seth was still worrying about Rebecca's answer. The sound of a rider coming in fast drew his attention. There weren't any Pony Express riders scheduled. He stepped out his side door and watched as the sheriff entered the yard.

He walked over to him. "What brings you out this morning, Sheriff?"

The sheriff leaned on his horse's saddle horn. "Just thought you'd like to know we caught our road bandits. It was thanks to your quick shooting."

"Who are they?" Jacob asked, coming to stand beside Seth. The other boys crowded around them, too.

The sheriff tipped his hat back. "Jake Edwards."

"Mr. Edwards that owns the general store?" Clayton asked.

"One and the same. Seems he and a couple of his old buddies were making extra money on the side by robbing stagecoach passengers. Seth here put a bullet in Edwards." He grinned. "Those things smart when they get infected. Bring a man to tears and to the doctor."

"How'd you catch the other two?" Seth asked.

"Seems the pain was pretty bad and he told Doc everything while the bullet was being removed." He rubbed his chin. "Who knew Doc could get information like that just by taking out a bullet?"

Seth was glad the men were behind bars. "Thanks for letting us know, Sheriff. We'll breathe a little easier around here."

The sheriff nodded. "Well, I best be getting back to town. I have prisoners waiting for breakfast this morning." He spun around and headed back to town.

All the way into the house, the boys talked about Mr. Edwards and the fact that they knew he was no good all along. Seth listened but didn't add to the conversation. His thoughts were on Rebecca and how she was going to answer his marriage proposal.

Rebecca listened to the boys repeat what the sheriff had said. She watched Seth's reaction to the news. He seemed distracted and she couldn't help but wonder if he was thinking of Charlotte.

They hadn't had their nightly meeting the evening before. Seth hadn't bothered to come in for dinner. Had he been packing a bag? Even now, was he planning on leaving after breakfast?

The boys lingered over breakfast longer than normal. She noticed that they watched Seth, too. Were they concerned that he would be leaving soon?

It was Andrew who finally said, "Seth, are you doing this today or should we go on and do our chores?"

Seth looked startled for a moment and then he swallowed hard and stood to his feet. He walked to Rebecca's end of the table and offered her his hand.

Unsure what was going on, Rebecca allowed him to

pull her up. She opened her mouth to ask what he was doing when he laid a finger over her lips.

"Rebecca Young, I have known for a while now that I love you, but because of Charlotte and my promise to marry her, I haven't been able to tell you. Until today." He stopped and searched her eyes.

Had he just told her he loved her? In front of her kids, Fay and Emma? She looked around the room. The boys all just sat watching expectantly. Fay covered her mouth with her hand and Emma and Joy sat staring with big eyes. She looked back to Seth. "I…"

Seth kneeled down on one knee in front of her. "I love you, Rebecca Young. Will you marry me?" His warm eyes held all the love that was within his heart.

"I do love you, Seth, but I can't agree to marry you."

He stood. Pain reflected in his eyes. "Why not?"

She looked to her children. "I need their permission."

Smiles broke out over the boys' faces.

Jacob laughed. "Ma, we've already given Seth our approval."

A smile began to touch her lips. Seth had respected her and her boys enough to ask their permission. "What about you, Joy?"

She felt Seth's arm snake around her waist.

"I like Seth. I want to keep him."

Rebecca turned to face Seth. His eyes now held understanding, but uncertainty at what her answer was going to be. "I want to keep you, too. Yes, I'll marry you."

Seth didn't give her a chance to change her mind. He pulled her close and kissed her lips. The boys hooted, the women laughed and Rebecca relaxed in his arms.

When he pulled away from her, she whispered against his lips, "I love you, too, Seth. I have for a while now."

He hugged her close. Rebecca savored the warmth of his arms as she thanked the Lord for bringing Seth into their lives. And for helping her to realize that God was in control and it was all right to love again.

Epilogue

Rebecca looked at her reflection. The full-length mirror had been a wedding present from the boys. She admired the soft cream-colored dress Fay had presented her with the day before. It was much prettier than the blue Sunday dress she'd intended to wear. Tiny pearl-like beads lined the sleeves and the train of the gown.

"You are beautiful, Ma."

She smiled over her shoulder at her eldest son, Jacob. He was to walk her the short distance to her groom. He wore a blue suit that looked snug about his wide shoulders. No longer was he the twelve-year-old boy she'd adopted. Jacob was a man.

"Thank you, son." She looked back at her reflection. Like her, Jacob had a right to start his life again. He needed to know about his mother.

He placed both hands on her shoulders. "Ready?" Their gazes met in the glass.

"Almost." She turned and gave him a hug, then pulled away. "But first I have to tell you about your real mother."

His back straightened. "Today's not the day for that,

Ma. We can talk about her another time." Jacob held his arm out for her to take.

Rebecca placed a gloved hand in the crook of his elbow. "I know where she is and I want you to go to her. If for no other reason than to find out why she abandoned you."

Jacob led them to the door. He pulled it open and nodded. "All right. Where is she?"

She swallowed hard. As soon as he knew, Jacob would leave. Rebecca was sure of it. "In California. A few years ago, she married. I'm not sure where in California they live, but she was last known to be somewhere in the vicinity of the Pony Express station called Twelve Mile Station."

He patted her hand. "Thank you for telling me, Ma."

Rebecca pulled him to a stop. "Aren't you going to go find her?" She studied her son's face, wanting to know and yet not wanting to know if he was leaving.

Jacob turned her to face him squarely. "Yes, I am, but I will come back. This is my home. You are my true mother. Nothing will change that." He used his thumb to wipe away a tear that had slipped down her cheek at his words. A smile touched his lips. "But first we have a wedding to attend. And I can't take you in there with tears on your face. Seth would have my guts for garters."

His words caused her to chuckle. Rebecca nodded. "Promise you'll say goodbye before you head out?"

"Promise." He kissed her cheek. "Now let's get you married." Jacob turned and offered her his elbow once more.

Rebecca took it. She pushed all thoughts of Jacob and his future aside and focused on her own future.

A future filled with Seth and the rest of the boys and little Joy.

Jacob walked her to Seth, who stood in front of the fireplace looking handsome in his dark pants, light blue shirt and cowboy boots. His smile was for her alone.

She couldn't pull her gaze from his. He was all she'd ever wanted in a husband. They shared friendship, as she and John had, but they also shared so much more. His touch made her feel warm and safe. His smile brightened her day and his voice sent shivers down her spine like no other man's ever had. She'd loved John and nothing and no one could take from that. But now she shared a special love with Seth.

Rebecca thanked the Lord that she could love both men without taking from either of them. They were both special to her in their own ways. Loving Seth would be a new chapter in her life, one she intended to savor.

As she repeated her vows and looked into Seth's strong face, she remembered the day he'd come racing into the yard to help put out a barn fire. Unbeknownst to him, he'd ignited her heart with flames of love. She silently thanked the Lord above for bringing such a wonderful man into her life.

"You may kiss your bride."

Seth pulled her close and gently kissed her lips. She ignored the wedding party and focused solely on her new husband. He was all she'd ever hoped for and so much more.

* * * * *

Dear Reader,

Thank you so much for picking up the first book in the Saddle and Spurs miniseries, *Pony Express Courtship*. I hope you enjoyed Rebecca and Seth's story.

Dove Creek is a fictional Pony Express Home Station but based on a real one. As far as I know, there weren't any home stations like Rebecca's, but my imagination didn't stop me from creating it. Also, as far as I know there were never two riders who went together on the trail, but again for my story, I created that possibility. What allowed me to create so freely is that there are many things that aren't known to be "facts" about the Pony Express.

I hope you will continue this journey with the Young family with me. The Pony Express changed many young and old men's lives. Let's explore some of them together. Please join me for the ride.

Warmly,
Rhonda Gibson

SPECIAL EXCERPT FROM

Love Inspired **HISTORICAL**

Booming Cowboy Creek has everything a man could need—except for women. But when a group of mail-order brides arrive, town founder Daniel Gardner is shocked to see Leah Swann, the girl he used to love. She's a widow now, needing a husband to care for her... and for the baby she has on the way.

Read on for a sneak preview of
Cheryl St.John's *WANT AD WEDDING,*
the exciting first book in the new miniseries
COWBOY CREEK,
available April 2016 from Love Inspired Historical.

"Gentlemen, please make a path and escort our brides forward!"

A smattering of applause followed his request, and from the outer edge of the platform, the crowd parted unevenly, allowing three figures in ruffles and flower-bedecked hats to make their way through the gathering to the stack of crates. Daniel jumped down beside Will and they stood on either side of the group of ladies.

Daniel removed his hat, and every cowboy doffed his own. "Welcome to Cowboy Creek." He glanced aside. "We're still missing someone."

"Mrs. Swann was with us a moment ago," the petite young woman beside him said. "She must have become lost in the crowd somewhere."

"Let the lady through!" Daniel called, standing as tall as he could manage and peering above the crowd. He was thinking that perhaps he would need to get back on the stack of crates, when he spotted a blue feathered hat on a pale gold head of hair. "There she is. Mrs. Swann! Let her through."

The poor woman steadied her wisp of a hat atop her head with one white-gloved hand and turned this way and that, speaking to men as she choreographed her way through the crowd. Disengaging herself from the attentions of an overeager cowboy, she nearly stumbled forward. Daniel caught her elbow to steady her.

"Oh! Thank you. This is quite a reception!" She glanced up. Cornflower blue eyes rimmed with dark lashes opened wide in surprise. The world stood still for a moment. The crowd noise faded into the void. "Daniel?"

Daniel's gut felt as though he'd been standing right on the tracks and stopped the locomotive with his body. "Leah Robinson?"

She was as pretty as ever. Prettier maybe, her face having lost the roundness of girlhood and her skin and bone structure having smoothed into a gentle comeliness.

Mrs. Swann was Leah Robinson, one of his best friends before the war. Will had once shown him a wedding announcement from a Chicago newspaper, and all these years Daniel had pictured her just as she had been back then, full of youth and vitality, and married to the army officer she'd chosen. That had been a lifetime ago. So what was she doing traveling to Cowboy Creek with their mail-order brides?

Don't miss WANT AD WEDDING
by Cheryl St.John, available April 2016 wherever
Love Inspired® Historical books and ebooks are sold.

www.LoveInspired.com

Love the Love Inspired book you just read?

Your opinion matters.

Review this book on your favorite book site, review site, blog or your own social media properties and share your opinion with other readers!

HLIREVIEWSR